Praise for Peter

THE LAST RANGER

"Heller writes in lean, descriptive, contemplative prose that often reflects a spirit of solitude. . . . Ren, like his literary creator, is a philosopher at heart; you get the feeling he'd do just fine hanging with Thoreau at Walden Pond."

—*The Boston Globe*

"Heller's style is Hemingway with the machismo scoured out of it. He can linger romantically on Yellowstone's atmosphere. . . . But his observations and dialogue are typically as clipped as Papa's. Still, his tension within the natural setting is more psychologically nuanced."

—*Los Angeles Times*

"Heller's best books have a lickety-split pace and archetypal characters whose behavior makes sense to us partly because he keeps them mysterious, forcing us to fill in their motivations. . . . Throughout the novel there's a sense that good and evil aren't as easy to separate as we'd like to believe. Maybe Heller's point is that the 'good guys' are the mountains and the streams and the 'bad guys' are all the people who think those things were put here for us."

—*Minneapolis Star Tribune*

"Both a warning about man's encroachment on the Western wilderness and another variation on the solitary-man theme [Heller] does so well. . . . Wonderful writing about endangered wolves and the obsessive behaviorist who studies them."

—Air Mail

Peter Heller

THE LAST RANGER

Peter Heller is the bestselling author of *The Guide*, *The River*, *Celine*, *The Painter*, and *The Dog Stars*, which has been published in twenty-six languages. Heller is also the author of four nonfiction books, including *Kook: What Surfing Taught Me About Love, Life, and Catching the Perfect Wave*, which was awarded the National Outdoor Book Award. He holds an MFA from the Iowa Writers' Workshop in poetry and fiction and lives in Denver, Colorado.

ALSO BY PETER HELLER

FICTION

The Guide

The River

Celine

The Painter

The Dog Stars

NONFICTION

*Kook: What Surfing Taught Me About Love, Life,
and Catching the Perfect Wave*

*The Whale Warriors: The Battle at the Bottom of the World
to Save the Planet's Largest Mammals*

Hell or High Water: Surviving Tibet's Tsangpo River

Set Free in China: Sojourns on the Edge

THE LAST RANGER

THE LAST RANGER

A Novel

PETER HELLER

VINTAGE CONTEMPORARIES

VINTAGE BOOKS

A DIVISION OF PENGUIN RANDOM HOUSE LLC

NEW YORK

FIRST VINTAGE CONTEMPORARIES EDITION 2024

The Library of Congress has cataloged the Knopf edition as follows:
Name: Heller, Peter, [date] author.
Title: The last ranger : a novel / Peter Heller.
Description: First United States edition. | New York: Alfred A. Knopf, [2023]
Identifiers: LCCN 2022046772 (print) | LCCN 2022046773 (ebook)
Classification: LCC PS3608.E454 L372023 (print) |
LCC PS3608.E454 (ebook) | DDC 813/.6—dc23
LC record available at http://lccn.loc.gov/2022046772
LC ebook record available at http://lccn.loc.gov/2022046773

Vintage Books Trade Paperback ISBN: 978-0-593-46851-7
eBook ISBN: 978-0-593-53512-7

Title page art by takahiro/Shutterstock.com

Book design by Soonyoung Kwon

vintagebooks.com

Printed in the United States of America

10 9 8 7 6 5 4 3 2 1

To Becky Arnold. And to her sons, Landis and Thor.
And to her husband, Andy, in memoriam.

THE LAST RANGER

Prologue

The night of the buffalo it rained. Hard, flooding the creek for hours as if trying to wash away the stain. He let them in—at first he thought the knocking was the limb of the pine at the corner of the cabin; too bad it wasn't. The two were panicked, cold, she was hyperventilating. They talked over each other. He smelled of probably bourbon. He let them lie about the accident for ten minutes while he gave them blankets and made them coffee. He built up the fire in the stove, and then he shrugged into his slicker and pushed out into the downpour and took care of it. Poor guy. The bull had been smashed at speed in the left hindquarter, and the force had spun him into the side of the van and crushed the left side of his face but not enough to kill him or knock him out. The cruelty of the thing. The bison was on his right side in the gravel of the shoulder, breathing in rapid strained snorts, and Ren put a hand on his neck and said, "I'm sorry, bud. I'm so sorry. Better them than you," and he meant it. The animal's eye was intact and in the headlights it shone black and wet, wide with desperation maybe, or simply pain. Ren unholstered his SIG .45 and gave the animal a coup de grâce. The bull heaved and scrabbled his front legs and lay still.

The van was crushed along the right side and askew on the shoulder, just into the lane. In the lights of his truck he could see skid marks to the west of the bull, and the broken glass of the mirror, making it clear that the van had been traveling east. But where he found the van was again well west of the wreck and aimed west—away from help, from the nearest town by far, from the ranger station just up the road, which the couple clearly knew about because they had walked straight there in the rain. Ren swore. They had left the poor bull alive and suffering and tried to drive away, but the van had not cooperated.

Ren ducked his head into the driving rain and glare of headlights and hustled back to the truck. Had the carcass been farther from people and the road, he would have left it for the wolves and bears and ravens. Instead, he radioed his friend Pete in Cooke City and told him he was point-nine miles south of the station at the fishermen's pullout and asked him if he needed help and Pete said, "No, take off. Aliya and I got this. Thanks, Ren." Aliya was Pete's sixteen-year-old daughter, and together they would skin the huge carcass and quarter it with a cordless meat saw and debone the quarters with knives by hand and load two hundred pounds of meat into plastic tubs in the back of the truck. They would do it all in the sheeting rain, under the floodlights mounted to the rear of the ladder rack, and in three hours they would be heading home.

Ren drove back in a blowing squall. The manic wipers couldn't keep up with the downpour and he had to drive slowly, and as the truck crawled his anger welled. It was the second unwarranted kill that day. In the afternoon, his neighbor, Hilly, had reported that she had found the fresh carcass of an uncollared female wolf from the Junction Butte Pack. She had been shot in the head and skinned yards from the bank of Soda Butte Creek, just inside the park. The slaying bore all the signs of a trained sharpshooter using a rifle with probably a noise suppressor.

Inside the park. It was brazen poaching and it was a Fuck You to anyone who cared about the wolves.

When Ren returned to the cabin, it was overheated and smelled a little of the alcohol and something else unwanted, something rancid or unwholesome. The man—Dave was his name, wasn't it?—knew enough to open the damper on the woodstove to make the cabin warmer, and the fire rushed in the flue, and the base of the stovepipe was cherry red. Way too hot: they could have burned the place down. A serious fire might have been seconds away. Ren stepped fast across the rag rug, pushed past their knees in the rocking chairs, and shut the vents down.

He hadn't been going to do it before, but now he did. He said, "How fast did you say you were going?" She started to speak, but the man spoke over her.

"Forty. Less. Thirty-eight."

"How do you know?"

"I could see the speedometer, I was dri—"

She had said she was the driver when they first told the story in a rush at the door.

Ren took the pad from his breast pocket and wrote it down. "Stand up," he said.

"What?"

"Stand up, please."

The man handed his mug to his wife and reluctantly stood. "Walk to me, please." Ren had backed to the front door. He didn't need a painted highway line. Panic blurred the man's face, then a reddening of anger. He stepped, put one hand out as if on a high wire.

Ren tugged the compact breathalyzer from his belt, handed it to the man. "Blow," he said.

"Whoa, look—"

"Blow," Ren said.

After Ren read .12 on the screen, he put his hands on the man's shoulders and spun him around and cuffed him. The woman was in the rocker, crying. It was too late to drive the three hours to Cody. He called Ty from the handset charging on the counter and said he was bringing someone in. He could be there in forty minutes. Ty was the Park County Sheriff's deputy stationed part-time in Cooke City, twenty miles to the northeast. A ranger from Yellowstone headquarters would transport the man in the morning. The man's wife was sobbing openly now, and he let her use the landline to book a room at the Super 8 that was right across the street from the two-room jail.

Chapter One

It was the anger in him that scared him. The more time he spent in Yellowstone, the more he wished that people would just go away, leave the bears, the herds of elk, the foxes, the hawks alone. The wolf packs. Yesterday morning he had issued a summons to a man and his nine-year-old son for walking across the shallow Lamar River to within sixty yards of where the Junction Butte Pack were trying to feed their pups.

The river ran through open meadows here, mostly wheatgrass and sage, and on the far side they were hedged by woods that climbed steeply. The four hunting wolves had loped in from a fresh kill down-valley, and the rest of the pack had run to meet them. Nineteen, twenty, strung out in the tall grass—the image frozen like a photograph in Ren's mind, a portrait of how the world ought to be—the wolves lean from summer, grays and blacks and buffs, one big male nearly white, sprinting flat out in what looked to be a joyous line beneath a wall of trees. They didn't have to run. But it was daybreak on a brisk mid-September morning, and the pack was all together, and there was meat. The sun had just cleared the pass, and it burnished the grass and threw the shadows of the runners ahead of them.

If he himself could feel joy, it was now. And then, through the binocs, he saw the two figures. Man and boy already over the far bank, through the willows, stalking for a better look. Already too close.

Integrity, Honor, Service. He would run. Splash knee-deep across the river, and in forty more yards he would hail them. Yell. The pack, which had known the two were coming since well before they crossed the river—and decided to ignore them—had tumbled together in an exuberant moil, yelping, wrestling, but now, at the shout, they would freeze and stand and look. The father and son would turn, confused. Ren would wave them back, retrieve them, as he was trained to do. Back at the road he would give a stern lecture about harassing wildlife and the safety of the boy and the wolves themselves, and write the man a summons that would result in a five-hundred-dollar fine. He would tell them that the wolves would have tolerated their proximity only so long and so close, and maybe within seconds the entire pack would have raised the alarm and moved into the trees, and that every calorie they spent retreating from the boy and the man was another calorie closer to starvation. Which was true.

But it was not what Ren wanted. What did he want? In a parallel life, the wolves would stand all together and turn and decide enough was enough. They would fan out in an arc, eyes steady and fast on their prey, and they would flank the father and son. And one of the fast females would feint a charge, and one of the big males would dart in behind and hamstring the man, and in minutes it would be over.

Wolves had never once attacked a human in Yellowstone. In Ren's fantasy they would spare the boy. And when Ren had shaken himself from his reverie, he thought, *Jesus, what the hell has gotten into you? Do you think you're the last ranger that puts the animals first?*

But that was the anger that frightened him. In his world lately, the life of a wolf, or a hawk, might be worth more than the life of a man.

Now, with the rain gusting against the roof of the cabin, he left the door to the porch wide open for a minute and filled the kettle in the steel sink and set it on the woodstove. He'd make tea. It was late, and he was amped from the night, more from what he'd seen in the buffalo's eye than anything else. The animal was one of those huge, scarred old bulls who had lived a life of hardship and battle and now browsed alone, and dozed in the open, sometimes skylined on a grassy spur because he feared nothing now, not wolf packs nor storm. As Ren squatted over him in the rain, he had thought he saw, beneath the confusion and fear and raw pain, a sadness: after wolves, lions, drought, snowdrifts so deep the calves drowned in them . . . had it come to this? Or maybe the depthless black eye was only a mirror for Ren's own bafflement and grief. In any event, he needed to open the cabin door wide and let the gusts smatter the screen door and fill the room with the cold of the autumn night. On the wind he could smell the faint sweetness of aspen turning and the unmistakable scent of snow, which must now be falling on the highest ridges. It was already past midnight. He wouldn't sleep much.

He picked a smaller stick of firewood out of the box and knocked the chrome handle of the woodstove and let the door swing open. He stuffed in two more chunks of aspen—not the best firewood, it burned hot and wouldn't bank all night, but there was plenty of it standing dead on the pass above Cooke City, and it was easy to cut a truckload. Part of the deal for him to stay at the research station: he'd supply his own firewood. He didn't mind. He liked it. To get out of the park and onto a highway whose speed limit wasn't forty. Where nobody was gawking. Where the pickups going too fast were the parents fetching their kids from the bus stop down in Ranford, and where sometimes a passing teenager flashed him the finger, because Ren's truck had a green stripe and "U.S. Park Ranger" on the side, and all things park were bogus because they wouldn't let the boy or his father kill the wolves in there, or the trophy elk that wandered the clearings so close to the road you could slay them with a shovel. He didn't mind. Life in Cooke City was hardscrabble. In the summer the tourists came in tidal floods, a local could work sixteen hours a day for thirty days straight, and in winter moms took their schoolchildren over the pass on snowmobiles in the dark. And so, having this enforced Eden right next door, enjoyed by mostly privileged folks from away who were *on vacation*, and where idyllic herds roamed and the lion practically lay down with the lamb—it galled. More than a few people along the park's borders would abolish Yellowstone in a heartbeat. Ren got it. He didn't mind. He usually met the flipped birds with a smile. He liked to leave the park, and then he loved to drive back in. There was wildness going in either direction.

But once in a while a resident in Cooke City did kill. There was today's wolf. And now Mink Man was back. In the same wooded canyon, and in another creek one drainage over, never far from the park boundary, seven leg traps had been discovered in the last few weeks. Each trap had had a red ribbon tied to the chain ring. It had baffled Ren and the other rangers. A taunt or a brag, who knew. A fisherman had reported the first, and after that Ren had made a point of fishing that stretch and scouting, and he had found the rest. In the silt of the creek at water's edge he had photographed a single boot print. Ren laid his Pilot pen next to the track before he took the picture. The foot was large—size fourteen, it turned out. How many trappers out of the handful in Cooke City had feet that big?

There had been other disturbing incursions. Outside of Mammoth, along Lava Creek, an enforcement ranger named Jim Lefevre had his tires slashed. Farther upstream, in plain view of the road, a nesting osprey had been blasted with a shotgun. A growing sense of organized harassment had begun to percolate slowly up the park's chain of command; but the chain of command did not at all like making a decision, especially one that carried a smidgen of political risk. And so the rangers' reports were tucked into a Review in Six Months file and ignored.

And then the note. A week ago, he had been fishing up Slough Creek, and he'd come back to his truck, and tucked under the wiper blade was a cash receipt from the general store in Cooke City. Someone that morning had bought ten dry flies for twenty-five dollars cash. It was folded in half, and Ren opened it, and on the back was scrawled in scratchy ballpoint a stick figure hanging from the inverted L of a gallows and in capital letters below it, each letter underlined, his name: *H-O-P-P-E-R.?*

Question mark after the period. A barb like an uncrimped hook. Ren on reflex took a step closer to the side of his truck, the protection of it. He looked down the line of seven pickups and SUVs still parked at the edge of the gravel road. Backpackers and fishermen, mostly. He glanced at the trail climbing steeply into the aspen. No one.

Tonight Ren wouldn't sleep much. He knew. The kettle would boil and whistle and he'd steep a chamomile and sit in the chair where the woman had listened to her husband lie. He'd let the buffeting wind from the open door chill his back, and then he'd get up and step onto the porch and let it truly freeze him. Until chest and hands were numb and he began to shake. And then he'd sing—"River in the Rain" or "Guantanamera"—just so he could listen to the hard quaver and chatter, and finally something clean and good would rise in his torso and warm it. "Stop whining," he would think. "This is fun." *Not whining.* "Well, you're something. This is the best place and one of the jobs you always wanted." He'd end the song with a loud "Brrrrrr" and body shake, then step inside and close the door and stretch out on the bunk in back and drift.

It was true. It was one of the jobs he'd always wanted. But then he'd been one of those kids who had wished he had a dozen lives to try out. Game warden had been one aspiration—among more conventional careers like cowboy, salvage diver, and founder of a new country—but when he landed the job with the NPS and was assigned to Yellowstone his fifth year, he had felt like he'd come home.

◖

Day broke nearly clear and washed clean. He slept in, which meant not being out in the dark, and he stepped onto the porch with his first cup of coffee just as the sun balanced on the black timber of Beartooth Pass and warmed the valley. Wolf Running Time. How he would think of it from now on. It was his day off. Must be a Tuesday, then, though out here he had to look at a calendar to know. He thought maybe Hilly would show up on her way through. He hoped she would.

Rich scents of wet earth, swollen creek water, rain-sweetened grass. Above him, mist spumed in tatters off the rocky cap of

Druid Peak, and off the wet black cliffs farther north. The sky looked scrubbed. The few clouds splayed like empty linens blown off a line. The gusting rain had torn leaves from the aspen across the creek and flecked the ground with yellow like a flight of songbirds just landed. Maybe the simile occurred to him because he could hear the meadowlark trilling what sounded like a glad song, an after-rain song. He was resident, Ren was pretty sure, his own cabin was in the bird's territory, and Ren had been hearing him improvise and embellish all summer and would miss him when he flew south in the next few weeks. Ren couldn't see the bird now, but at one of his caesuras he whistled a few responding bars and raised his cup. Did the glad singer pause a beat longer, as if trying to interpret his regular interloper? Ren always thought he did, and then the bird warbled on.

Still brisk, but he left the solid door open and stepped inside. He unhooked the skillet from over the gas range and scrambled eggs in an enamel bowl and poured them, hissing, onto a skim of clarified butter. No toaster, but he rolled the eggs onto a plate, pried two more fat chunks of butter from the plastic tub and into the pan, and laid two pieces of bread onto the *beurre noisette*. What his mother had called it. Twenty seconds a side, and he plucked out the ranch toast with two fingers, fetched a jar of huckleberry jam from the fridge, poured another cup of coffee, and carried it all out onto the porch. He sat in one of the two cane rockers, and used an upended wooden ammo-crate for a side table. It had been used to ship tranquilizer darts. Why the government sent a thousand rounds of darts at the beginning of every season, and why they came from Agriculture, he had no idea.

He ate. Three ravens flew over, just clearing the roof, and croaked a greeting. Below, over the broad meadow sloping to the river, he could see a harrier hunting, gliding just over the browse and hovering abruptly, wings beating—flushing mice, probably, or voles. And farther out, across the stream that now ran low and clear, over stones of a hundred colors, blues and greens and burnt reds, a herd of elk grazed, heads down. He knew the wolves would be watching them from the deep shadows at the edge of the woods.

Again the sense of the world working as it should. He tore off a piece of jam-covered toast and closed his eyes against a current of air moving down-valley. It came off the pass, night cold, and flowed downhill as the river did, and if he listened closely he thought he could hear it in the tallest grass. He breathed. He thought he could sit like this for the rest of his life. This time of day. He loved the stillness and awakening together. He fluttered open his eyes and used the toast to slide eggs onto his fork. Sipped the coffee. *What could be better than this?* What he often told himself, especially when he needed convincing. And he thought, not for the first time, that though there was no hour that held more stillness and peace, it was also when the hunters in all this country were most active. The night hunters might still kill, and the diurnal predators were just getting started. Wolf and meadowlark, lynx and harrier . . . and trout.

Trout. Did he want to fish today? Maybe. He might drive down to the confluence with the Yellowstone. The good fishing was a two-hour walk in. Or he might hike straight out the back of the cabin, over the flank of Druid and down into a creek that he never named, a stream so alive with green-gold cutthroat that the grizzlies fished it, too; or they swiped at the thickets of serviceberry that grew along the banks. When he fished there, he almost always encountered a bear. By now he knew that the big male with the scarred face was 631, the sow with two cubs 570.

When he saw her he would move fast away and fish another bend, but the battle-scarred boar was never bothered. Plenty of food for everyone. Ren had often fished a run while the huge grizzly foraged and dug on the slope above. Once, the two of them fished the same long riffle—Ren at the very bottom, where he knew he could beat a retreat around the corner.

He was tired, though. He felt hungover, though he had not drunk. He didn't want to get out of the chair. He would, in a sec, hoist himself up to get more coffee, but this morning he wanted to be in no hurry. Which meant that he would probably just drive a few miles down to Slough Creek and hike up to the second meadow, where he could fish into dark if he wanted; it was a good wide trail, and after nightfall he could find his way down by feel.

Ren always thought that planning a day was almost as good as spending one. Which meant he was in no hurry now. It had driven Lea crazy. She was his first and only wife. She ran a small nursery-and-landscape business in Denver, with a fiercely loyal clientele who loved her no-nonsense positivity and generous laugh as much as her work. Ren had thought about it often, and he concluded that one of the traits people adored in her was her literalness. That could always cut both ways, but in her it was endearing. When she said she and her crew would show up at seven and be done by noon, she meant it. When she thought your wild English garden looked slovenly and sad and you'd be better off with a few more parking spaces or a basketball court, she buttressed her impression with a "You know, a landscape, more than any other feature of a home, reflects the character of the owner." And if that stung, and you asked why, she would tell you that it was because it was evolving and aging just like you were, and how you handled it was how you handled yourself. God. Her candor could leave the more tender humans in tatters, but somehow it usually just made the clients love her more. She had no patience for hothouse flowers. Ren marveled. Well, he had loved that in her, too. As much because it was so much the opposite of the way he navigated the world—he who spent half his morning daydreaming, and who, among all the other aspirations, had wanted to be a writer. A writer of the wild, like Merwin or Dickey or even Conrad. Well. He was a bad poet, or at least unexceptional, which was pretty much the same thing. Poetry is like hunting, he thought: you either come home with the kill or you don't.

They had met in a coffee shop in his neighborhood in Northwest Denver. He was twenty-four, working a job at a brick-warehouse art gallery in the River North district, where his appreciation of art history was channeled into transporting sculptures and hanging pictures and repainting walls. Down at the gallery, they had been preparing to hang a new show by the well-known cowboy artist Maddie Caldwell. The show was a departure for her: most of the paintings, which were large, were of silos or empty landscapes. Empty of her usual subjects, which were mostly wranglers on horseback herding cattle through every kind of weather. These new pieces were insistently quiet. A quiet so pervasive it spilled into the gallery. The usual conceits of drama were wholly absent; there were no wheeling horses, or lowering storm, or driving wind, or even the flattering long light of early morning or late afternoon. The silos and barns and rail fencing stood above their own short shadows, the grass barely stirred, the hour felt no need to explain itself. Ren was transfixed. On a break, he would stand before one or another and feel the curious pull of an ecclesiastical silence. He wondered why a hugely successful artist—one who had delighted many and raked in the bucks with a dependable genre of nostalgic work—why she would make such a departure. What in her life had prompted it? He thought it her best work and wondered at that, too—that, in taking what seemed a step back, she had entered exciting new territory. And . . . how could that be? There were a billion paintings of barns in the world, and silos, too.

In any event, the gallery staff had been busting ass to hang the show before next Friday's opening, and they had nearly finished, and the owners had given everyone an afternoon off. Ren never had an afternoon off in the middle of the week, and so he walked up the hill to West Highlands with a book of short stories by Gogol, his favorite nineteenth-century Russian. His favorite because, of all the towering intellects of an intellectually top-heavy empire, Gogol carried his brilliance the most lightly and was the most brazenly satirical, and . . . he made Ren laugh.

He got a café au lait and sat at a table facing the window and was buried in his book when the door jingled and in walked a tall young woman in torn Carhartt work pants followed by two equally ragged minions who wore hand shears and Leathermans in leather holsters on their belts. Clearly a work crew of some kind. The tall girl took off her safari hat, and Ren, more curious about her just now than the comings and goings of Nevsky Prospect, saw high tanned cheeks smattered with freckles and smirched with mud, a strong jaw, and the forthright amber eyes of a husky. Her cotton work shirt was rolled to her elbows, and her forearms were grimed with dirt, and tendoned. She moved with the balance of someone very strong. Ren had not dated in many months, and suddenly he was more than intrigued. He knew his verbal pickup game was lame at best, and so he slid his napkin toward him and took a pen from the jacket hanging over the back of his chair and jotted his number. Beneath he wrote: "Wish I had the nerve to say Hi but I don't. BTW you have dirt all over your face. Ren."

As she passed his table he cleared his throat and said, "Excuse me." The husky eyes came around, fixed him, maybe mildly curious, maybe holding no expression at all.

Ren said, "Here." He held out the folded napkin, and she cocked her head barely, touched the tip of her tongue to the corner of her mouth as if she were reckoning how many yards of soil she'd need to cover a plot, and took it. No word exchanged. The crew got their coffees to go and left and she never looked back, not once. And so it was kind of a shock when his cell rang the next day with an unknown number. He was on a stepladder adjusting overhead spot lighting; he heard a woman's voice, clear, direct, but with a resonant raspy edge, say, "I'm having a glass at six tonight at the BookBar. I might not have dirt on my nose, so you might not recognize me." And she hung up.

That was Lea. He was already head over heels. He got to the bookstore/café/wine bar ten minutes early, and she walked in the door at six-zero-zero *en punto*. Also Lea. And she wore clean jeans and a clean button-down rolled to the elbows and her hair was brushed out, and as she scanned the room he noticed how broad her shoulders were. In truth, thinking back on it, he would have taken her hand and gone to the altar right then. How did he know? He knew.

Ren sipped the strong coffee and thought that he would give almost anything on earth to have her in the chair beside him now.

The memory was interrupted by the faintest click of stone.

His cabin was one of five that were built into a grove of Doug firs. His was at the bottom, at the edge of the clearing, and had the widest view across the valley. The largest was behind him, up the gravel drive, and had served as lodge and common dining area when the station was most active, in the late nineties, when wolves were first reintroduced. It was boarded up now, part of a package of deep cuts that had swept the National Parks across the country. Ren thought it was just another waste of resources in hand. Managed well, the lodge could have been thriving all summer and fall, hosting college groups and grad students studying ecology and wildlife management and, of course, wolves. It could have paid for itself and for a lot more, including, he thought, another resident ranger to help handle the swelling flow of tourists that poured into the valley. The other cabins were now empty except the one at the top, farthest up the creek. Hilly lived there. She had been a college intern when the first wolf pack was established in '95, and had gone on to study under Bob Ream at Missoula and Doug Smith at Michigan. She was now one of the country's most respected experts, and she held a professorship at the University of Montana but never taught, preferring instead to spend her time with four-leggeds and pursue research funded by grants.

And now she appeared at the corner of the porch, presto, and leaned her head around, asking for permission. Her thick black braid, threaded with silver, swung off her shoulder. She wore binoculars around her neck. He lifted his cup, summoned a smile. "Come up. I've got a pot on."

"Bad time?" Hilly said. She hovered, poised to move. Ren thought she was spring-loaded, like the wolves she studied. And, like them, she carried not an ounce extra. Her eyes were alight with green flecks, her high cheeks deeply burnished by years outside.

"No. Yes. But it's never a bad time to see you."

She didn't ask what the trouble was. He liked that about her. Because she loved wolves much, much more than people, her dealings with humans were pretty much on a need-to-know basis. He was already standing. "Black?" he said. She nodded. He opened the screen, stepped inside. She came up the steps without sound, as if she were weightless, and sat in the chair farthest from the door. She flexed her ankles and let it rock. Her eyes roved across the river and up the valley. Then she halted the chair, lifted her binoculars, slowed her breathing. As he came out again with the two full mugs, he thought that she held the exact poise of a hunter about to take a shot. But of course she wasn't. Her reason for being, entirely, was about protection. She *was* a remarkable markswoman, he knew—he had seen it and marveled—and it was with a bolt-action rifle modified to take a .30-caliber tranquilizer dart. If she wanted to tranq a wolf and get a radio collar on him, and she had to do it leaning out of a helicopter with her Remington, very few could elude her.

She laid the binoculars against her sternum. He handed her the coffee, sat.

"What do you see?"

"A new kill. Looks like a bison calf. Wanna see?"

He held up a hand. "I've had enough dead buffalo for a few days," he said.

She didn't ask. He had his job and she had hers.

"Are you going to bring in the man who killed my wolf?" she said.

My wolf. That was Hilly. "I'm going to try," he said. "Try hard."

"Thanks."

They sipped the coffee. Ren thought that whoever the poacher was might be lucky if Hilly didn't get to him first. Word going around Cooke City was that she had started bringing her rifle—the *un*modified one, the lethal Winchester that shot bullets, not darts—with her into the field, and not for grizzly protection. And an outfitter whose truck door advertised legal wolf and bear hunts in Montana had emerged from the Lamar Trailhead restroom to find two empty bottles of Karo syrup on his hood. The syrup had evidently been poured into his gas tank, because the truck would no longer start. When Ren had asked Hilly about it, she shrugged, eyes alight, and said, "Gosh, there's corn syrup in just about everything now."

Now the sun warmed the grass below the cabin, and the creek burbled. Ren felt no desire to move anywhere. Hilly said, "Your day off, right?"

"Yep. I was thinking about fishing."

"You're always thinking about fishing. Sometimes it makes me wonder about the state of your intellect."

"Well, wolves are always thinking about food, aren't they?"

She actually cracked a smile. A bona-fide grin. Her hazel eyes danced. "No, not always. Sometimes they think about fucking. And I wouldn't be surprised if once in a while they thought, *That ranger dude really stinks. He should stop using cucumber soap and Old Spice.*"

Ren choked on his laugh. He didn't get the mug down fast enough, and he spilled coffee all over his hand.

They sat side by side in the chairs and didn't discuss the weather or the surprising stream of post–Labor Day tourists. Most people would have, just to hear themselves talk. Nor did they range into gossip, which would have been easy, since the young host couple at the campground a few miles downriver was going through a difficult split. Robbie and Kelli were thirty-ish and from Tahoe, where they had sold their bakery to come to the wilds to host the Slough Creek Campground. One night recently, Robbie was making his late bedtime rounds—he joked with the guests about turn-down service—checking that everyone was okay and where they were supposed to be—when he discovered someone not at all where they should have been. He was passing Kyle's place. Kyle was a bearded wildlife guide for an elite tour company based in Jackson Hole who liked to spend the few days between groups camping at the creek. He was a mountain-man devotee. Whenever he met anyone new, Kyle inserted into the conversation that he was born two hundred years too late. That he would have been more comfortable in elk hide than Gore-Tex. Robbie thought that, for a mountain man, Kyle had a very slick mini Airstream trailer with heater and shower. And Robbie grew nervous whenever Kyle pulled up in his truck, elbow out the window, and regaled them with stories of his latest face-to-face encounter with a bear. Robbie concluded—after later hearing some of the tales confirmed by people who were there—that Kyle probably never lied, and he actually had deep knowledge of birds and plants, as well as the charismatic megafauna popular with park visitors. And he was the only person Robbie knew to get a close-up photo of one of the few mountain lions in the park. What made Robbie nervous was how Kelli shone whenever Kyle swung by, how she would set down her clipboard mid-check-in with a new guest and come to the truck. How she laughed at almost everything Kyle said. Well. That night, Robbie was making his turn-down service rounds and, through the gap of a hastily drawn curtain in Kyle's trailer, he spied Kelli unbuttoning the guide's shirt. That was all. No *in flagrante delicto* or *coitus interruptus,* no *fellatio.* No Latin involved, no nudity, just that simple act. But in the way she touched him, the way she spread her hand on his chest before undoing the next button, and the tenderness and lust in her eyes, which Robbie could see even in the frugal light of the LED over the sink—the image was more painful somehow than if they had been engaged in anything more vigorous and banal. "I mean," Robbie cried, "you could almost expect *that* from a young person cooped up in a sixteen-site campground in the middle of nowhere for five months."

Robbie had related all this to Hilly. He had found her one afternoon at her tripod and spotting scope in the first meadow, two miles up the creek. He talked, then gushed. He spilled everything, maybe because she never lifted her eye from the scope and because he knew she didn't care a whit about anything he was saying. And because he was young. He would have forgiven Kelli, probably—they were churchgoing Christians, it was how they had met—but when he confronted her, she had declared her intention to leave him for Kyle. "Well, he's big and handsome and knows a lot about everything," he said to Hilly, and slumped heavily on a rock. "Also, he says he belongs to some club of millionaire ranchers. Go figure. Me, I'm just me. I guess Kelli is bored."

Hilly withdrew herself from the eyepiece and turned. "How can you guys feel cooped up out here?" she said with a sweep of her arm. "Do you really think this is the middle of nowhere? This is the middle of *everything*."

Robbie stared at her as if she were clinically insane, probably dangerous. She softened. "I'm sorry, Robbie. It hurts, huh? You know, the legendary female o6—I'm talking about a wolf—she had two mates. Two brothers. It could work. Or you might tell Kelli you'd like to take a break, too, tell her you understand it's a bit . . ." Hilly hesitated, looked around the Slough Creek Valley as if asking its forgiveness. "Maybe it feels a bit claustrophobic. And when she's done playing around with John Colter, Jr., who, BTW, to my mind is a mega-sized fuckwit, she can come talk to you about renewing her vows. Just a thought."

Something snagged in Robbie's grief-torn mind; she saw it. Some kind of bafflement and relief. She smiled. "My hunch is, she comes back," Hilly said, and returned to her scope.

She had related all this to Ren last week, but only to say that if Robbie seemed less than his enthusiastic goofy self, this was why. And they only talked about it once. They did not indulge in *Schadenfreude* or gossip, because there was enough pain in the world. One night about a month before, Ren had heard her truck in the turnaround below and he came out with two cold beers. When he met her on the path, he could see the streaks on her face. She had been crying.

"You okay?" he said.

"Oh, yeah," she said with conviction. And then she told him how she had just witnessed a male from a rival pack slay an entire litter of pups. She was close enough to hear the yowls and frenzied barks of the mother, who was trying to defend her young, and whom he had almost killed, too. She took the beer, held it up, clinked his bottle. "To life," she said. "One part wonder, three parts pain."

Now Hilly sipped her coffee and followed the transit of a fox along a berm on the far side of the river and said, "Edgar's back."

"Yeah?"

"Yep. He went viral again."

"Oh, no."

"If you go up the creek today you might see him." She dug into the pocket of her cargo pants and pulled out a phone. She tapped it and handed it to Ren. The video began with a wide trail through yellow aspen and the sound of heavy breathing. Then a woman's panicked voice: "Oh, shit, here he comes. He's *running*. He's *charging*. Oh *God*." Jerky picture, and here, around the bend, comes Edgar, trotting. A two-year-old black bear, small and so plump that most of his parts are round—even, it seemed, his legs. Trundling toward the freaked-out hiker in what is clearly a genial amble—no change in pace at all, no alarmed lifting of the head—a bear fairly used to intruders and heading from A to B, minding his own business, and using the good trail as anyone would. More jostle and panic from the filmer, and then the unexpected hand in the picture, holding the can of bear spray, and then, when Edgar is maybe twenty feet off, a yell and the audible hiss and jet of pepper: Edgar's head jerked, his whole body shied sideways, he gave a cry like a human child, startled. Ren knew it was always a mistake to anthropomorphize a wild animal, but he couldn't help it. Edgar flinched back and whimpered and ran off into the trees as if more than his eyes stung.

He handed back the phone. "Well, that was dumb. Why didn't she just step off the trail?"

Hilly shrugged. " 'Cuz it's more fun to post something dramatic on TikTok?"

Ren stood. "More coffee?" he said.

"No, I'm good. Thanks. Catch you on the flip." She handed him her cup, and tripped off the porch as lightly as she'd come.

And Ren almost reluctantly started his day. The part where he didn't just sit and listen to the wind rushing in the pines and think again how sometimes it sounded like surf, how the ticking of the aspen leaves in the same wind was prettier than chimes. He knew himself: how he loved to hold time in abeyance, or try. He never could, of course, because time, like everything else, flowed through his cupped fingers like water, and he knew he could rarely stave off anything that was already in motion.

He made a sandwich with thick slices of cheddar and the last of the roast beef and wrapped it in a produce bag from the grocery store in Gardiner, thirty-five miles away. He disciplined himself to go every other Wednesday, and sometimes on day ten or eleven he'd begin to keep the trout he caught. There was no limit on rainbows or browns or any other non-native fish, and, in fact, anglers were supposed to kill any they pulled in. They were invasive. So, every couple of weeks, when his provisions got thin, he ate trout. Now he filled a stainless two-liter water bottle at the sink, and took a fresh can of Copenhagen out of the freezer drawer below the fridge. He packed his vest, waders, boots, and rod in an old Lowe rucksack, checked again that he had bear spray, and headed out the door. Halfway to the steps he stopped, turned back. He snagged his badge off the table and retrieved the .45 automatic handgun from its hiding place behind the fridge. He swung down the pack and slipped them into the top zippered pocket. He was required to carry them even on his days off.

(

He drove. Down the gravel drive to the paved park highway, which was more like a country lane. It was narrow and winding, with no shoulder and regular turnouts, designed to encourage drivers to go slowly but not just pull off anywhere. It didn't work. The sportier visitors, who had places to be, became impatient with theme-park speed and treated the sinuous, smooth track like Le Mans. Ren wondered why they had come to the park in the first place, or even gone on vacation. They gunned past lines of three or four creeping cars, or tried to, and killed themselves with great efficiency on a regular basis. When they lived, and were *compos* enough to speak, he often found out that they had a bucket list of sights to tick off and had only eight days of vacation and were understandably in a hurry. Productivity over time. If that's what fifty weeks a year demanded, it made perfect sense that one would approach the remaining two in the same way.

The pavement of the park roads was built up in most places a good eight inches off the sloping grade, sometimes more, and when gawkers tried to pull halfway off to take a picture of a swan or a marmot they might scrape their mufflers from the undercarriage, or simply get stuck. The wrong vehicle might just tip over. The ever-popular tall and boxy Sprinter vans were the best candidates. Pete from Cooke City did a roaring business in hauling them back to their feet and cutting temporary plexiglass windows to replace the ones that had been broken so that the grateful campers could continue their tour.

But no road engineer with a zest for social control could keep drivers from simply stopping in the middle of the highway. A herd of buffalo trying to cross was the best. Traffic might back up half a mile from Specimen Ridge in both directions while visitors parked themselves square in their lane, opened doors, and attempted to get gored while taking selfies. The bison huffed and snorted and wherever there was a gap they crossed between the cars. A festive, circuslike atmosphere, unless you were trying to get across the park for your bimonthly groceries in Gardiner, or transport a perp to the police station in Cody. In any other jurisdiction in the Lower Forty-eight, the drive from his cabin to Gardiner would take an hour and a half, even at forty MPH, but if it was daylight—light enough to see a marmot— Ren always added an extra hour.

He rolled out of the Lamar station driveway and onto the pavement and turned right and followed the river downstream. Grassy bottomland here, with broad meadows climbing into the spruce forests on either side of the river, and islands of aspen on the open slopes, their canopies shimmering gold in the sunrise wind and loosing flurries of yellow leaves. Higher up were rimrock outcrops and the wooded ridgelines and a hard featureless sky. And the river itself, on his left, running low through the gravel bars and cut banks, lens clear over beds of colored stones. He could bitch all he wanted, but in truth he could drive this stretch of road every day for the rest of his life.

He slowed and rounded the last tight bend that led into a narrow granite canyon, and stopped. He pulled over, two wheels on pavement, and got out. Across the river, in a wide swale, were maybe two hundred buffalo, heads down and grazing. They spread like a cloud shadow across the depression between the humps of grassy hills. But that's not what caught his attention. He lifted his binocs from the passenger seat and focused. Moving toward the herd from upstream was a line of wolves. They came at an easy lope—not running, as they had been the other morning, but at a determined trot, single file, contouring along the hillside. Ren slowed his breath, held the binoculars as still as he could. He counted twenty-one, all adults. Before they got to the muscular hump of meadow that looked down on the herd, they slowed and bunched and gathered. Four broke away—two blacks, a big fawn, and a gray—and continued to a rock outcrop with a view of the bison. They did not crouch. They stood tall, with the downstream breeze ruffling against the grain of their fur and carrying their scent to the grazers. Ren thought that in their proud stance on the bluff they looked like four generals planning the strategy for an assault. They probably were. And now everything began to move. Not hurriedly, but the way clouds merge and spread when there's little wind. The mass of dark bison coalesced, the outer edges drifting inward, and it was as if there were currents of movement within the swarm, a stream of animals flowing into a tighter bunch closer to the river. Ren saw that these were mothers with their calves. And as the herd moved, the wolves came on, as if on some signal. The four scouts hopped off the ledge to grass and the pack followed, no one in any hurry, lined out across the slope and maybe fifteen yards above the throng. Animal to animal, the wolves looked agile and small and valiant. And then Ren saw something he'd never seen: as the file of wolves made to flank the herd, four massive bull buffalo broke out of its upper edge and challenged them. It looked to Ren coordinated, almost like a drill team—the humped and shaggy bison, with their massive heads and lethal horns, stepped up at the same time, almost evenly spaced along the flank. It was a bias, Ren knew, to give the IQ points to the predators. And as the lead wolf neared the first guard, the bull dropped his head and lunged and swung his horns, and the gray shied and feinted higher, and the wolves strung across.

All the way across. They would have their eyes and noses on the huddle of calves farther down, but the risks, just now, were climbing. They loped and stayed well clear of the huge bulls and convened again on the hump of the next spur. They gathered all together and turned to survey what seemed now an enemy army, and Ren thought they were discussing it; and then, on no signal he could see, they all swung downstream and went on. Over the hill, away from the rising sun.

He lowered the binoculars and breathed. He was moved. Not sure why, except that what he'd just seen seemed an ancient dance, enacted probably for millennia. Hilly had told him once that a wolf's failure rate on a hunt was 85 to 95 percent. He didn't know whether to laugh or to cry. He felt a little like doing both. And he never knew who to root for.

He drove on downriver. Entered the tight little canyon. The current spilled through boulders that gleamed in the long light, and he came out the other side into open country again and could see the turnoff for Slough Creek up ahead. Slowly, through the loginess, and a hangover from the events of last night, he could feel his blood rising. He was going fishing.

Chapter Two

It was his mother who had taught him. She had grown up fly fishing with her father in the Adirondacks and Michigan's Upper Peninsula, and her love for the pastime was as much about connecting to her old man and maybe her youth as it was about catching fish. What it seemed to Ren. Because as soon as she stepped into a river or brook—no, before: as soon as she neared the bank and could hear the current, as soon as she unhooked the fly and began, as she walked, to strip line from the reel—she was at home. Her movements were fluid, her eyes brighter, her body was quicker. And she grew. He thought later how magic it was; his mother was petite by the yardstick, and elegant, but, knee-deep in a stream, she was neither. Elegance carries a social aspect. She shed it. It was as if Laura Hopper were freeing herself from the encumbrances of gender and age, and channeling something more primitive and essential, which might have simply been her own childhood. He knew how much she had loved her father and the places they had gone, and he could see as she fished that the love fueled her. She became as devoted and single-minded as a warrior. Sometimes he leaned his rod against the limb of a willow and just watched. And marveled that love could foster such grace. He supposed there never was one without the other.

Did he love to fish in the same way? No. There had been some hard years between his mother and him. He did not invite her to the wedding, and when Lea died she showed up at the service unannounced, which somehow doubled his grief. And so now he thought he fished in spite of her. Or to remember, in the way movement and muscles remember, a time when he held no grievances and seemed to love all things.

◖

He turned onto the side road and waved at Tenner, who was rolling a mop bucket out of the single-pit restroom at the pull-out. Tenner lived in Cooke City and was the happiest mainte-nance man on earth and looked most like Santa Claus. He had a flowing white beard and a round belly and twinkling bloodshot eyes. When he put on his wire-rimmed granny glasses to read a work order or supply list, Ren conjured elves, a sleigh, reindeer, a Mrs. Claus. There was a Mrs. Claus, but she did not wear a bonnet. Sandra ran a bar in Cooke City called the Crooked Moose and wore short shorts even in winter, and had a jade-green python running down the side of her neck and into her snug sweater. No drunks, not even bikers, gave her shit when she politely asked them to leave.

Tenner adored his wife and his job—which allowed him flex-time to go fishing as long as he got his restrooms cleaned—and so he was generally in a good mood. Ren pulled off. His window was already down. Tenner leaned the mop handle against his own tailgate and walked to Ren's truck. "Did you stop to give me a dip?"

"Yep." No. He stopped because Tenner made any day better. The man was congenitally generous. When Ren's old black Lab, Carl, had died last March, Tenner showed up at Ren's cabin with a loaf of banana bread Sandra had fashioned with ears and a tail and a dog collar, and he also carried a fifth of mezcal, which the two finished. Tenner had slept on Ren's bed, because Ren would not let him drive home, and Ren had slept on the porch in his sleeping bag, because Tenner's contented snores vibrated the floorboards. That was the last of dogs for Ren: the word from HQ was no more staff pets at remote housing inside the park.

Ren snagged the tin of Copenhagen out of his breast pocket and handed it out the window. Tenner peeled off a blue rubber glove and shoveled about a fifth of the tin into his mouth. When he got it all tamped into his upper lip and handed the tin back and spat once, a perfect dark jet, he said, "I swore to Sandy I'd never buy another can. So I depend on you, you know."

"Awesome responsibility," Ren said.

Tenner half turned and looked up the dirt road that hugged the creek through slow flats to the parking area. From there a good trail climbed the stream into the mountains. "Should be good today," he said. "No moon, and I've already seen a couple of hatches. It's like they get stirred up by the storm."

"Wanna come?"

"Ha. I got a late start. Where're you going?"

"Secret."

Tenner grinned. He knew exactly what that meant: Ren would hike to the first meadow and, instead of climbing higher, he would walk back downstream and follow the creek as it dropped away from the trail and enter a short rock canyon. Nobody fished there, because the going was hard against the rock walls, and the pools were deep and difficult to wade. Also, it was remote. Tenner had stopped fishing the stretch when he was in his thirties; somehow, as he got older, the slab rocks at the base of the wall got slicker. He could easily imagine losing his balance along the bank and, well, drowning.

"'Kay, be careful," he said.

"You seen Edgar?" Ren asked.

"Nope, he's staying up in the woods, where he belongs. Plus, he got his feelings hurt yesterday."

"I saw it."

"I'm just scratching my head half the time."

Ren waggled thumb and pinkie, *hang loose,* and restarted the truck. "Hey to Sandy," he said.

"You should go up there and see her and Lauren this evening. You need to get out more."

"I might," Ren said, and pulled away.

❧

He fished. All day. Not in the canyon, but out in the broad meadow, whose grass had turned tawny and was crisscrossed

with the trampled paths of single browsing buffalo and pock-
eted with beaten patches where they had lain. They would
be the lone bulls, wandering up this high, unassailable and
unafraid. Ren had seen them much higher. Once, he had stumbled on one grazing among the rocks above tree line. Here in
the meadow were signs of elk, too. He could smell their particular musk and see where they had tracked the thick grass
in a small herd and left piles of droppings. He walked across
open ground. The creek twisted through it, taking its time on
this wide bench. In the afternoon, he was sure he would share
it with other fishers, but now, so early, he had it to himself. He
walked to the bleached carcass of a single black cottonwood that
had been toppled by storm or flood. It lay parallel to the bank
with one broken limb gesturing over the water. *Fish here*. Ren
liked to use it as his seat. He dropped the pack and straightened
and stretched and looked upstream. At the top of the meadow
the creek flowed out of a rocky cut, and beyond it were pine and
spruce woods and ranks of climbing hills, and beyond them, in
a blue distance, the rugged ramparts of the Absarokas. Some
of the most rugged and remote country in the U.S. outside of
Alaska. He liked to fish here despite the scattering of others
who often came, because he could look up from casting and see
those mountains and feel their wildness leaning into him.

He took out the canister of his water bottle and drank, and dug
out a Clif Bar and ate it. Peanut butter, pretty good. He sat on the
smooth toppled trunk and pulled on waders and boots. Buckled
the webbing safety belt that would prevent his waders from filling if he slipped in deep water. Other fishers had taken to shoulder bags or waist packs, but he still liked to use a fishing vest,
so he shrugged into it. Then he slid his four-weight rod from
its tube and unwrapped it from the flannel cloth and pieced it
together. He tightened the reel to its seat with the locknut, and
strung the line through the rod guides, straightened the leader,

tied on fresh tippet and a single beadhead prince nymph. No strike indicator. He slipped the handle of the net into the belt at his back. Then he sucked in a long draft of air, more invocation than breath, and hopped off the eroded soilbank onto a gravel bar and waded in and began to cast.

Nobody he'd ever heard of fished a beadhead prince the way he did. The weighted fly was made to roll along the bottom and imitate a blue-winged olive or caddis in its nymph stage. Easy pickings for a hungry fish. But the cutthroat trout in this creek, especially here, had seen every fly known to man, and they were discerning and mostly unimpressed and seemed to have a sense of humor. He could watch them rise in smooth, dark water, the rings dapping like rain, and they would hit the hatching insects. Ren would have in his fly box the perfect match, size and pattern, which he would throw. And the trout would ignore it and feed around his floating dry fly, often inches away. Seemed like a taunt. He would swap flies, trying stimulators, attractors. He would retie and tie again, casting eight, nine dry flies in a row. If a trout could laugh. He would switch to a nymph, roll it along the bottom. A leech. A streamer that he would strip in like a wounded minnow. And then, one night, in desperation, he tightened up the line to his tiny prince and began to twitch it, retrieving it slowly, and—*wham!*—a strong tug, the rod bending, and a fish on. He started catching trout. He wasn't really sure what he was mimicking, and maybe the fish weren't either. It was goofy. He thought maybe they hit the thing because it was so outrageous it pissed them off; they couldn't help themselves.

So now he went straight for his tried-and-true and had a cutbow on with the second cast.

He fished. Slow water here, nearly black in the deeper pools and slipping over lighter gravel in the shallows. The sun warmed his back, and the wind stirred downstream. A hatch of may-flies drifted off the water, out of the shadow of the bank, and sparked softly in sunlight. He closed his eyes. He could smell the warming grass, bison manure, the tang of pines; water and cold stones. And hear the lip of current, the rattle of a grasshop-per. He cast again, waded a step, looked upstream, and noticed for the first time that Cutoff Mountain had a fresh dusting of snow above tree line. He caught fish in an irregular rhythm, brought them in patiently, netted the larger cutthroat, slipped the barbless hook out easily, and released them. He switched flies to a floating ant and caught more. Sometimes, if the fish was exhausted, he held it gently into the current with a lightly cupped hand and let the gills work, and let it rest until it wriggled free and lost itself in the shadows of the stones. He lost himself, too. Who knew how long he fished. He didn't keep track—not of the path of the sun or how many fish; or of the quiet elation. He forgot the conversations of the morning, the night before, forgot even his name or that he should own one. Why should he? For a while he was movement only, and sensation, and a circle of awareness that encompassed the ridges, the mountain, the meadow, and in which his own distinction vanished.

Is that what he wished for after all? To vanish? Maybe everyone did. He would think later that the sensation was the closest thing to becoming pure spirit. Which, oddly, brought a sense of fullness and relief. Why, then, did we fight death so hard?

But now he thought of almost nothing except how not to spook the large cutthroat he could see idling in quiet water beneath a riffle, just off the safety of an undercut bank.

He fished and the day dwindled, and by the time the sun went over the ridge across the little valley he realized he was cold and thirsty and hadn't had a sip of water or a bite of anything but the Clif bar all day. Nor had he seen another fisher. He waded onto gravel, hooked the fly to the keeper, found a notch in the chest-high wall of bank, and clambered out. He walked back to his pack and the log and sat on it. Pried off boots, tugged off waders and damp wool socks, and enjoyed feeling the chill breeze on his bare feet. He was in no hurry, still. Even when darkness came, the pale meadow would be luminous, as if lit from within, and the trail at the edge of it was wide and smooth. Trace of a moon if any, but there would be stars, and they would cast a wan light. He'd have no trouble finding his way down. Also, he had a headlamp.

He was thinking that and chewing on his second power bar when he saw movement at the bottom of the clearing. It was on the trail where it emerged from the woods, a black shape moving fast. His compact binocs were in the top pocket of the pack with badge and gun, and he pulled them out and followed the shape with naked eyes and brought up the field glasses. Edgar. The little bear was hauling ass, straight up the trail. Why? Then Ren heard the single bay, a rising bark cut short. He slid the binocs back along the trail and saw the dog, a blond figure, big, weighing probably as much as the bear and in full charge. It was a massive male golden retriever, maybe seventy yards behind Edgar but closing. Fuck a duck. He swung the binocs farther to his right and saw the third figure, a large man stepping out of the trees.

The man carried a rifle. At three hundred yards, Ren could see it was a bolt-action with scope. He slung the binoculars, grabbed his handgun from the open pocket, and ran. Not to the man but across the grass on a straight diagonal to the top of the meadow. He might not beat the dog, but he'd be close. He sprinted. Dodged the dried patches of rabbitbrush, jumped over a tuft of sage, nearly buckled and fell in a hidden dip, recovered, lungs burning. A sprint he could not sustain, but he needed only a little longer. He was less than seventy yards from the bear, who normally would have registered him and swerved into the trees, but Edgar was running for his life, his rounded limbs moving with a surprising speed of terror; the dog had closed to thirty yards. Ren could see the bulky collar now, probably a shock collar, why the bark was cut short. Whatever the man was doing, he didn't want it advertised. Ren thought it all in a flash as he stopped abruptly and raised the SIG in a shooting stance with both hands and fired. He meant to shoot just ahead of the dog; he let his hands swing and led it like a running elk—if it didn't work, the next shot would be in the body mass.

A yelp and cry and the dog tumbled and fell over. And then scrambled to his feet, howled in a high whine that again cut short, and stood in the trail shaking. Ren could see now a leash trailing from his collar. He let out a long breath of relief. He managed to turn his head in time to see Edgar flow up the trail and disappear into trees. Phew. He guessed a stone had ricocheted with the shot into the dog's chest or head. Now he trotted toward it. So did the man. Ren looked back down the trail and saw him coming, hitching along with a swinging limp, no rifle now. He recognized the man, thought he did; he had seen him in Cooke City and remembered him from a photo . . .

When he was within earshot, the man slowed to a walk. He was big, barrel-chested, and he had huge feet—like size fourteen. He looked from Ren to the trembling retriever, who was rooted to the ground. "Come," the man said. The dog looked back. Did

Ren see fear in his eyes? The golden came. Gingerly, it walked, as if testing each step, and then it loped, leash dragging, to its master and sat at his feet. One huge hand came to the dog's neck, felt in the fur for blood, then down to shoulders, chest.

"What'd you do to my dog?" the man snarled. Heavy face, hard jaw, mussed black hair, no cap. Deep tan couldn't cover the broken veins of a drinker on cheeks and nose. Had to be Les Ingraham.

Ren had no patience now for the brazen bullshit of a poacher. "What were you doing running bear?"

"I never ran bear in my life."

Ren met the man's eyes. They were muddy and hard, staring back with impudence and no remorse and zero fear.

"Dog off leash. Dog in the backcountry. Both illegal."

"I had him down in the parking lot. Totally legal. He yanked away from me and ran."

"You chased him all the way up here."

"Yep."

"He seems extremely well trained to me, especially with the shock collar."

"He gets randy; sometimes he needs a tug on the reins."

Ren was thinking the same thing about the man. "Where's the rifle?" he said.

"What rifle? Anyway, if I had one, that's legal, too."

"*Anyway,* when I find it, I'm keeping it, along with a bunch of traps I found last week along Soda Butte."

The man's eyes didn't waver. "Suit yourself," he said. "If I had a gun, it'd be a Ruger American bought used—say a hundred fifty dollars—with a thirty-dollar scope. Merry fucking Christmas."

Ren felt the checked grip of the SIG in his right hand. He had not tucked it away anywhere, like into his belt. He wanted, in every cell, to raise the gun and shoot the man point-blank and leave him for the coyotes and crows.

"You have ID?" Ren said.

"ID?" Now the man's mouth twisted into a smile. "Who the fuck do you think you are?"

Ren looked down at his chest. The badge on its lanyard was not there. He'd left it in the pack. Crap. But he guessed that the man knew damn well who he was. He was screwing with him every which way.

Ren said, "My name is Officer Hopper. And you know who the fuck I am." And he must have. Because this guy and he had been at the Crooked Moose at the same time more than a few nights. "I'm an enforcement ranger with the National Park Service. Next time I catch you pulling shit like this, we might forget about the regs."

"Whoaaa . . ." the man said, in mock awe. "Off duty and off the books, *damn*. Well, Ranger Rick, no badge, no uniform, I don't fucking believe you. But if you were some Dudley Do-Right, you might be friends with the little cunt who studies wolves. Who should watch her step. Just saying. Have a nice day."

And the man turned his back on Ren and walked back down the trail, the dog heeling with perfect obedience at the end of a six-foot leash.

Ren needed a drink. Not the alcohol so much, though that would be nice about now—the warmth of a shot blooming in throat and chest, the cold effervescent sluice of a beer-back. All good. But more than that he wanted to hear loud music over crappy speakers and the cluck of racked pool balls, and, even more, Sandra's guffaw and her unmodulated "No shit? That is seriously *regal*," as she cocked her head at some BS'ing customer and dunked a beer glass in Cloroxed water and pulled the cock of the Corona tap at nearly the same time; and then see her big smile when she registered his entrance, and watch her bite back the old booming "Ranger Ren! Law of the Wild!" which she learned that he hated and that made him shy. Lately, she just beamed and winked and pulled the Knob Creek off the shelf behind her.

He wanted all of it because his quiet day off had not gone as planned. After the man walked away and Ren restrained himself from shooting him in the back, he collected his rod and pack from the broken tree. *Why?* he asked himself. *Why would a poacher want to kill a little black bear? In the park?* Because Edgar was easy pickings, he decided. Everyone knew where to find him. And because the black market for bear gallbladders was hot. Chinese buyers actually traveled to the States to buy them for use in traditional medicine. Last May, Fish and Wildlife had conducted a seminar in Mammoth for enforcement rangers on the illegal international trade in wildlife and wildlife parts, with a focus on species in the Greater Yellowstone Ecosystem. It had shocked Ren, and sickened him.

Les Ingraham had been on the park's radar. Ren had seen his photo once, during an investigation of elk poaching. And he had seen him in town, he was sure. He'd heard the stories— drinkers at the Crooked Moose loved to spin out the details. Les was huge, maybe six foot five, and his claim to fame was that he had played linebacker at Missoula. He had a mean streak, but there was no better trapper or hunter anywhere.

Now dusk was thickening. Ren could see two stars high in a luminous blue, and the temperature was dropping. In the gathering dark, he walked down to the edge of the trees and searched for the rifle. He knew he'd never find it. Les would have covered it hastily in leaves and duff, and tomorrow he'd be back to retrieve it. Nothing illegal in having it in the park anyway as long as it wasn't fired; it was just that, together with the bear and the dog, it painted a picture that might aggravate a judge.

Ren snugged the shoulder straps on his pack and hiked out under a bowl of sky that held the last light very high. He concentrated on the faint windings of the trail, and on his footing, and when he looked up again, the night was suffused with stars.

Chapter Three

The Crooked Moose was packed. Approaching nine on a week-night, and it seemed the visiting fishermen, the fall tourists, the well-to-do wolf watchers from Jackson Hole, the road workers at the Super 8—all were there. Along with Jim and Carol from the general store and Kaylee from Pilot's Perk—who had just finished inventory and payroll, respectively—and 70 percent of the town's twenty-somethings, and a whole bunch of the thirty- and forty-somethings, and a few octogenarian stalwarts bravely representing . . . they were all packed in, competing in overloud conversation with the clatter of pool balls, the clamor of beer glasses hitting varnished wood, and the vintage jukebox playing a vertiginous mix of Bonnie Raitt, Luis Fonsi, and Walker Hayes. Perfect. Half the drinkers were standing in bunched groups and were just happy to be out of the wind. The clear night had turned cold, and an exuberant gale—wind without clouds—poured out of the Beartooths and shook the windows and eaves.

Ren made his way through the crowd, nodded at Kaylee from the café and her Kiwi boyfriend, Roy, smiled at Lena the Bulgarian waitress from the Polish restaurant, fist-bumped Lucas, who fixed his truck, and squeezed into a spot between stools at the bar. Lauren, Sandra's top bartender and all-around lieutenant, finished pouring the sixth shot on a round cork-bottom tray, which was whisked out of sight by the server, and pivoted, ponytail swinging, and caught sight of Ren mid-spin, so she grabbed the bourbon off the shelf as she replaced the tequila. She was filling the shot glass in front of him before it even hit the bar. She had a rhythm and it was a dance, and she never slowed or paused, and she managed to say, "Hi, Ren! Somebody bite you in the ass?," which made him laugh. He needed to laugh. It was why he still had wet waders in his truck, and had driven straight past his cabin in the dark and on into town. Just what he needed. Lauren held up a finger to a fisherman yelling for a pitcher, and drew Ren a glass of IPA and slid it over.

"Thanks. Where's Sandy?" Ren said. He almost had to shout.

Lauren lifted her chin. "Somewhere out in that mess. She's serving with Sybil. If I never see her again I'll call the state police. Or the rangers." Her brown eyes sparked, and she touched his hand. Ren felt the heat in his face, and he hadn't even drunk the shot. "Hey!" she yelled at the gesturing fisherman. "I *told* you. Be patient or you get milk!" And she was gone.

Ren breathed. His pulse was running exactly as it did when he felt the first hard tug on the nymph. *Go figure,* he thought. *I do need to get out more.* And then he tossed back the Knob Creek and the hot current ran into his chest and he heard Tracy Lawrence on the jukebox ask the artist to paint him a front porch, make it early spring, and on the swing a girl in a calico dress, and Ren was surprised by a rush of grief, which he blinked away.

Someone bumped his shoulder turning on a stool, and as the man stood, another slid onto the seat.

"Heya." It was Pete. Reliable Pete. The one whom Ren had called the other night to come take away the buffalo. Pete wore his perennial grease-stained Carhartt, which might hide his thin frame but not the animation and humor in the man. He said, "Doesn't anyone here have a job?"

"What I was wondering. What're you drinking?"

"Sprite. Someone has to wake up with a clear head."

"How's Aliya?"

"Shot her first grouse yesterday. Two. Boom-boom. Flushed and going different directions. What a natural. It was like the twenty-gauge did it for her and she just stood there amazed." Ren clinked his glass. "Thanks for the meat last night," Pete said.

"Was that just last night? Jesus."

"More fun today?"

"Yep. Ran into a guy running a black bear up Slough Creek. Dog and a gun."

"Edgar. Jesus. They oughta leave that little dude alone. He's going to need all kinds of therapy."

Ren laughed. Pete had a twisted take on everything; Pop would have said he was pixilated.

Pete pinched the brim of his Diesel Cat cap, which Ren noticed he did to ward off evil or gather strength for a big decision. It was like a rosary he wore on his head. "Did you arrest him? Guess not, I would've heard."

"Couldn't."

Pete sipped his soda and searched Ren's face. "He had a big fat story, huh? Watertight enough."

"Yep."

"Big guy?"

"Yep."

"Had a dog, you said?"

"Yep." Ren felt like he was playing Twenty Questions.

"Golden retriever?"

Now Ren swiveled on the stool.

Pete pinched his hat brim. "Was it Les Ingraham?"

"I guess. Had to be."

Now Pete was perplexed. "Didn't you ask him?"

"Day off. I didn't have my badge, I couldn't demand it. When push comes to shove."

Pete took a swig of beer. "With that guy, push will always come to shove. You can bet on it. I better get you another beer. Wanna hear a story?"

Ren wasn't sure that he did, but he nodded.

Pete took a long swig, set both forearms on the edge of the bar, leaned into them, and turned to Ren. He said, "Les was a genius."

"What?"

"That's what they say. Maybe that's a little strong, but he was crazy about math. Top of his class in Butte, every year. I mean, valedictorian."

"How do you know?"

A big unshaven guy in a Patriots knit hat jostled Pete as he squeezed onto a stool. Pete readjusted and continued. "My sister-in-law dated his roommate at Missoula."

"No shit."

"Yah. So he was recruited for football, but he enjoyed classes, go figure, and was just a monster on the field. Coulda gone pro, what they say."

"What happened?"

The Patriots fan on the other side of Pete stood off his stool and waved a hand, almost blocked Lauren as she passed. She veered around him, left him blinking. She leaned into Ren, said in his ear, "This guy is driving me nuts. Thinks he owns the place. Calls me Lala. *Whoo.*" She shuddered. And was gone. Ren noticed that on her way back down the bar she veered again and did not acknowledge the guy or take his order. Good for her.

Ren turned back to Pete. "Sorry. You were saying Les coulda gone pro."

"Yah, but then there was an accident. Junior year. A bad hit in the showdown with Montana State and he broke his back."

"Jesus."

"Yah." The big man to Pete's right turned away on his stool and knocked Pete again. Pete squeezed the brim of his cap, said, "Don't mind me. Jeez." Turned back to Ren. Ren noticed with affection that Pete wasn't really bothered, that his essential good nature was much stronger than his pride.

"Oh, yeah, I was saying," Pete continued. "For months he couldn't feel his legs. Then a year of painful therapy. He walked again, learned to run, slow. Kind of a miracle. But he was broken."

Lauren breezed by and clapped down two more glasses of draft beer and was gone. The beer brimmed and ran down the glasses and puddled on the bar. The two men sat up straight and clinked glasses, and Pete resumed. He told Ren how Les had gotten an undisclosed settlement from the U, drew disability, moved to Cooke City, and got serious about killing animals and drinking. He ran traplines, built sniper rifles, and fixed snow machines and other small engines, as Pete did. Whatever he earned he took in cash, so as not to jeopardize his government check. He also poached. Probably. Bull elk that could have only come from the park were seen hanging in his shed. Coyotes, too. But no one could ever prove it, or much wanted to. Because the bright, curious, physical kid that had nearly made it to the pros had turned sour. Dealing with him was edgy at best, scary at worst. He married a local, Gretchen Waggoner, who managed the gift shop, and Pete said the word was she had come to work at least twice with heavy concealer on her throat and neck. She had had a hysterectomy at nineteen and could never have kids, which many in the town now thought of as a blessing. And Les applied himself to Stoly with the same dogged focus with which he assembled a rifle or rebuilt a carburetor.

Pete said, "Nobody's ever really had the balls to cross him. Except your pal Hilly. She's made it known that he's suspect number one in the wolf killings. The recent one, and the one a few years ago, the 'White Ghost' female that was gutshot in the park." Pete shook his head, and Ren wasn't sure if it was with admiration for Hilly or concern.

By the end of the next round, they were off Les Ingraham and talking about the best places to cut firewood. Just what Ren needed. "I guess," he said finally, and stood. "Thanks, Pete," he said. "Any day I see you is a good day."

Ren stepped out into the gusting night. Who knew what time it was. The wind poured off the pass and blew the stars around. He pulled open the door to the pickup. Was he sober enough to drive? Felt like it. He'd blow a test on himself. If he wasn't, he'd go back in and drink coffee at the bar until he was legal.

Why would a man who wanted to be left alone taunt law enforcement? That's what Ren thought while he drove through thick woods and past the unmanned gatehouse and into the park. Because, he decided, the man has nothing to lose.

The black cliffs of Baronette bulked against the stars on his right. There would be a score of mountain goats up there, curled on tiny ledges; the gusts that had almost knocked him down outside the bar would buffet their dreams. They lived precarious lives. What it seemed to the watchers who flocked with spotting scopes below, but not, apparently, to the mountain goats themselves. Ren had watched, gripped, while a ewe with a gangly kid had hopped from one ledge to another, the baby knocking stones that clattered down a thousand feet. Jesus. What were the odds? To watch another navigate their life and surmise motives and emotions was a guessing game at best.

The next day, Ren fished again, but in a place where he was certain he would meet no one. He left in the dark and hiked up Rose Creek and over the steep ridge and dropped into Hornaday and fished the little stream in and out of thick willows and caught the hungry cutthroat on dry flies and forgot himself again. He kept two pan-sized rainbows for dinner and hiked out the last two miles with the sun riding the ridge.

It had been a good day, physically exhausting, and still he felt uneasy. He had his camp stove and a pan in the back of the truck, a plastic bottle of olive oil, and salt and pepper. He thought he'd head up to Mom's Cabin on Specimen Ridge and fry up the trout on the porch, and keep the stray dog company. What he called it: Mom's. It was a boarded-up ranger cabin two miles up a dirt road to the east of Slough. He went there sometimes for solace because it took him back to the cabin he and his mother had always used when they fished the Ausable and the smaller streams in the Adirondacks—when he was a boy and nothing yet had soured between them. The two cabins were almost twins—squared log walls and a steel roof and a wide porch with ornately lathed posts.

The dog he called Lucy squirmed, whining, from under the porch when he bounced to a stop in the clearing. She was a small brindle mutt, and she bumped his legs and whimpered, and he thought she looked heavy in the belly and hoped she wasn't pregnant. He unfolded a ball of aluminum foil and gave her the scraps of steak and ham, and then the two of them climbed to the porch and he made his own dinner. He carefully deboned the fish and gave her most of the second fried trout, and they sat on the porch and watched the darkness thicken together. "See ya, girl," he said when he left. "Be good. Be back in a few days." She curled on the porch and refused to look at him. But he knew she had a full belly and he felt much better when he drove home.

Hilly's truck was not in the turnaround. Sometimes she stayed out late to observe nocturnal hunting behaviors and didn't get in till the middle of the night. He dropped his pack on the porch and pulled out his wet gear. He hung his waders from a nail on a porch post and left his fishing boots on the top step. He had his hand on the screen door when he heard it. Very faint. He held his breath and turned an ear and listened.

Far off but clear: the strain of a single wolf. Two barks testing the night. Almost like a tuning, the confirming plucks of a string.

And then a rising resonant howl that froze the stars in place, and dropped and hollowed like a woodwind, and crescendoed again. The night went taut, like a drum skin, as if the solitary wolf had willed all of creation into a sounding board or bout for his song. That's what it was—music. It rooted Ren to the floorboards. The cry climbed and thinned and wavered. It held desolation and yearning and joy all together. Somehow. The hairs on the back of Ren's neck stood up. He wondered if it did the same for the others in the pack, raised their hackles but not in anger, in ferocious love. Because, as another wolf lifted her voice in answer—she was much closer, somewhere at the base of Druid Peak—and as another and another loosed a pitched cry from across the valley, that's the way it sounded. Like the most desolate, life-affirming love.

He was back out on the porch at daybreak, with coffee, dressed in a down sweater and ski hat. A hard frost lay on the grass. He drank with pleasure from the steaming mug and watched the sun break over the mountains and stream into the valley and ignite the freeze on the meadows to a white fire. He couldn't stop thinking about the note on his windshield. The pink receipt with the gallows word game on the back. What the hell. Was it a threat? Felt like it. And why did the punctuation after his name feel so sinister? The period was like a hammered nail—it affirmed the identity of the hanged man—and the question mark pried it out, at least partway. Ren felt like it was meant to hurt him, but who would do that? It didn't feel like the same level of encroachment and poaching that had been going on in the last few months—the killing of animals, the vandalizing of a ranger's truck. This felt much more subtle and personal.

He was hoping Hilly would stop by again, but she didn't. Nor did she pass and wave on her way down the drive. Odd. Even after the rare nights she stayed out late, she was unfailing in her schedule: she rose before the wolves began their dawn hunting. Ren set his insulated mug on the ammo box and walked down the track to where he had parked his white ranger pickup the night before, but her black Tundra was still not there. Or she had come in very late and gone out very early.

Since the Junction Butte Pack had moved its rendezvous site right across the river from Wolf Watcher Hill—what he and Hilly called it—she had moved her own observation post. The new spot was a fine place for the wolves, no doubt. The meadow was broad and ran for a good way along the left bank of the Lamar. The grass was high, and the pups and their minders and injured adults could rest there, mostly hidden and unmolested. Any intruder—grizzly or man—would be seen from a long way off. It was backed by dense woods that climbed the ridge. And at the downstream end of the clearing there was a long, low flat moraine, a bench of gravel and silt deposited by some flood, behind which the pack could find even stouter shelter.

It was also a prime spot for the cohort of wolf watchers, because it was clear viewing from across the river. They showed up in droves every morning at very first light, and before. If one faced downstream on the Lamar, the bank on one's left would be River Left. That's where the wolves were. Along River Right, there was more meadow, maybe a quarter-mile in width and clumped more thickly with sagebrush. Farther back from the river was the park highway, running parallel, and two low hills standing just off the pavement at the base of a climbing ridge. These hills offered enough height so that a Kowa or Swarovski spotting scope on a tripod could pick out a black wolf sleeping in the tall grass a half-mile away. So why did the wolves choose a gathering ground directly across from avid tourists? Half a mile is not far. They would nap and feed and wrestle their pups to the wafting of complicated human smells, to the constant thuds of car doors slamming, of engines cutting and starting again, the cries of unruly and probably delicious human children. Hilly knew of many other meadows within the pack's range that were much more remote; they offered similar prospects and protections, and proximity to water.

It was almost as if the wolves wanted to be observed. Hilly—who told Ren at their first meeting that she was a card-carrying misanthrope and preferred to be as far from where humans gathered as possible—wondered at the choice. She also knew that there was very little room for whimsy among a pack of wolves. The margins of survival were very thin. If precious calories were budgeted in wrestling and play, it was because, in the hard calculus of natural selection, survival demanded that pups get strong and learn to grapple and bite and then hunt. So was there some survival advantage in hanging out near people?

She had an old friend from the wildlife program at U of Montana who went on to study polar bears and wolves along a stretch of western Hudson Bay that bordered a wilderness ten times bigger than Yellowstone. The wolves there were some of the largest on earth, and were the only nonhuman animals on the planet known to hunt polar bear. Once, when she met Jad Davenport at the Rhino in Missoula—it was a testament of her love for the man that she would venture out to happy hour—he told her that these Hudson Bay wolves stood up to three and a half feet at the shoulder. Point being that the polar bear were under a unique hunting pressure that they faced nowhere else on earth—that of being occasional prey. Jad, who studied the bears, was also a fierce advocate, whose activities included taking visitors on tours of the animals. He told her that on these tours he had begun to see the strangest behavior: Often, when his group encountered a mother bear with, say, two cubs, she would leave her young close to the photo-snapping tourists and go off to hunt by herself. She did it, he realized quickly, because she knew the cubs would be safe from wolves whenever they were close to a group of humans. She was leaving her cubs with the nanny while she took a little Me Time.

Maybe the Lamar Pack was doing something similar. Who would attack wolves, maybe eat a pup? A grizzly. A lion, of which there were very few. But grizzlies in Yellowstone were not very shy. They killed, fed, foraged, and slept in plain view of sightseers. Mountain lions were reclusive—maybe the pack was here because the proximity to the hordes kept them safe from at least this one predator. Hilly had to admit that the theory was thin and that maybe wolves were simply a lot more gregarious than she was. Were they exhibitionists? She was never quite sure.

In any event, she never observed the pack with the throng on the hill. Her research would not allow it. Hilly had written many papers on the Yellowstone wolves and, despite her aversion to most human culture, she had appeared in a slew of films and in *Nova*, and National Geographic and Discovery Channel specials. Her latest focus was on pack configuration and how the number of individuals and their distribution according to social order, age, and sex affected hunting success and pack viability over time. So, even though the two hills were excellent viewing platforms, Hilly worked alone and needed to observe the pack from a much closer vantage.

But she was glad for the *Lupistas* and their passion. Some drove every morning in the dark all the way from Gardiner. They stuck together in their own pack, and they were the wolves' biggest fan club. They were patient and assiduous. They could stand at their scopes for hours, murmuring in hushed, excited tones, "It's a black adult and a gray coming over the hill . . ." "Yes, that's two pups from the new litter. Over against the berm . . ." "The black moving east is 41's great-granddaughter . . ." They were of every age, class, race, and gender: Great-grandparents and college kids. Retirees and professional photographers. All bound together by an intense love for nature and for their subjects. Pretty cool in this day and age. They were generally sweet to newbies, got initiates interested, and shared views through their scopes with curious tourists; many had deep knowledge of the packs and their natural history. A handful were dedicated pros who had done valuable research and even written popular books. Their observations often added data to existing sets, and their passion helped create advocacy.

Hilly had her own observation nests. In the past few weeks, she had parked at the Lamar River Trail parking lot and hiked in three miles to a spot in the trees on the same side of the river as the wolves, and at the upstream end of their meadow. She was often within two hundred yards of the pups and could document feeding behavior and delineate family groups by the most subtle markings. They were all aware that she was there, of course, and over the years they had come to know her well— her scent and her movements. If culture is learned behavior passed from one generation to the next, then wolves had culture in spades. Young mimicked the songs of adults, which they later taught to their offspring. The legendary female alpha 06 developed a method of stalking and bringing down adult elk that she passed on through her mates, and Hilly had seen 06's granddaughter use the same technique. The famous alpha male 08 had taught something like compassion to his son, who, like his father, granted mercy and life to vanquished wolves from warring packs. Hilly thought the adults probably communicated a lack of concern about her presence. All of it created certain scientific challenges, as the observer inevitably affects the outcome. She believed that, though her observations might not be as pure as, say, if she were watching via satellite from space, they were, over time, season after season, a good baseline. It was like, she thought, when documentary filmmakers move into a household or community: the family or village eventually forget that they are there and live their lives as they would with or without a film crew.

So she set up her scope in the same spot at the edge of the trees every morning or evening, depending on her goal; pulled out binocs, a camera, a notepad, and a thermos of sweet tea; laid the binder with laminated genealogies of the pack and the photographs of individuals beside her; and settled in. Ren once remarked that her pack diagrams with photos looked like FBI mob charts, which she did not think at all funny.

Now Ren stood in the turnaround beside his truck and looked at the spot where Hilly's Tundra ought to be. He thought it strange: Hilly, it seemed, had not come home at all. Two nights ago, on his way back from town, he hadn't noticed her truck at the Lamar River Trail parking lot; but, then, he had been thinking hard about the bear chaser and wondering if all the recent poaching came back to one man. Plus, her Toyota was black.

He was standing beside his truck and the spot where Hilly's Tundra ought to be and his antennae were humming. He did not have his badge or gun, since he had planned only a stroll to the parking spots. And his coffee mug holding the coveted first cup was on the porch, but fuck it. At least he was wearing boots and not his sheepskin slippers. He climbed up into his Ford, found the key under the seat, and pulled out of the drive. He turned upriver.

❯

Four miles to the trailhead. He took the first bends at over sixty. And had to brake hard for the crowd of wolf watchers up ahead. Twenty minutes past daybreak and the pullout on the riverside was already crammed with vehicles, and he could see the brake lights of new arrivals pulling off, stringing back along the road. Wildlife enthusiasts carrying tripods were crossing the lanes. Already a circus. He hit the lights and siren. Hated to break the mood, but was relieved to see them scatter and to have the pavement open.

Ahead on the right was the trailhead, up on a bluff. View down to the grassy valley, the dark river winding through. A wide track dropped to the Lamar, crossed it on a footbridge, and disappeared around the base of a ridge. No one on it. No cars in the lot yet either. Squat restroom, trash can, someone's fleece hat on a pylon. He turned off the siren, opened his window, and idled. If she was anywhere, this is where she would be. And then he saw her truck at the far end of the lot, black against dark trees. It had to have been there all night.

He grabbed the first-aid pack from between the seats, pushed out of the truck, and ran. Past the wooden trail sign with its large topo map—"You are here"—onto a path that dropped steeply over broad steps and thumped over the plank bridge. On the other side of the river, the path bent left around a wooded spur and he found the game trail forking right and tracing across the broad river bottom to the line of woods. A game trail and Hilly's trail. Easy to follow but rough. In and out of stiff sage that snagged and scratched at his pant legs, over burrow holes made by rodent or badger. To the wall of spruce and fir and through the gap, in and out of the trees, maybe a mile to where the edge of the forest dropped down close to the river. Downstream and across the valley he could see the cluster of cars on the rise and the two hills smudged with watchers, and he knew he was close. He hopped around a big Douglas fir and down into a hollow screened by alder brush and boulders, and there was flattened grass, a daypack, an open notebook. Also, dried and twisted wolf scat. And then he heard it, the rasp of a fine file but halting, a squeak or moan, metallic. He went through the boulders, and there, five feet below an outlier pine, was Hilly, curled. Right shin above the boot crushed in the flat jaws of a #15 leg trap.

Flash of Lea on the kitchen floor. He froze.

The rasping was her breathing. The squeak her scream. She did not shake. Bad sign, Ren knew. Out all night in the freeze, the exposure, core body temp way low, she would die unless warmed. Good God. He shook it off.

He got to her, put a hand on the side of her face. "Hey, hey, I'm here, it's Ren. It's Ren." Eyes barely opening. Acknowledgment, good. Fingers to throat, pulse weak. "I'm gonna open the jaws. It's gonna hurt like a mother. I'm getting you out of this." A creak, almost a moan. Good. He slid down to her feet. She had bled above the boot. Of course. Had not had the strength to open the jaw once in it. Why hadn't she dug out the stake? Who knew. Her can of bear spray lay on the grass, the trigger guard off. He found the long flat springs on the jaws and he shoved down hard, stiff, maybe thirty pounds pressure, shoved to the catch, and she was free. Gingerly, he slipped the open jaws past her boot. He tossed the trap. It jerked. Its stout chain, rusty, snaked up out of grass and leaves where it had been covered, and he saw that it was wrapped around the base of a pine and locked with an old padlock. Jesus.

Her lips were blue. Blood crusted her pant leg and sock, but the flow had stopped, good. He put a hand on her shoulder. *"Hold on, hold on,"* he said. "Gonna get you warm."

He gathered her up and carried her the fifteen feet to her nest behind the big rocks. He whipped off the pack, dug out the survival pouch. Ten hand warmers, thin plastic packets. He squatted and cracked and shook one after another. The chemicals mixed and heated instantly. "Hilly, Hilly, we're gonna warm you up with these warmers first. Here." He uncurled her enough, took off his fleece, and propped it under the side of her face, undid her belt. He stuffed two of the warmers into her groin, top of her legs, both sides. Tucked two against belly and retightened the belt. Two on her back and two on her chest under her soft-shell jacket, and he worked two under the jacket into her armpits. "Okay, hold on, we're gonna make a fire."

In the same pouch was a jet lighter, a tube of fire starter. He climbed the slope five steps to the base of an old orange-barked spruce and reached up for the dead underbranches. They fanned out like desiccated feathers, best tinder on earth. He broke off two limbs and crumpled the fine dry lace of twigs. Scraped a hasty firepit to dirt with his boot and crushed the fistfuls of twigs into it. Went back up for more and tore off an armload in seconds. Broke the limbs apart and piled them and flicked the lighter. Yellow flame spread and crackled. Dead aspen limb barkless and gray at the edge of the boulder. He stretched, grabbed it, snapped the ends, laid it on. Pops and flames, a campfire, thinking, *Careful, now, you sure as hell don't want to start the Hopper Complex Forest Fire*. At least the rain of two nights ago had dampened the woods.

He moved back to her again and scooped and slid her close to the fire, then found the emergency blanket in the pack, like a great sheet of foil, and wrapped her. Warm liquid would be good, sweet tea if she could get it down, but he didn't have a pot. This would have to do.

He prayed. He never prayed. He had, maybe three times in his life: once that his mother would make it through rehab and become his mother again, once that Lea's pulse would return, and now.

Now he would call for help. And now he realized that, in his casual wander down to the parking spot below his cabin, he had left his handheld radio charging on his counter. Fuck. Well, how could he have known? He had his phone, but the only cell service around was the pile of rocks below the Slough Creek campground. God. He should have another handset, another gun, another badge, that he could stash always in this pack. No, that was stupid. A radio, maybe. He shook himself: focus on Hilly. He fed the fire for over an hour. Lost track of time, again. He took off her boot and sock and checked her leg, it was gashed, clotted, probably nothing broken. He poured iodine into it and wrapped it tightly with gauze, worked her sock back on. She began to shiver violently, rustling the emergency blanket, painful to watch but a good sign. Her eyes remained shut, but the blue in her lips faded to pale and little by little was tinged with pink. He was sitting beside her, talking to her the whole time, and now he stood, stiff, and looked over the boulders and down the meadow. Wolves, half the pack, curled in the long grass; he counted eleven. Nap time. They were maybe three hundred yards away. Two were standing at the edge of the trees, noses lifted, and they looked right at him.

No surprise. If they hadn't heard him, they smelled him. Hilly had told him that a wolf's nose has 280 million scent receptors compared with a German shepherd's 225 million. She said that, though researchers were certain that a wolf could smell prey at least a mile and a half away, a radio-collared female with pups in Alaska had once been documented making straight for a fast-migrating herd of caribou sixty miles distant; had somehow calculated the very shortest route to a moving target. Ren knew he was not prey, but still—he had seen the twenty-one stalk the bison, and if these sentries roused the pack he wouldn't stand a chance.

Hilly's was a perfect observation post; she could sit on a hump of ground and watch between the rocks and see the whole meadow, the river. Close enough not to need a spotting scope: her binocs would do, and if she needed a closer look, her Sony compact with zoom would bring wolf faces into full frame. The sun had broken over the Beartooths and was pouring a warm light into the valley. Downstream and across the Lamar he could now clearly see the line of parked cars, the watchers on their hills.

Time to go. If he carried her back the way he had come, it was three miles. From here straight down to the river was maybe a quarter-mile, then maybe a half-mile to the road. He could get help. He was not in uniform, but he had a flare in the first-aid pack. He could shoot it off, but he knew it would confuse the wolf watchers, they wouldn't know what to do about it—probably piss them off more than anything. They would see him soon enough.

He pulled sticks to the edge of the fire and let it collapse, and found a flat hand-sized rock embedded in earth and scraped up dirt all around the embers and smothered them. As best he could. Still hot, still coals, but it would have to do.

"Hilly? Hilly. We're going to move." Her teeth chattered. "Hilly? Can you hear me? It's Ren. I'm going to carry you."

She half opened her eyes. Shook violently. Her core still frozen but blood working to extremities, the sensation of coming to life much more painful than sliding into death. The inner cold the worst. He had been there.

"Okay, just a sec." He gathered up the first-aid kit, found her boot, stuck it all in the pack, and tightened down the straps and slung it. Buckled the waist belt to help support the weight he would add. Then he wrapped her tightly in the reflective mylar blanket and said, "Hilly, here we go," and lifted. He was not strong enough to carry her in his arms, not such a distance, so he squatted and worked his arms under her and scooped her up and turned and slid the bundle onto his right shoulder. She groaned, cried out. "Okay, okay," he said, "I got you," then worked her belly to the back of his neck and shrugged her higher so she was jackknifed around him, and he crooked his right arm over her legs and his left over her arms, and he walked.

Down out of the trees, and as soon as he did, fifteen wolves stood out of the tall grass and turned.

They moved. The wolves. The pack with pups loped downstream to the long bench of the berm and disappeared. But five swung up and trotted toward him. Them. They were wary. They spread out and loped a few strides and stopped and lifted noses, cocked them to the downstream breeze, smelled the blood maybe, smelled Hilly—familiar—and him, the stranger, and then both eyes front, the stare, trying to figure out this odd, top-heavy shape. Ren was close enough now to see the colors of the eyes: the two grays' were amber, the buffs' gray-green, the black's yellow. They spread farther in the grass to flank him and Hilly. Nothing for it, keep moving. The one thing he had on his regular belt was his own bear spray. He always had it. He yelled, "It's just us! We're moving through!"

It stopped them in their tracks. Okay, this strange shape with the hitching walk that smelled human and of human fear *was* human after all. No wolf has ever attacked a person in Yellowstone. Not ever. The five big adults halted, stood stock-still, lifted noses again, and then, as if by silent mutual agreement, turned and trotted after the pack. Whew. Ren adjusted his arms and tightened his grip on Hilly and let out a long breath.

The wolf watchers that morning were treated to the strangest sight: The pack alerted as to a bear and alarmed. A shape emerging from the woods across the valley, not bear at all, or wolf or coyote. Someone would have exclaimed, and all spotting scopes would have swiveled, and the first to focus would have cried out, "Hey, that's a man! Carrying a woman! Who looks dead. Whoa! Not dead, injured." Hand it to them: three of the younger women and two men all said some variation of "Watch my scope, please!" and skidded down off the rise and ran to help.

Chapter Four

They got Hilly to one woman's Sprinter camper van and laid her on the back bench and cranked up the heat to near sauna temperature. Ren stayed with Hilly and held her to the seat, and the woman drove as fast as she could up the Entrance Road toward Cooke City, which was only eighteen miles away. There was no doctor in town, but there was a volunteer ambulance crew and five certified EMTs. Pretty good for a hamlet of 150 souls.

But she couldn't drive fast enough. It was already close to 9:00 a.m., and the tourists were on the move. Also, before they hit the Lamar Trail, they encountered a herd of buffalo, maybe eighty photogenic shaggy bulls and moms with calves, and the traffic backed up, and they had to slow to a crawl in a line of a dozen vehicles. Cammi was the driver's name, and she honked and honked the horn and tried to work into the oncoming lane, and received in return a flurry of fuck-you fingers and angry yells out windows. The traffic crawled. Hilly shook and moaned. They got abreast of the Lamar trailhead and Ren shouted, "Pull in. Into the lot!" and she did, and he carried Hilly to his truck and laid her on the back seat and thanked Cammi with an "I owe you," and found his key under the seat. He hit the lights and siren and stomped the gas in reverse, slid, and smoked out of the parking lot. He forced the entire line of cars over and then had clear sailing till the Baronette pullout, where there was a mother moose down in the pines, and he simply goosed it to eighty and passed four slow vehicles on the straightaway. He was on the radio now. Flew through the entrance gate, slowed two miles farther on at Silver Gate—three rustic motels, a log-cabin café famous for its pancakes, a general store—and blasted into Cooke City, where Ty and three of the EMTs met him with the ambulance outside of the Perk.

Chapter Five

Hilly had explained to Ren once how the reintroduction of a top predator can revitalize an entire ecosystem. How it can swiftly improve even the geology of a region, even its climate.

They were in their usual spots at the usual time: sitting side by side in the rockers on Ren's porch as the last stars faded and a gray light moved in the trees. Drinking coffee from insulated mugs. It was late spring, warm enough for a thick sweater only, and Ren had asked what was so great about wolves, anyway, aside from their charisma. "I get that they make the best T-shirts, hands down," he said. He loved poking her.

The creaking of Hilly's chair had stopped. She swiveled her head slowly and extended her neck like a heron about to strike. "You really want to get me started?" she said. She seemed to glow with intensity.

Ren hesitated. "I guess not," he said. "I'm just an enforcement ranger."

"Get us a refill," she ordered. He never knew if she was onto him. She had the same seriousness about her work, about life, that Lea had possessed. He could count on her that way, and sometimes it made her easy prey. He brought out the pot and filled their cups and dutifully sat back down.

"Once upon a time," she began, "there was a grand national park in the Rocky Mountains from which all the wolves that historically thrived there had been extirpated. Shot, poisoned, trapped. And guess what? The herds of elk and deer that had been kept in check by these social, highly intelligent predators flourished and overpopulated. Meaning that the deer and elk exceeded the carrying capacity of their range. You with me, kid?"

She was five years older than he was and lorded it over him. "No T-shirt models howling at the moon. Sales are down. Bummer," she added.

"Got it," Ren said. Okay, she had been onto him.

"Well, the deer and elk overgraze the meadows, and browse the willows and alders and young aspen off the riverbanks. And guess what happens?"

"The banks of the rivers and creeks erode?"

"Correct. All the vegetation, all the root systems that held them together, give way. And the streams cut the banks and straighten. They lose the sinuosity and the structure like gravel bars and big eddies that sheltered so many species. And guess what?"

"Fish die?" Ren said.

"Yep."

"Beaver who depend on willows die?"

"Yep."

"Osprey and bald eagles who feed on fish die."

"Correct."

"Muskrat die. And insects who need pools and bars to develop and hatch die. And the birds who feed on them and nest along the banks die."

"You get the idea. It's called a trophic cascade. You're pretty smart for a cop."

"Hey."

"So you let this run for decades and you get a degraded eco-system. System-wide." She fashioned a sphere in the air. "Now along come some radical enviro biologists who somehow convince the U.S. government to let them"—she dropped her voice to a whisper—"reintroduce the wolf."

Ren did feel a little excited, like a kid in class transported by a big idea. He raised his hand.

"You in the back," she said.

"So now it all gradually reverses."

"Yes."

"The wolves cut down the deer and elk, and the willows come back, and the alders, the saplings. The riverbanks hold. Here come beavers!"

"Not only that: The beaver dams slow the rivers and get them to meander again. Which forms riffles and deep pools. The fish love it. Insects, too. Riparian birds. Osprey and eagles. Not only that: The beaver dams back up ponds and sloughs, which grow rich with willows and create even more habitat for all these others. The wetlands change the microclimate, make it cooler and wetter. And here comes Mr. Moose again, who now has a perfect home. And the overgrazed meadows replenish. And the aspen saplings grow up instead of being browsed down, and now you have groves and new forest. And the wolf-kills leave carcasses that are scavenged by grizzlies, black bear, coyotes, foxes, ravens, crows, vultures, eagles. All these benefit. There is a redistribution of nutrients . . ."

She stopped. She had been seeing all this in her mind's eye the way a religious zealot might imagine the construction of a soaring cathedral. Now she remembered her pupil. He looked dazed. Not fake-dazed but truly dazzled. Good.

"Is it getting through, Renito?"

"Oh, yeah." He raised his mug.

"Can I trust you?"

He blinked. "What?"

"Now, if a visitor asks you what's so great about wolves, will you try not to hash it up?"

◖

Ren remembered the conversation as he walked with Deputy Sheriff Ty Kokocinski up the single main street / highway to the sheriff's office at the east end of town. On both sides of the street were elevated covered boardwalks that ran in intermittent bursts outside of one or two businesses and gave up. So the two men stuck to the frost-heaved pavement. Neither talked much; they'd wait until they were securely inside the small outpost. Ty did not live in town, but spent about a week a month in Cooke City, as much to broadcast a presence as to work on anything particular.

Tenner drove slowly by in his big truck, white beard flowing, and they both waved. He was heading home at midday, either for lunch and maybe a roll with Mrs. Claus—who might just be rising after the hectic night at the Moose—or he might just be picking up his dog, Nellie, on his way into the hills. Ren and Ty walked in tandem, their boots crunching the gravel sprayed over the road. Ren was thinking about what Hilly had told him, how an apex predator changes everything, how the wolves had helped save the park. But there was another predator above the wolves, and this species walked on two legs, and one of the two-leggeds, it seemed, was more savage and ruthless than the rest.

The sheriff's office was a clapboard saltbox with false front, not much bigger than a storage unit. Desk, three oak chairs, two bunks in back behind bars with a bucket to pee in. Mandatory corkboard with rows of Most Wanted flyers. Once they had hung up their coats, Ty said, "The jaws didn't cut her Achilles and nothing's broken, it looks like. Just bruised. She should be okay. Jenna said she was warming up."

Ren nodded.

"The clinic in Mammoth is waiting for her."

"Thanks, Ty."

"You and she pretty close?"

"She's a good friend."

"Want some coffee?"

"That's all right. Unless you make a flat white with a fern in the foam."

Ty stared at him. "Show me the pics," he said.

They sat on either side of the desk. Ren handed him his phone and Ty scrolled, handed it back. "You want to go to the crime scene?" Ren said.

"There is no crime scene."

"Come again?"

"Well, there's poaching in the park, that's you guys. I'm not goldbricking, I'm just saying." Ty had a point: wildlife crimes within the park were the purview of U.S. Fish and Wildlife and the park rangers. Set one foot outside the park and you were in somebody's county and belonged to the sheriff.

"What about attempted murder? If the perp lives here, you're definitely on the investigation. On the team."

Ty leaned back with a creak of oak, rubbed his ear with a knuckle. "Attempted murder how?"

"You tell me how not."

"A poacher was going for bear or wolf. No way to prove otherwise."

"That was Hilly's observation nest. Practically had a plaque."

"No plaque. You told me before, the trap was not in her nest but out in the grass. In what looked like a bed, beaten down, with wolf scat nearby."

"The trap was not staked down. It was slung around a stout tree and padlocked."

"I see that. Not uncommon to use a tree in rocky ground."

"A padlock? If your wolf trapper was going for an animal, he would've used a carabiner or gated link."

"Maybe a padlock was all he had. Imagine the scenario: he's in his garage, he grabs a trap, says, 'Damn! I ran out of carabiners and gated chain links. Well, bless my hide, here's a padlock!'"

Ren felt the vein in his forehead throb. "Ty, seriously? Are you sandbagging me?"

Ty leaned forward in the chair, put both scarred hands on the desk. Ren liked Ty. He had known him for two and a half years, since his first days on the job. Before becoming a deputy, Ty had worked the Continental Pit mine in Butte. The scars were from fixing diesel excavators.

"Look," he said. "You and I both know this was a setup." He pointed to Ren's phone on the desktop. "No argument there."

Ren took a deep breath, relieved. "So—let's move."

Ty shook his head. "Like I said, there's no crime. It's a dead end."

"But . . ." Ren, breathed, backed up. "I ran into Les Ingraham running a black bear up Slough Creek the other day. With a dog and gun."

Ty raised an eyebrow.

"I couldn't cite him because: (A) I was off duty, and (B) he hadn't discharged the rifle. And (C) the dog was loose but towing a leash, which Ingraham said he'd yanked out of his hand. Said he was just running after him to get him back."

Ty pursed his lips.

"We got into it a little bit, and he said something that gave me a chill. He said something like 'Tell that little cunt friend of yours who studies wolves to watch her back.'"

Now Ty squeaked back in the chair and sat up straight. "That's interesting," he said.

"I guess Hilly's been getting into it with him, big-time. Pete told me at the Moose two nights ago that she hasn't been at all shy about spreading around that she thinks he's the one who's been poaching in the park."

Ty reached for a pen and memo pad on the desk, opened it, and wrote something. "Okay, threat noted. We'll file it."

"*File* it? What gives?"

"*What gives* is that I've been through this before. Like ten years of it. Like since my first month over here. I know his mind, and it's how I suspect, as you do, that the trap and padlock came right out of his twisted sense of fun, maybe, or retribution. To me, personally, he might as well have engraved his name on it."

"So. Well?"

"Well, I've gone to a judge more times than I can count on one hand. Half a dozen times maybe. Sometimes I think he does shit just to screw with me." Ty tapped a toothpick out of a shaker and rolled it to the corner of his mouth. "There's reasonable suspicion, sure. There's always reasonable suspicion. All you gotta do is watch the guy walk down the street. But there's never enough for a warrant. Not then, not now." He offered the toothpick shaker to Ren, who held up a hand.

"Like I said, I'd bet money he set the trap, but . . ."

"But what?"

"Thing about Les is that there's just as much possibility that he set that trap for a wolf. That he would be mad at himself for almost killing Hilly—from a coward's distance. He can get bank for a tanned pelt, and that spot is the easiest and most reliable access to the pack without walking right across the river. And you can say a lot of things about Les Ingraham, but being a coward is not one of them. If he wants to mess with you he's more likely to get right in your face."

Ren thought about the man in the meadow. He'd certainly had no fear the other day, and no problem at all with confrontation.

Ty said, "He skates. Skates right along the edge like it's the funnest thing ever. The closer the better." Ty grimaced at Ren. He had a look like he smelled something sour. "I could use a chew." Ren reached for his chest pocket, but now Ty held up a palm. "I swore to Kacey."

"You and Tenner."

Ty wasn't listening. His gaze went past Ren. "I've known perps that wanna get caught. Just want it so bad. That's not him. He's a different animal."

"Ty, someone's gonna die."

Ty was still looking past Ren into some bitter distance. "Tell you the truth, I'm kinda surprised he hasn't killed someone already. The man definitely has it in him."

"Has what?"

Ty shook himself, as if from a dream. "Nothing. You want me to buy you one of those fancy coffee drinks?"

Ren considered the deputy for a half-second and stood. "Nah, wouldn't want you to step out of your comfort zone."

Ty said, "Well, then, I'll be heading back over the pass," and they shook hands, and Ren went out into the blustery, sunny late morning.

The laptop bolted to Ren's dash had a satellite connection. He could unlock it and carry it into the cabin, and that's how he did most of his office work. But he figured getting data by satellite was probably expensive, even for nps.gov, and the Wi-Fi at the Perk was free. That's what he told himself. It seemed half the town parked in front and used the café's Internet from their cars. An open Wi-Fi signal was a watering hole. Those sitting on the deck were willing to pay the price of admission and buy a cup—usually the tourists. Kaylee had tried having a password but gave it up when her staff spent half their working hours giving it out.

So sometimes Ren did sit in his truck outside the café and work there, and he found it a pleasant interlude. It was a mini-vacation, where he was out of his jurisdiction and folks were less likely to interrupt him. It was good people-watching, which he loved. And he did, always, pay for a cup; the flat whites were world-class delicious, and he even sometimes ventured onto the deck and sat in the sun at a little table and chatted with whoever stopped by. He was very grateful for the place.

Now he wanted the espresso drink, and he wanted to let his fury cool, and he also wanted to run a search on Les Ingraham.

There were no gaps in the line of cars parked nose-first to the Perk. Half of them had fly-rod racks on the roofs. Late morning, why weren't they fishing? Because people who were camped in this corner of Yellowstone at this time of year were usually retired or on some kind of extended vacation, and they were in no hurry to do anything. In the campgrounds Ren had met a Silicon Valley CFO who was between start-ups and could think of nothing better to do with a quarter-billion dollars than buy an RV and head with spouse to the Serengeti of the Rockies. He had met a Michelin three-star French chef who had a restaurant in Vincennes and one in Malibu, and who said in a heavy accent that he got vertigo now whenever he walked into a commercial kitchen; he said he thought it was God telling him to take a break and go back to his first love, which was fishing. "When I was a boy," he said, "we had a pole maybe three meters, no reel, just the string, and we fished off the bridges. It was the Loire, the river of silver fishes. It was fantastic." Ren had asked if he thought he would ever cook again, and the chef put a hand on the hood of his Jeep as if for reassurance and said, "It's easy to fall in love. Falling out of love is hard."

If they were experienced fishers, they also knew there was no point in rushing to the river at the crack of dawn: dawn was mostly freezing now, and trout are a little like people in that they like to wake and warm up a little before eating breakfast. Lately, the best fishing had been in the afternoon.

Ren parked across the street at the outer limits of the Wi-Fi signal. He couldn't see the deck from his truck, which meant the customers there couldn't see him. Good. He didn't want the attention. He was not in uniform, he was unshaven, and he had Hilly's blood on the arm of his sweater, so when he did step up onto the deck the tourists who were standing with their coffees made way as they would for a homeless person—a fast glance, a step back, a turning of attention elsewhere. Good. Good enough.

Ren stepped inside the café. It was a very small room, no tables, just a few shelves of guidebooks for sale, and the order counter. In a month, when the bulk of tourists were gone and it was too cold to sit at the outside tables, Kaylee would close for the winter. That was always a sad day. She was at the register. She had dark half-moons under her eyes, and her skin was blotchy. She must have closed down the Moose last night. She had one hand on the humming receipt printer, ready to tear off the slip, and with the other she swept up a pen and rested it on the open cash drawer. She didn't look up. "Gimme just a sec," she said, irritated.

"Sure," Ren said. "No rush."

Her eyes came up. Recognition, a flicker of a smile, sad, which vanished.

"Ugh," she said.

"Ugh."

"Flat white?"

"Thanks."

"That is *low*. I know there's a bunch of wolf haters in town, but that is definitely a new low. Lucky she didn't die."

"Yep."

"Hilly's got, like, a mystique." Kaylee tore off the receipt, initialed it, and stuck it on a spindle. She called over her shoulder, "One flat white, large, for you-know-who." Paul, the young barista from St. Lucia, shouted back. Ren held out his credit card. Kaylee waved it away.

"Get out of here."

"Mystique?" Ren said. "Hilly?"

"Yeah. Half the town thinks she's some crazy wolf-whisperer."

"You mean a witch?"

"Sort of. Whatever they think, who would wanna hurt her like that?"

Ren thought he'd try out a theory. "Maybe it wasn't set for her. Maybe it was set for bear or wolf."

Kaylee leaned back to get a better look at him. "Yeah, right. You and I both know that there are folks around here that hate everything about the park. Including biologists."

Kaylee the stolid business owner still carried the rebelliousness of a teenager. How old was she? Twenty-nine? Thirty? Younger? Ren thought how she hovered between youth and middle age as if she couldn't decide where the greatest virtues lay. She said, "I hear it was padlocked to a tree. When someone sets a trap like that at my front door, maybe I'll just think, 'No prob, this is probably just for a beaver.'"

How did she know about the padlock? Ren made himself smile. "Thanks for the drink," he said. She touched two straight fingers to her forehead in salute. She said, "Paul will call you at the window. He's scared shitless, BTW. He said to me just now, 'Me, I'm sticking to the good trail from now on!'"

Ren walked between the tables occupied by chattering patrons and went to the far corner of the deck and into a patch of sun. He turned into the railing and let the sun warm the back of his neck, and he looked down-valley to the gleaming cliffs of the Baronettes. He watched Bert, a shepherd mix, wander up from the general store, skirt the backs of the cars, and clamber up the steps to the deck like he was going to work; the tourists were guaranteed to make a fuss over him and feed him ham from their breakfast sandwiches. Ren closed his eyes. The day was warming. He could drowse right here, fall asleep standing, like a horse. He felt like he could sleep for a week. That first image—Hilly curled in the dried grass, face white and lips blue—it had knocked the wind out of him. He hadn't been able to breathe. The conversations behind him, punctuated by laughter, formed a pleasant drone; even in half-doze he found himself pulling out the threads: what had looked like a girl with her grandparents was talking excitedly about hiking up to see the little black bear. Was Edgar that dependable? The memory of the young bear running in terror for his life intruded, and he pushed it away. For a minute he did not want to be so angry, he just wanted to stand in the sun and smell the mountain breeze and the pines behind the café.

The patter of the girl reminded him of his own excitement when he had come west as a boy. He was twelve. He lived in southern Vermont, on a wooded hill overlooking the Connecticut River Valley and the blue ridges of New Hampshire on the other side. One true mountain stood in the haze to the east, Mount Monadnock, and it acted as a landmark from which he could always get his bearings. Not that he ever really needed to; he grew up in the woods.

Below the house was a hay meadow, and below that Sawyer Brook ran through the deep hardwoods. The stream was full of excitable brook trout, and it's where his mother had taught him to fish. Behind the house was what seemed to Ren the wilderness of Putney Mountain. One abandoned track wound its way up through a forest of beech and maple and huge creaking pines, and skirted old hayfields, and ancient sugarbush. The track only had a name, Ren thought, because someone in the middle of the last century had hauled a green aluminum camping trailer up there and abandoned it; such a landmark had to be recognized. So what was once a logging road was now referred to simply as "Green Trailer," just as one of the trails was called, without fuss, "Blueberries." Ren knew all the traces the way city kids know their block. He ran over them when he trained for soccer in middle and high school, he camped off them alone when he was much smaller; on spring breaks he helped the farmer Frazer Cooper-Ellis gather sap when the woods were soggy with melting snow. And he and his father had cut firewood on the mountain together since he could remember.

When he was maybe ten, an old man named Ed Hedges moved into the green trailer with his little Aussie terrier. He patched the hole in the roof with a scrap of sheeting and installed a woodstove made from an oil drum. No one objected. He was friendly enough and kept to himself, and had no vehicle but a coughing four-wheeler which he drove the five miles down to the village for groceries and church. After many waves and shouted hellos as he ran by, Ren began to stop and knock on the tinny door and chew the fat with EH for a few minutes mid-run. He liked how happy the old man was to see him, and how Squirt never barked at him but reared up and scrabbled at his shins and grinned. And he liked Ed's stories. It turned out he'd been a dairy farmer in Dummerston and had gone belly-up when the market turned bad for farms his size. And he'd lost his wife and two kids in a bad winter wreck on the steep road down to West River. So he'd sold what was left for a song, and now here he was, one mountain over from both the old farm and the switchback with the scarred maple tree where his family had ended. He said, "I thought of moving upcountry, but this is as far as I could bear to go."

Ren's mother, too, was taken with the old coot and would sometimes bring him half-casseroles in her daypack, or pieces of pie, or bags of cookies, and even fifths of bourbon, on her way around one of the loops.

So Ren was already well versed in the outdoors and most happy in wild country by the time his mother took him to Montana. They flew through Denver to Missoula, where one of her college friends had bought a horse facility at the edge of town. "Facility" is a sterile word. The place was on the edge of the Clark Fork, just above its confluence with the Bitterroot at Kelly Island, and it had a log lodge looking over the river where Missy lived with her husband, Dave; and back of the river were red barns and white rail fences and horses and pasture and more horses. To Ren it was a ranch, and paradise.

Ren and his mother stayed for a week. Dave was some kind of financier and a great cook, and they had dinner every night on the back porch, and Ren had his first glasses of wine—half-glasses—and his first taste of how the stuff lubricated the story-telling. Which fascinated him—the tales did, since Missy and Dave were well read and well traveled and they had senses of humor and could spin a good yarn. He noticed that his mother mostly listened with deep appreciation, and he saw how her eyes grew shiny and her listening more avid and her laughter looser as the dinners wore on. It was the first time he noticed how many glasses of wine she drank. One after another.

It was late July, and the rivers ran clear and every morning he and his mother took off after breakfast and fished the Clark Fork. They brought lunch in small daypacks, and they would eat their sandwiches in the shade of the massive narrowleaf cottonwoods on the island and wave at the passing drift boats, and Ren recognized the lingering smell of deer from the beds back in the trees. His mother was so at home and so peaceful she didn't say much as they ate, but she leaned into him and tousled his hair and complimented him on his fishing, and when the wind shifted upstream it blew strands of her hair across his face and he felt something that he could name as simply as those trails back home: Joy. Unadulterated joy. Joy undulled by fear or any anticipation of collapse. Joy sufficient to itself and at home in the world, and so entwined with the beauty of the spot and the warming breeze and the sounds of water it was almost too wonderful to bear. But he did bear it. And they would wipe the crumbs from their mouths on the arms of their lightweight shirts and pick up their rods and wade into the cold current once more. Sometimes they were out until the sun hit the mountains, which was very late, and they would have to run home, sticking to the game trails away from the banks.

Ren leaned into the railing of the Perk's deck, and the memory of the trip was sweet but burned going down—like single-malt Scotch, which was his mother's drink of choice. Because he would never feel joy like that with his mother again.

After they returned home from that trip to Montana, things changed. First of all, Ed Hedges got sick. He began to cough, and he grew thin, and Ren noticed over the next couple of months that he was weaker and trying to hide it. His mother brought him food more often, and one afternoon in mid-October Ren and his father dropped off two pickup loads of cured and split firewood, about a cord and a half. Pop, who didn't spend as much time with Ed, wanted to take him down to the hospital in Brattleboro or, barring that, have his friend Dr. Dixon come up and see him. His mother, on the other hand, was adamant: Ed didn't want to see a doctor, he refused, he'd rather die, he'd attended to both parents and a sister in deathbeds in that very hospital, and there was no way on God's earth he was going out with tubes and beeps, he was just fine where he was, thank you very much.

"We can't just let him wither up and blow away," Pop insisted, and his mother shot back, "Yes, we can! That's exactly what we're going to do if that's what's in the cards."

There was also Aileen, the ex-nurse who worked at the co-op where Ed and everybody else got their groceries. She had befriended Ed at the store when he'd first moved over from Dummerston. He came in on Thursdays, and she nudged him to share his story, and little by little, over the stainless deli counter, he told her. She was about thirty, rawboned, with a tight mouth and flat blue eyes, and had left nursing for undisclosed reasons. Ren's mother hated her. She had overheard Aileen once tell a co-worker that Oprah was a pig and a communist, and suspected Aileen of being rabidly racist. But Ed didn't—hate her. He gravitated to her, maybe because it seemed she just wanted to listen. It turned out she was a deacon at the Baptist church in Brattleboro, and after a few months she convinced Ed to get his groceries on Sundays so that she could drive him to the bigger town for church. When Ed got sick, Aileen somehow got him pills for the pain, and dedicated herself to his care. If Ren's mother was on her way up the hill with a casserole and saw Aileen's Explorer parked at the end of the good dirt, she turned around.

One day, a week before Thanksgiving, Ren's mother came back from a walk in the first snowfall. She was carrying Squirt, and she stood inside the door and forgot to set him down, and the snow melted on her shoulders and hat. Ren saw that she was sobbing. She said that Ed had shot himself, that he was dead.

No ambulance could climb the rutted track and exposed ledge rock to the green trailer, so that night the sheriff drove his own ATV up the mountain and took the body down. He and his deputy loaded it into a department Suburban parked at Florence's—the last house on the county road. Many neighbors had gathered there. The deputy pulled away, and the sheriff asked Ren's parents if he could have a word with them. So they all drove back to Ren's house, and his mother made coffee, and they sat at the kitchen table. Ren sat, too, and made himself quiet; nobody seemed to notice or mind that he was there.

The sheriff said, "It's my understanding that he was quite ill."

"He was," Ren's mother said. Her face was still tearstained, or tearstained again. "It almost seemed like tuberculosis. Does anyone get that nowadays?"

The sheriff didn't answer. Pop said, "We tried to get him to see a doctor, but he wouldn't have it."

"You all visited him often."

Ren's mother nodded. "We brought him food sometimes. More lately."

"That pile of cordwood?"

Pop nodded.

The sheriff nodded, too, but to himself, Ren thought. The sheriff worked his jaw. His eyes lingered on Ren's mother and back to Pop.

"He shot himself," the sheriff said. "Appears he'd had enough."

Ren's mother trembled, a wave of body shudder. She said, "It looks that way, Sheriff. I think he was suffering a great deal, but he'd never say it."

The sheriff said, "You were bringing up a Tupperware of mac and cheese. On a late-afternoon walk, as you often did—is that correct?"

"Yes."

"How was he when you found him?"

Ren's mother closed her eyes. "Shot," she said. "Lying back on his bed. Blood and bits of him were on the ceiling."

"Was he dead?"

Ren's mother's eyes sprang open. "Of course he was dead. He'd propped the shotgun under his chin and pulled the trigger—Jesus."

Now the sheriff studied her. He worked his jaw and he watched her, and if he wanted to say something he didn't. Then he said, "Did you hear the shot?"

Ren's mother hesitated. "No."

"You were too far down the hill."

Now Ren's mother sat up straight in the chair. "I don't know where I was, Sheriff. I didn't hear it."

He nodded. He sipped his coffee, set the cup on the grained cherry. And said, "How do you know he set the shotgun under his chin?"

Ren felt a pressure drop in the house. Silence. The woodstove cricked with heat. Outside the windows, gray snowflakes fell and swirled in the last light. Almost no wind.

"Thing is," the sheriff said, "he shot himself with a Beretta White Wing over-under with a twenty-eight-inch barrel. Mr. Hedges was not a tall man by any means." He let that settle. He put two fingers through the handle of his coffee mug. "There's no way he could reach the trigger. There was nothing like a forked stick near the body, or a crescent wrench, or anything he might have tried to use to extend his reach."

Now Ren saw his father turn to his mother, and Pop's face lost color. His lips trembled. He didn't say a word. But the sheriff did. He said, "Now I'm gonna ask you again, Mrs. Hopper: how was Mr. Hedges when you entered the trailer?"

She wasn't looking at any of them now. She was staring out the window at the snow falling in the dusk. "Dead," she murmured.

That night, Ren lay in his bed and heard his parents arguing. He'd heard it before, but not for a while. And unlike the other times, this argument did not resolve but intensified over the next days. Frustrated, angry voices slipped into his dreams. His father, who had always laughed so much, now laughed less and came home later. She, who had spent every waking hour outside when she wasn't teaching math at the elementary school down the hill, came in earlier and poured a Scotch.

Two weeks after Ed died, there was a service at the Baptist church in Brattleboro. Ren's family attended, although with some reluctance. Ren's mother believed that Aileen, the former nurse, had gotten Ed addicted to pain pills and so made him dependent on her and her God.

It was not a long service, thank goodness, but the minister had compared Ed to Job, which Ren's mother thought was over the top and had railed against on the drive home. She said that pumping Ed up into something saintly obscured the rare courage and decency of the man. And during much of the service, Aileen had twisted her head and glared at the three of them.

In January, Ren turned thirteen and insisted on no party. Two weeks later, near the end of the month, he came home from a cross-country ski meet and the house was dark and empty. His father must have been still at work—he was an architect at a firm in Brattleboro. His mother must be taking a night walk on the road up to Dusty Ridge. Or maybe drinking wine in the dark, or maybe napping. Ren called out. No bark and scrabble of little Squirt on the slate floor. No Mom. Ren switched on the kitchen light and saw an envelope on the round table. His name alone on the white field, in her script. He remembered now that his hand had shaken hard as he picked it up. So hard he had to open it and lay it again on the cherrywood to read it. Because he realized that he had feared this moment and known it was coming. For months, maybe. He read. And the gist of it was that she loved him more than anything and that she couldn't tolerate it anymore and was not coming back. And that she took Squirt because she needed a companion in her grief and he had Pop.

Ren had no idea what "it" was. The thing she could not bear. Ed Hedges had died—that seemed to be when things turned—and it was heartbreaking for all of them but not something to leave over. When he asked his father that night, Pop just looked away and shook his head.

She moved to Keene Valley in the Adirondacks, close to the Ausable River, where her father had taught her to fish. And though she made efforts to see Ren, and invited him to come fish with her, or to canoe Long Lake and the Fish Creek Ponds, he always refused. It was not so much the idea of the trip, it was that when she called she was indulgent and sentimental and her words slurred.

And he did not forgive her then or later, for stealing the possibility of a family in which he might have experienced again the kind of happiness he had known on the banks of the Clark Fork and the Bitterroot. Also, he'd grown attached to the dog.

◖

His reverie was broken by the shout of his name from the Perk's little window. He made his way between the tables, thanked Paul, brought his drink back to his spot in the sun, and turned into the railing. Just a few more minutes here; it was so intensely pleasant, even if the memories were painful.

He pried the plastic lid off the cup and inhaled the sweet milk and bitter espresso and sipped. Yum. He made an effort to think nothing. The clamor of conversations behind him intruded again, but he didn't mind. He heard the four fishermen he had noticed at a table on the other side—their voices carried. They were from the Midwest somewhere, maybe Minnesota—they had the flat inflection—one was talking about his "firstborn" moving to Colorado to be a fishing guide, they were proud of him because he walked in Christ. From the table just behind him in low murmurs he heard just snatches: "Pretty proud of their coffee, ain't they? . . . Some ranger found her in the trap . . . the prick that's been harassing . . ." Ren held his breath, turned his ear barely. One had an accent, maybe Arkansas or West Tennessee. The one who had called him a prick. He heard the scrape of a chair pushed back. "Let's roll," the other said.

Ren turned as the men stood. One was tall, athletic, broad-shouldered, with a trimmed black beard. He wore duck work pants and a battered cap bearing the POW-MIA black patch: *You Are Not Forgotten.* The other man was short, in thick black-framed glasses, clean-shaven, soft at the edges, in a Realtree camouflage windbreaker with a large Livingston Archery logo on the chest. The words were crowned by a recurve bow. The man was forty-something and maybe ten years older than his buddy.

He nodded to the two, said, "Mind if I snag your table?" The tall man barely glanced, said, "Have at it." Yep, Tennessee accent. "Thanks." Ren watched the men climb into a cement-gray late-model F-250 dually with a compound bow racked into the rear window. The short man drove. Ren noticed the license plate. It was easy to remember: it said "BRDHED2." A broadhead is a hunting arrow, a shaft tipped with tapered razors.

He'd been planning to enjoy his flat white on the deck in the sun but now he was wide awake and impatient. He crossed the street and started the pickup and nosed into the space the men had left. He'd get the best Wi-Fi signal right here. He drank his espresso and steamed milk in the front seat, with a good view of the coffee drinkers on the deck, and he opened the laptop mounted to the dash.

Ren did not mind the investigative side of his job. In truth, he didn't get to exercise it much. Most of his law enforcement duties entailed handing out summonses to tourists for doing dumb stuff. When there was a traffic accident, it was not usually hard to tell who was at fault; if the accident involved a death, he took photos of everything and took statements, and a special team came over from Mammoth. The poaching was his domain also, but if he needed immediate help, the two Montana game wardens posted in Gardiner were cross-commissioned in the park and would drive over. There was also U.S. Fish and Wildlife in Bozeman. The feds had asked to be kept in the loop on the shooting and skinning of the wolf last year, but they had only actually come in once on a wildlife crime: it was Ren's first year, and a poaching ring out of Salt Lake had killed three grizzlies in the park and had taken only their gallbladders.

Now Ren brightened the screen of the Toughbook and opened the National Crime Information Center database and searched for Les Ingraham. He pulled a memo pad from the center console and slid the pen from the wire spiral and began to jot a string of notes. Then he unclipped the mic from the radio mounted to the headliner and keyed it and called for Ty.

"Yuh," he answered.

"You on the pass?"

"Almost to the top. What's up?"

"Did you know Les had a sheet?"

"Yeah. Misdemeanor assault, when he was like eighteen."

"No, aggravated assault. There's an arrest but no prosecution."

"Happens a lot with teens. If I remember, it was a fight."

"You're not sure what it was?"

"Before my time. I knew him at Missoula. Only reason I know at all is 'cuz I was mad once or twice, just like you are, and looked him up."

"Okay. You got another minute?"

"I'm just driving. Shoot."

"What do you know about Livingston Archery?"

"It's an archery shop . . . in Livingston."

"Ty?"

"Sorry. What did you want to know?"

"Who owns it?"

"Lawton Krebbs."

Ren made a note. He said, "Pudgy guy in thick black glasses?"

"About right."

"He into anything?"

"Boston cream donuts, mostly."

"No sheet?"

"Don't think so, never checked. Why?"

"He have a good buddy, six two, two thirty, fit, broad-shouldered, short black beard, accent maybe Tennessee?"

"Dan Chesnik. Whole different story there."

"How so?"

"They've got a club in Livingston. The Pathfinders. Advertised as a men's club defending and fostering traditional values. Whatever the hell that means. Not your typical. Bunch of wealthy ranchers belong—seventh-generation ranchers with big spreads. It's basically a militia. Not on the watch list yet, but it should be. Don't have to tell you that they have an issue with federal land. Protected land. Think all of it should be opened to grazing, hunting, mining. Logging. Or else privatized. But that's not an uncommon view. Truth be told, I wouldn't mind myself if the park opened an itsy-bitsy elk season. Anyhow, Chesnik is one of the founders."

"How come I've never heard of them?" Ren had been in and out of Livingston, and he liked it well enough. There was good food and coffee and a couple of art galleries, and one of his old college buddies ran a woodworking-and-furniture shop on the north side of town.

"The club is pretty new," Ty said. "I'm thinking this summer and last, so maybe two years. They stay buttoned up."

"They ever cross the line?"

"Not unless it's the cough of full-on auto in fifty-round bursts coming over the ridge. Nobody's issued a warrant yet for noise."

"Would any of them set traplines in the park? Marked with red ribbons, like a taunt?"

"Ribbons?" The feds and the states and counties surrounding the park were evidently not talking to each other. Or the reports of recent disturbing incidents hadn't made it much past the ranger stations.

"Forget it," Ren said. "Okay, thanks."

"You just have coffee with those guys? At the Perk?"

"Pretty much."

"Stay clear. They hate park rangers."

That was Ty, Ren thought as he keyed off the mic. Plainspoken, but you never knew if he was being understated or hyperbolic.

A talent, if you thought about it. Ren plucked the shades from the brim of his cap and put them on, started the truck. What now? Sure had been fun so far. It was almost noon. Well, he'd like to see Hilly, and get his groceries, which he'd neglected to do yesterday. He'd drive the two hours over to Mammoth, which had the tiny health clinic and triage center. It's where they'd taken Hilly, and he'd go and pay her a visit. Then he'd do his shopping in Gardiner and pick her up if she was okay to come home. But before he did any of that, he wanted to stop in at the Gardiner Public Library. It was a tiny, one-room cabin, but they would have online access to archives of all the Montana papers. He was interested in the Pathfinders, and he was interested in Butte.

Chapter Six

After Ren's mother left, he found himself turning more and more inward. He started high school as a day student at the Putney School with a handful of good friends—Jeremy Dine from Saxtons River, Geordie Caldwell from up the ridge, Will Backer from down the hill at Four Corners. It was a boarding school and except for a few other locals, the two hundred students came from around the country. But the four friends had all come up from kindergarten together, all played on the middle-school soccer team, all enjoyed reading, especially adventure tales, and they all talked about moving to Alaska one day and buying a fishing boat together. At least two of them usually had a crush on the same girl, and it was a testament to the resilient camaraderie of the group that those early romances didn't tear them apart. In soccer, they had played together for so many years, they had an instinct and rhythm that allowed them to move the ball fast and pass with a speed and precision rare in high school. They seemed to play without much thought—Geordie and Jeremy played forward at left and right striker, and Will and Ren were midfielders—and many who came to the games remarked that it was beautiful to watch. So, after one season on JV, the whole cohort was promoted to varsity and drove the team for three years to Triple-A State, two as champion and one as runner-up. That was Ren's godsend: the soccer, and the three other boys who shared a history and sense of place—who had run the same trails, knew the dirt roads and orchard ponds and quarries. They formed a kind of net that protected Ren from his most perilous falls.

And he had them. The falls. The night the sheriff left his parents and his house, Ren walked out into the steadily falling snow. At the door, Squirt pushed through his legs and rocketed down the stone steps and up the lane of sugar maples that led to the mailbox and the county road. Ren watched the pale streak vanish in the thickening dusk. He knew where the little dog was going. He uttered a mandatory "Crap!" but he didn't mind, and followed.

Not a frigid night, just snowy and mostly still. The flakes fell straight down and silent and melted on the dirt of the road and whitened the leaves gathered in the ditches and along the shoulders. He climbed past Shumlin's clapboard farmhouse, Florence's tea house designed by his father. He turned the bend past the hayfield and into thick woods where the county road ended and the Green Trailer track steepened to wet slab rock and gullied dirt. In some places the defunct road became no more than a cobbled creekbed. The only light came from the snow itself, where it began to spread on the forest floor. By the time he'd climbed almost a mile and was standing outside the trailer and listening to the whines and yelps of Squirt and the frantic scratching of his claws on the aluminum door, Ren had almost forgotten why he came. But now, standing on the patch of level dirt that was Ed's front yard, and seeing the thickening snow gather on the handlebars of Ed's four-wheeler and the two-by-four railing of his three front steps, Ren untethered. For the first time in his life he experienced the unassailable absence of someone he truly loved. The pure vacuum. When his mind unfroze, he berated himself for not understanding how much pain Ed must have endured. All he had known was that the man was getting thinner and coughed more.

Ren was not stupid. He had just not heard, or been willing to hear, the sheriff's insinuation. He propelled himself forward and scooped up Squirt and clutched him tight to his chest and trotted back down the mountain.

The three things of value that Ed owned, aside from Squirt, were his four-wheeler, his shotgun, and a folding knife with deer antler inlay, all of which he left to Ren. The deputies found the note with last testament on the night of the shooting. Ren began using the four-wheeler right away. On days he didn't walk to school, he drove Ed's Steed. That's what Ren called it. He would eschew Aiken Road, which turned to pavement, and just head straight into the woods on a wide track, and over a log bridge at Sawyer Brook, and up a long rough trace over a shoulder of Putney Mountain to Banning Road, and then down. He really loved driving the thing. He pretended he was on a mountain pony. It was not strictly legal on the paved road, but that was only a mile.

The shotgun he set into the gun rack above his bed that Pop had made for him. It was a beautiful gun, if guns can be beautiful. The receiver was unblued bright steel and engraved with doves flushing from a thicket. Walnut stock over-under with single trigger. Ren had managed to transform the thing in his mind from the malevolent instrument of Ed's death to a finely crafted gift meant for him alone, and bearing the last wish of his friend.

One September afternoon as he had just begun his freshman year, a fierce lightning storm had overtaken their soccer practice. Maybe he was remembering it now because it was just the same time of year, with the same sense of transition, of everything moving and changing, and many of the same smells: of falling leaves and new mud and woodsmoke. The field was on top of a hill, like most of the school. The clouds had darkened fast, and everyone's hair floated from their heads the way it can do with the static of a rubbed balloon. Then the first crack and flash, and a giant maple at woods' edge flared and broke, and the rush of a downpour swept the pitch.

Needless to say, the coach canceled practice and gave everyone a free afternoon. Ren left his book pack in the cubby in the field house and drove the four-wheeler home. He drove through woods gone eerily dark, and under the constant barrage of rolling thunder. He was half blind most of the time as he tried to shield his eyes and cheeks from the slashing rain, but he knew the way by heart and puttered up into the carport twenty minutes later, chilled and shivering but somehow elated.

He changed fast in his room and was reaching for a light sweater that he'd hung off the rifle rack when his eyes were pulled to the gleam of gunmetal as they would be to an open fire. He noticed again the fine engraving of the doves, and he pulled the shotgun off the wall. He sat on the bed. He broke open the breach and checked each barrel as he had been taught, and then, with the same curiosity with which he had tossed a running shoe into the brook to see if it floated—and lost it—he propped the butt of the gun on the floor and tried to get the two stacked barrels under his chin. The bed was too low. He went to his desk chair, tried again. Now it worked, barely. The ends of the barrel pried hard into the V of soft tissue back of his chin. Ouch. Then he

worked his hand down the barrel and let his fingertips find the
fine tracings of the engraving, and he reached for the trigger
guard and couldn't. Couldn't reach. And he was taller by half
a head than Ed. *No forked stick, no wrench, nothing like that to
help him reach the trigger . . . We didn't find anything.* The sheriff's clinical words, spoken with the willed neutrality of a doctor delivering bad news. Letting the blows land with their own
force. And the sense Ren had then of his mother's stillness.
And the sudden blanching of his father, the way he looked then
at his wife, a sort of fleeting horror. And he remembered the
awful woman Aileen, the way she had glared at them during
Ed's memorial, the stark hatred on her face.

The next day, Ren was suspended for striking a teacher to the
ground. And he would have been expelled, surely, but for the tes-
timony of witnesses who attested that they had seen the French
instructor Monsieur Blanc drag his bulldog by the leash and
a choking collar the entire length of the language building's
walkway—half the distance the strangled dog was on his side—
and they attested that, had Ren not intervened, the dog would
surely have died.

❯

It was not that Ren had understood in a flash that his mother
was a killer. Or that the entire Windham County Sheriff's Office
knew it, too, as well as the DA's office in Brattleboro, and had
declined to prosecute for reasons probably more to do with PR
than with the law. Euthanasia was not legal in Vermont, and the
law did not make fine distinctions between mercy killing and
just plain killing. Nor, apparently, did the Bible. To Ren it was
none of that. It was that she had taken up the mantle of fugi-
tive. Used it, Ren decided, to inflame her own guilt and have a

reason for leaving. For shattering their family. For robbing him of more of those days fishing. So that she could go away and isolate and drink, probably, which Ren decided was what she really wanted to do. That's why he couldn't forgive her.

He drove and tried to clear his mind. Every fall, the memories came back to him; they came with the smell of autumn the way some people recall the cries of geese flying over in the dark decades before. He did not enjoy reliving them. Off to his right, down in the precipitous canyon of Lava Creek, he could see the painted colors of antelope grazing. The near reds and flashes of white.

A mile out of Mammoth, the traffic was backed up, wagons and SUVs and rental cars and campers. Labor Day was past and gone—who were all these people? He shifted his mind into neutral and drifted, let the snaking traffic tug him through town, past the sand-colored buildings of the Park Service and federal courthouse; the two-pump gas station / general store with lines out into the road where they clogged traffic; the bungalows and hotels and scores of fat elk loitering on the lawns and posing for photographs. Another afternoon in the park. He passed the turnoff to Lower Mammoth Street and the clinic where Hilly was recovering and took the sharp turn north up the Entrance Road and out of the park.

Good cell reception here, and he tapped on a speed dial.

"Ren? Is that you?" A soft singsong. Karen Logan was a transplant from Rocky Mount, North Carolina. Ren could listen to her all day just for the accent and tone of voice.

"Karen, hey. I really—"

"*Hush.*" She cut him off. "How many minutes out are you?"

"Fifteen."

"I'll be ready. There's really nothing I'd rather do."

◗

Ren didn't mind Gardiner. It sat on the banks of the Yellowstone in a grassy valley flanked by the modest escarpment of the Gallatin Mountains. Like Cooke City, it lived off the tourist trade, and it was the expected jumble of saloons and restaurants and fishing shops, motels and rafting outfits and hokey Old West false fronts. Country music spilled from the open windows of the taverns and competed with the diesel thrum of idling tourist buses. The town had a certain jubilance, as if it was well aware that it was one of the few gateways to the greatest national park on earth—and if the money poured through it, as did the currents of the mighty Yellowstone, and if its residents raked it in for half a year and could still wear flannel shirts and steer the hordes away from their secret fishing and camping spots, how cool was that? Whereas Cooke City seemed to take the responsibility of being a gateway maybe too seriously, Gardiner seemed to be giving the world a big wink.

But now he was not in the mood for slinging a beer at the Antler. He turned up Main and took it west away from the river. He passed the Comfort Inn and the road turned to dirt, and he pulled in at the low-slung shed of the community library. A wooden plaque by the front door said "Open Tuesday 10–5 6–8

Thursday 6–8." Well, it was Thursday, not yet six o'clock, and there was one other car parked in front, a rusted green Subaru Outback. There was a dog in it, a massive fluffy white Great Pyrenees sticking her head out an open window and grinning. A silver sticker on the bumper traced the reclining nude mud-flap girl, but this one was reading a book. Ren pushed open the door and Karen was standing behind the checkout desk, hands flat on the counter in official ready position. She wore a braided Irish wool sweater and frameless hexagonal glasses, and her long silver hair was held back by a sterling band. "What can we do for you today, sir?" she said. And flashed a mischievous smile. "And are we unshaven and out of uniform? Has the world so devolved?"

There were two stacks of freestanding shelves in the single room, and two computer terminals under a window, one of which Ren put through its paces over the next thirty-five minutes. What he had seen in the criminal record of Les Koren Ingraham was almost nothing. He had a clean sheet, nearly. Remarkable, Ren thought, for someone so brazen about breaking laws wherever he went. Clean except for one intriguing mark. What Ren wanted now was the story of an assault that had been dismissed, and anything else about the man's past that could help him with Hilly's attempted murder. Because, no matter what Ty said, that's how he thought of it.

Ingraham was thirty-five, one year and one week older than Ren. What had aroused Ren's curiosity back in Cooke City was Les's arrest for aggravated assault. The incident was on May 10, 2002, two months after Les had turned eighteen, in the spring of his senior year. So he was a promising football star then, by all accounts bright and on his way to Missoula with an athletic scholarship. A weapon was used, or a fist, probably. In Ren's experience, people are usually arrested for aggravated assault in the middle of a brawl or an attack, or just after, when the facts are not in dispute. It was a serious crime for which Les could easily have gotten prosecuted. But the case had been dismissed.

What gives? Ren thought. Maybe he was completely innocent, maybe someone fingered him for some reason out of spite. He could call the DA's office in Butte. The case was seventeen years old, but there might be something enlightening in the file. And in a smaller town, cultural and institutional memories tended to be long. The clerk you talked to at the courthouse might even have been a neighbor. But Ren wanted to stay under the radar for now. He didn't want anyone in Butte to get the impression that he had it out for Les Ingraham in any way, or was building a case against him. For now, this was simply all about trying to understand the man.

So on the library home page he clicked on the tab labeled State Library Resources and found the link to Montana newspapers, and he began to scan the pages of the *Montana Standard* from May 10, 2002, onward. The paper had a police blotter, but in the following days there was nothing. So Ren used the search tool and typed in Les's full name, and the screen filled with pages of hits, mostly a litany of school football stories. Ren skimmed. There was one about Les and two teammates raising money for the children's wing of the hospital, and one about a July Fourth If It Floats boat race on the reservoir that Les and a friend won in an outrigger fashioned from duct tape and bubble wrap.

Ren was now at the beginning of Les's senior year; he scanned forward again more slowly, and there, on February 3, 2002, was the headline, this time front page, below the fold: "Bulldogs Football Star Saves Three Teenagers from Icy River." The story told how Ingraham had been driving back along Grizzly Trail Road with three friends from the McDonald's in Rocker and how Ingraham, who was driving, pulled over when he saw a strange glow in Silver Bow Creek. It turned out to be the headlights of an overturned vehicle. Without regard for his own safety or the sharp ice along the banks, Ingraham dove into the water, kicked out the windows, and pulled three teenagers from the pickup. All survived. Ten days later was a story, now back on page five, that the Butte Board of Supervisors in conjunction with the Butte County Commissioners had voted to award Les Ingraham the Butte Medal for Civic Heroism.

That was it. Ren pushed back his chair, entwined his fingers, and stretched his arms over his head. Les was an honest-to-God hero. You couldn't make it up. The same selflessness and athletic confidence that had allowed him to dive into a half-frozen winter river to save others had probably forged him into a ferocious linebacker. He would tear through blockers and make the tackles with little regard for his own well-being. And he was smart and could probably read the opposing team's offense with a tactical keenness that would give him a jump. Ren didn't have to search any newspapers to know what happened three years later, when Les was a star at the University of Montana. Pete had told him: how Les had suffered a terrible accident in the U of M Grizzlies–Montana State Bobcats showstopper. He had broken his back and was lucky to walk again, and the kid's ferocity and intelligence had turned inward.

"Fuckin' A," Ren exhaled.

"I heard that," came the mellifluous voice from the front desk.

"I better buy you a late lunch, then."

"I was counting on it."

"One more search. Just a minute."

"I'm in no hurry."

Ren tabbed back to the search bar and typed in "Pathfinders" and got hits for a model of Jeep and a drug-and-alcohol treatment center in Colorado but nothing about a group of anti-government gun enthusiasts in Montana. They were either very small or very secret or both. So he searched "Livingston" and "Ranchers" and "Dispute" and "Conflict" "with Yellowstone," "with the U.S. Park Service."

"Gotcha," he murmured. There it was, one lead: Dan Chesnik, hunting outfitter, and a wealthy rancher named Cal Stephens were suing the federal government over what they claimed were historical grazing and hunting rights that predated the establishment of Yellowstone. The case was destined to fail, but the publicity was apparently galvanizing other ranchers, hunters, logging companies, and mining interests to organize and file amicus briefs. A photo of a group of local ranchers and sportsmen supporting the suit had been snapped on the steps of the Mammoth federal courthouse. The picture was grainy and the caption did not name anyone, but Ren counted seventeen men: lots of cowboy hats, a broad-shouldered dude that could have been Chesnik, and . . . He squinted. It looked like a tall, full-bearded guy with loose hair to his shoulders and a fringed leather jacket. *Kyle?* The mountain man? Jeez. Strange bedfellows for sure. He asked Karen if there was a way to print a photograph or an article, and she said, "Darling, I love you, but you make me sad," and led him to the printer. He finished his search with an article in *The New York Times* that mentioned the lawsuit in a larger story about a wave of sympathy in the American West for efforts to privatize public lands. The Bureau of Land Management, the U.S. Forest Service, and the National Park Service were all facing suits and loud grumblings at county commissioner meetings and town halls.

He took Karen to lunch at the Grizzly Grille, her favorite, and they took their double bacon cheeseburgers to a picnic table in the town park, overlooking the flurry of a rapid in a bend above the Yellowstone. They sat in the sun and tore open the greasy paper bags as a pair of bald eagles gyred over the river downstream, hunting their own lunch. Karen was telling him about her granddaughter in Charlotte who had won a first-prize medal at a seventh-grade science fair last spring for building a robot that would fetch slippers and a rolled newspaper. She and her three teammates were going to Washington, D.C., later in the fall. "I think it's witty, don't you? I mean, who reads physical newspapers anymore? It's an anachronism, as are, I'm guessing, slippers; as well as the old dogs who fetch them and will never learn a new trick . . . You have ketchup on your nose."

Ren could have sat at that table and listened to Karen all afternoon. Her big dog lay at her feet in the shade of the table. She was not normally gregarious or voluble, but she had known Ren now for almost three years, and she recognized another solitary when she saw one, and could sense when he needed to be told a story like an out-of-sorts child at bedtime. Even big bad park rangers sometimes needed a mom.

When they were done, and had wet their forefingers and dredged up every last crumb of French fry from the paper pockets, and had hugged till the next time, Karen said finally, "I never ask you when you come to do research, but . . . well . . . do you want to talk about it?" Translation: *I've never seen you so upset.* Ren found himself torn. He blinked away the hesitation and said, "I better not. But I love you tons." He walked her back to her Subaru and climbed into his truck.

He didn't go grocery shopping, and he didn't pick up Hilly. Not right away. There was something he needed to do first. He passed the Comfort Inn again and pulled over before he got into the clutter of businesses in the town center. He picked up his cell and dialed the ranger station in Tower. Now he could use some fast help. As the phone rang, he watched three paint horses and a gorgeous strawberry roan graze in the small pasture beside him.

"Tower," Inky said. He recognized the curt voice.

"Hey, Ink, it's Ren. Can you look up a couple of numbers for me? I'm a little tight for time."

"Sure."

"Who's the DA in Livingston?"

"Hold on."

"And just in case, I'll take the county court clerk and the DA in Butte."

"Feeling sociable, huh?"

He waited. The horses all faced the same direction as they grazed, like any herd animals. Ren wondered why they did that.

"Here you go. I've got the office number for Butte and the personal cell for Sherry Cotswoll, County District Attorney. Will that do?"

"You're the best."

She rattled off the numbers, which he jotted in his memo pad. "Here's the clerk, main office, Livingston."

"Thanks, Inky. I owe you a pitcher at the Antler."

"Nah, just put real money on the next game of darts. You suck."

" 'Kay." He hung up and called the courthouse in Butte and left a message with the date of Ingraham's arrest and asked the DA to call him with any information. Then he called DA Cotswoll's cell which went straight to voicemail. Figures. He had better luck with the clerk. She picked up right away.

"Livingston Courthouse."

"Hey, this is Officer Ren Hopper, I'm an enforcement ranger in the park. In Yellowstone."

Short laugh. "Where else is there?"

"Right."

"I might have seen your name on one of Ty's reports. What's cooking?" she said.

"Have you ever heard of the Pathfinders?"

Ren thought he heard the rustle of a gum wrapper or a pack of cigarettes. Couldn't be the latter in a county courthouse. "Nope," she said. "What is it, a sports team or something?" And there it was, the smack of chewed gum. The back of Ren's neck tingled. There was something deliberately blithe in the voice of the clerk, something that rang false. And he realized he had made a mistake. It was a blunder to call someone he didn't know and simply ask outright. Now he'd have to be much more careful. "I wish I knew," he said. "Thanks for your time." He hung up and pulled back onto the dirt road and headed into the tourist circus of Gardiner.

Grocery shopping was rote. He could grab a cart and do it blindfolded. He ran through the store with his cooler under the cart, and he added a bunch of stuff he thought Hilly would eat. When he cashed out, they packed everything in dry ice—standard procedure for a food store whose clients included a lot of remote ranchers and the entire winter population of Cooke City. Then he drove back into the park and Mammoth. The town that felt more like a campus or an army base or a movie set. The elk were all over the lawns, the tourists could not get through a green light without pausing to take another photo, most of the buildings were the same beige sandstone, and the rows of identical cottages had the feel of barracks. It was more than that: Whenever Ren drove past the gatehouse and re-entered the park, he had the sense he was entering a world that was make-believe. A corner of the Rocky Mountains where the natural laws were as different from those in the rest of the country as a snow globe was from an actual winter village. The other visitors sensed it, too, and it was maybe why nobody felt inhibited about stopping dead in the middle of a highway, or walking to within a hundred feet of a grizzly bear protecting its kill. It felt as if, once they were inside the boundaries of the park, nothing really bad could happen. But of course it could. The elk that the grizzly swayed over was really dead. Had really been clawed open and disemboweled before the release of oblivion. And people could really kill each other, whether by accident or murderous intent.

No one knew all this better than Hilly, who observed wolves every day, and now sat up in a vinyl-covered chair in the patient room of the emergency clinic. When Ren arrived, she was dressed and she was devouring her third butterscotch pudding.

"Want one?" she said. She looked exhausted, but her big smile answered his most pressing question. Her cheeks were flushed—good—and her eyes had the old brightness, but slow now, not quick. "These are really good," she said. "They said they'd cut me off at ten."

"Just ate, thanks." He sat on the bed. "Nothing broken?" She shook her head. "You sew the rip?" Ren nodded down to where the jaws of the trap had torn her trouser leg.

"My favorite hiking pants. I had to do something—you took your sweet time."

"Yeah, sorry."

Now she looked at him straight on. "Thank you," she said.

"Sure. You wanna go somewhere and get a milkshake?"

"Not really. I kinda wanna just get home." She looked down at the empty pudding cup in her hand, and it was like a shadow passing over a hillside, and he saw the cup quaver. When she looked up, he saw that her eyes were wet.

"Okay," he said gently. "Let's do that. I've got a bunch of great food in the cooler if you're hungry when we get there."

They drove in silence. The heavy traffic was coming their way, out of the park, and they had clear sailing. The sun was low behind them and lit the fawn hills and warmed the slopes of black timber to a hundred hues of green that refracted like iridescence as the wind tumbled through the spruce and pines. Where the swaths of aspen ran along a ridge, they wavered and flamed, and the creek bottoms were traced with red-stemmed willows. Only a few evenings like this in a year, Ren thought. They were in the company truck, and so they drove a steady forty. They drove with the windows down and smelled the tang of turning leaves and desiccating grasses. And sage. And the sudden scent of tumbling water and cold stones as they crossed the Yellowstone, and again as they dropped into the Lamar.

That was when they knew they were home. That smell. And the unhurried stony river on their right, and the valley both opening ahead and hemmed by the mountains and ridges on all sides. And Hilly sat up and turned and followed the transit of a blond coyote, skylined on a grassy hill and haloed in sunlight.

Home. That's when Ren sensed her shoulders relax and her strength return. She turned to him and said over the wind pouring through the windows, "The sonofabitch tried to kill me, didn't he?" It was matter-of-fact, as if the coyote had reminded her that there was nothing more normal than a predator and a food chain.

"I don't know," Ren said. "I think maybe not. The trap was out in the meadow, out below your nest."

She was quiet. He saw that she was looking out her open window, letting the air buffet her face and her eyes sweep the hills. "I went out there to get a better look at two pups," she said.

"If he was trying to kill you, don't you think he'd put the trap right in your trail? Or where it's all beaten down, where you sit?"

He saw her shrug. "I don't know. If not me, he was going after my pack." He could barely hear her over the rush of wind. Up ahead, across the river, was where he had seen her wolves line out above the herd of bison.

Hilly turned fully to him in the seat. Her face was unguarded and sad.

"I'm glad it was me."

"What?"

"I'm glad it was me in that trap and not one of my wolves. It's hard not to get attached," she said. "I try. I mean I try not to, but I always do. And I always lose."

"Telling me," Ren said. "I—" He stopped. What we do best, he thought: Lose stuff. Lose everything. Some get to do it when they die, and some have the opportunity well before then.

He felt that he had. Already. In the last year with Lea he had never been so happy. The joy he could never recover with his family he had found with her. Their lives were simple. He was working at the gallery, moving art and lights around, and he liked it. When Lea asked why, he said that the coming and going of art reminded him that the world is more than widgets. She had swiveled her head and looked at him the way an owl might look at a mouse: *I really don't understand you, but I value you immensely,* the look seemed to say. *You're gonna taste great.*

Every workday morning he went downtown and she went off to her nursery in a suburb south of the city. They got engaged on Thanksgiving, and then, one evening in late December, he came home from work and found her on the couch, icing her knees and lower back.

"What's wrong?" he asked.

She wouldn't look at him. Finally, she said, "Have a seat." He did.

"I have a family tremor," she said.

"What's that?"

"My aunt died of it. It's a neurological thing. Progressive. It starts with shakes, under stress usually, and then it hinders athletic stuff like running or swimming, and then it takes away your ability to walk and puts you in a wheelchair. And then your skin burns like it's on fire, and then you're done."

"Done?"

She nodded. Her blue-gray eyes did not flinch. "Then you're dead."

He winced. "Always?" he asked.

"I think so."

He had to calm his breathing. He loved her more than any person he had ever known aside from his father. "How old was your aunt?"

"Fifty-five."

They were twenty-four. When you're twenty-four you know that you'll never get to fifty-five. You see those folks hobbling around, gray at the temples, and you know that will never be you.

"Well," he said. "How do you know that you have it?"

"I know," she said. Then she turned away, looked out the window. They lived on a lake on the west side of Denver, and she seemed to be studying the spine of the Continental Divide. The way it was honed to a razor edge just after sunset on a December evening. "That's the thing," she said. "It's passed down. If a parent or a parent's sibling has it, their child has a fifty-fifty chance. It means we can't have kids."

That was a lot, four days before Christmas. They had already talked about where they would have the wedding—in the mountains, of course, way away from any duded-up "wedding venue."

No floral designer within a hundred miles. Their friends would play the music and they'd make a giant pot of Lea's killer green chili.

Ren cried. The tears spilled before he could hide them. She caught it, from the corner of her eye; she didn't miss a thing. "I don't blame you," she said. A tautness in her voice as she girded herself.

His hand reached for hers. He pulled her into him, and as soon as her head hit his chest she was sobbing, too. He whispered again and again, "It's not that, it's not that. I love you more than anything on earth." He held her and repeated it as she cried. "I'm so sorry," he whispered. "That you have been so afraid." And hugged her tighter, and said, "I love you. I will never, ever leave you."

Well, she left him. Only four years later. He came home from work and found her lying on the kitchen tiles, unresponsive. She died at the hospital, and they told him that she had overdosed on Oxycontin. She had trembled lately when they made love, a body shudder like nothing before, and he had had the vanity to believe it was because he was becoming a better lover. *God.* And he remembered that she came home from the nursery some days and iced her knees and thighs and poured three fingers of Jack. *God* again. He had driven home from the hospital and in a frantic search for an explanation he had discovered the prescription in her bathroom drawer. The Oxy was simply for pain. Unbearable pain. And she had been too proud to tell him. And he would go rigid, imagining the discipline it would have taken to hide it from him. Why did she? It must have felt so lonely. And scary. Why couldn't they have talked about it? Maybe because, if she had been so robbed of time, she wanted to give him a little more of it. Fifty-five was a long way off; none of this was in the cards. And he would burn with shame and go mute with heartbreak—that she felt she had to carry her pain alone.

He had found the prescription, but he found no note. No note? He had searched, frantically at times, at times in the middle of the night, waking from a dream in which he held her or walked with her, in which they talked quietly over after-dinner tea as they used to do—nightmares—and he would search and search the house in the dark, panting, his breath coming fast, a running dog, and he would end on the rug in their small living room, curled on his side, having to admit that she wanted it to seem an accident. That way he could never torture himself with questions of what he might have done differently to keep her from suicide.

It was no accident. He knew. He knew her. She would never make that kind of mistake.

He was driving, but on autopilot now, not really seeing the road or anything else, when Hilly said, "Did I ever tell you the story of 755?"

Ren shook himself. He was in his truck. He was on the Northeast Entrance Road in Yellowstone National Park, he was a ranger, he was driving; for a moment it seemed like a dream.

Hilly was looking at him, concerned. "You all right?"

"Yeah, thanks. What were you saying?"

"I was talking about a wolf, 755. He was part of the Lamar Canyon Pack. He mated with a beautiful black female, and she whelped five pups. And one day she strayed over the park boundary and was shot."

"Oh."

"I know. 755 seemed inconsolable. He ranged out alone often, but one day he encountered a young gray female and they paired and she whelped a litter of four pups, and within a year she traveled over the line and was killed. 755 was older now, but a good hunter, and he paired with a young gray female, but when a three-year-old alpha male from Slough Creek showed up, she dumped him. 755 spent a lot of time on his own now— one shies from saying he was brokenhearted—but he tried again. He mated with 889 and she bore four pups, and then, one day, three sleek young males from the Lava Creek Pack trotted in and drove off 755. *They* wanted to mate with 889. For months, the old wolf snuck over to the den when the three were off hunting, just to visit his pups. But the three caught him and they fought and nearly killed him and drove him off again. He ranged over the park boundary to the north and was never seen again. I have a picture of him at the cabin, and I look at it now and then. He's crossing a creek, coming toward the camera, and his fur is all flecked with gray and he looks haunted and sad and determined. He does. I'm not supposed to anthropomorphize, but it's clear as day. I love him. I don't know why. I love him more than all the wolves I've studied."

Ren made himself glance at Hilly, and he saw that she was crying.

Chapter Seven

A hurt wolf goes solitary. She will back herself into a spot that can be defended from one direction only, preferably close to water, and she will curl up and let her metabolism slow and let nature take its course. She will heal and grow stronger or she will die. Now and then, if destined to live a little longer, she will hobble or belly-crawl to a creek or a seep and drink. Hilly always marveled at the sense of acceptance that radiated from an injured wolf. Get close and you will trigger the deepening snarl, the ferocity and fear. But from a distance, through the scope, there was sun-gleamed fur ruffling in wind, yellow eyes when they opened not defiant but neutral, waiting for death with a hunter's patience, as the wolf would wait for the trailing scent of an elk. Hilly sometimes remembered Jeffers's stunning poem "Hurt Hawks," the line *He is strong and pain is worse to the strong.* Not so the wolf; to her pain is pain and comes and goes like weather.

She herself might have felt like backing in and curling up. But she didn't have that option. The next morning, a little later than the usual daybreak, Ren rapped at her door with a pot of coffee, and within minutes Tenner had pulled in with a sack of Sandra's butter cookies, and then Pete and Aliya showed up with a bacon-and-cheddar quiche Aliya had made, and Kaylee from the Perk soon after with a commercial thermos of hot Costa Rican French roast. Hilly came onto the porch with her brand-new aluminum cane the color of a cranberry, and Ren noticed that she did not carry her usual reticence but openly winced—her version of a big smile—and invited everyone up. They were part of her pack after all, her clan. She limped back inside and shouldered out again without the cane and the fingers of her hands curled through half a dozen coffee cups, and they all sat in the Adirondack chairs and on the porch rail and ate all the cookies and drank coffee and then devoured the quiche, which everyone swore was the best they'd ever had—to Aliya's painfully shy delight.

There was no mention of the trap or who had set it. No need. To mention it or dwell. Just as in a wolf pack, there is a pool of ever-evolving communal knowledge, communicated as much perhaps through scents—on fur, on air—as through anything else. It was like that. They knew.

Hilly, because she was Hilly, had probably not said as much as a hundred words to any of them save Ren, but they all moved around each other every day, and raised hands in waves, and voices in greetings, and all knew what the others were up to in a general way, and within a certain territory; and so, season after season, without any of the demonstrative expressions employed by people with less time on their hands, a web of trust was built. And respect. Hilly really didn't have much truck with people, or use for human society, but Ren noticed that this morning she was relaxed, if still tired. And she told them all that, three days before, just after she had left Ren to his day off, she had witnessed something she had never seen: a golden eagle striking a young badger in a meadow above Soda Butte Creek.

"It was a female, huge. Still," she said, "why would she do that? Hunt something that you know could kill you that fast, when there is so much else to eat?"

Tenner said, "I guess it's like me betting on the Knicks."

Everyone turned to him. He must have read the mix of expressions, because he hastily added, "Okay, it's not a thing like that."

Pete said, "Aliya and I saw a show the other night where the Japanese eat these puffer fish that can poison them. Like stone-cold dead in minutes. Didn't we, Al? Total crapshoot." He reached into the bag of cookies Kaylee held out for him. "Thanks." He chomped half in one bite and chased it with a swig of coffee. Then he pinched the brim of his cap for moral support. He said, "But, then, you'd think an eagle has enough adrenaline in her life, with flying around all over the place and stooping at a hundred miles an hour."

"A hundred fifty," Hilly said.

"Damn."

"I know. So then I watched her feed for over an hour. And guess who came over the hill?"

Ren noticed that Aliya was watching Hilly with a mix of curiosity, wariness, adulation. Starstruck. She had probably never been this close to the famous wolf biologist, who had been on television, on National Geographic and Discovery and History

Channel specials—the woman her father said couldn't stand TV people but did the shows in service to her wolves, to raise awareness. The girl now leaned so far forward from her perch on the rail Ren thought she might topple off.

"Two of the Lamar Pack males—493 and 507, a buff and black. She saw them before they crouched. Nothing like the eyes of an eagle. And she hopped and tried to fly, but she was too gorged. Too heavy with her feast. She hopped and spread her wings and tried again, and they charged." Hilly sipped her coffee and looked at Tenner. "Whaw, this story is making *me* hungry. Tenn, mind handing me a slice of that awesome quiche?"

Ren was astonished. Once again, he was amazed to see someone in their element. Was this her element, or one of them? He had no idea that Hilly the Recluse had it in her. He had never seen her hold forth or tell a story to an audience of more than one. No, that's a lie. He had seen her give wolf talks to highschool and college class visitors with reasonable aplomb. But. Front-porch storytelling is a different art, and she was a master, it seemed. Her timing was perfect. She had everyone canting forward now.

"They charged, low and fast. I'm guessing sixty yards. That's all the distance they had to cover. I don't think I breathed. She couldn't get off the ground, this huge engorged eagle. And then I saw her do another thing I'd never seen. She turned down the hill and half waddled, half ran with her wings spread, and finally she lifted off a little and coasted down the slope and right across the river. She had just enough glide. She settled on the cobbles on the other side, and the wolves stopped halfway down the slope and stood in the sunlight. Aw, beauties. The way the light sheens off those summer coats. And they had to decide whether to chase after a bony bird with razor talons or turn back for most of a fat badger who was no longer capable of clawing anyone. So they turned back."

Ren thought everyone was about to burst into applause, but they held back, it seemed, out of respect for the usually reserved misanthrope.

When they left, Ren took the seat beside her. He could see the roof of his cabin and a sweep of the valley through the widely spaced pines.

"Nice up here on the mountain," he said. Her cabin was 150 yards behind his.

"Suits me."

"Hurt?"

"A little."

They sat. The morning was still. A reedy cry drifted down from above and behind them.

"Cooper's hawk," she said. "Accipiter. Kills birds on the wing. Look out, meadowlarks."

"Look out, everything," Ren said.

"Right? I'm reaching my limit with this asshole." She picked up the cane propped against the chair and stubbed the planks of the porch with the rubber tip as if digging for tubers.

"I think it's my fault," Ren said.

She twisted around. "How so?"

"The other night, when I was fishing, when I caught him running Edgar, I got into it with him. I think it just egged him on. I mean, if he put the trap out that night."

"Well, I would've tangled with him, too. Or maybe just shot him right there and bypassed all the talk."

"Yeah." Thinking, *I was about an inch away*. And then, *We shouldn't be having this conversation*. "Well, you didn't take an oath," he said.

"I did," she said. "In a way. A long time ago." Her long hair was loose over her shoulders; she hadn't had time to get herself together before Ren had arrived with the first coffee. Now she dug into a pocket of her Gore-Tex shell and pulled out a frayed blue hair band. She reached behind her and twisted the thick hank and worked it through the band and doubled it and thumbed it through again. She turned to Ren. She had dark crescents of exhaustion under her eyes, but her movements were crisp.

"I promised myself I would defend the ones who have no voice. No voice in the human world."

And Ren thought about the howls he had heard the other night, the singing of the single wolf answered by another, and another far across the valley. The inhuman voices. And the hawk gyring somewhere up behind the cabin. The two crickets he could now hear somewhere in the warming grass just off the porch. Last night, when his head had finally and gratefully hit the pillow, he listened for too long to a bull elk bugling in the dark. An untuned fiddle bowed in an echo chamber, breaking high and so loud it blew all the thoughts out of Ren's head, which was not a bad thing. Those voices had been in these valleys for hundreds of millennia before the first human had muttered and yammered.

"I was just thinking of all those voices," he said.

Hilly winced her smile.

"I was thinking how I describe them to myself in human terms. 'Bugle,' 'fiddle,' 'song.' Funny, huh?"

"Not really," Hilly said. "And they only have value in human terms, too. Or cost. As when a wolf strays out of the park and kills a calf. Which is twisted."

They sat in silence. One of the big pines wheezed, its trunk flexing slowly in a wind they could not feel. "You know," Hilly said, finally, "if the earth were a meritocracy and we were graded on how much each species contributed to the well-being of the whole, we'd be fucked. God would blow his whistle at all the people and yell, *Everybody out of the pool!* It's why Paul Watson, the Sea Shepherd captain, once said that the life of a worm is worth more than the life of a man. Sounds nuts, but it's something to think about."

"Crazy," Ren murmured. But he was thinking that the other day he'd had almost the very same thought.

"You know I'm not," Hilly said. "Crazy. Don't you think you better get to work?"

He laughed, and as he was about to get up she said, "It was me."

"What?" he settled back into the chair.

"*I* egged him on."

"Who? Les?"

"Yep."

"How?"

Her mouth tightened and she looked away. "I . . ." She winced down her eyes and he could see the spray of crow's feet at the corner. "He killed one of my pack. I know it was him. So when you went fishing I drove to his house in Cooke City and taped a wanted poster on his gate."

Ren stared. "You did? A *wanted* poster? What did it say on it?"

"It said, 'Wanted Dead or Alive. For poaching wolves.' And it had his face on it. Don't ask how I got the photo."

Good God. He was going to have a bona-fide range war on his hands. "Is that it?" he stammered.

"I took out a Sharpie and I wrote on the bottom, *Better Off Dead*."

❱

There is a certain respite in work. Simply working. When Ren put on his uniform, which he did now, and strapped on his utility belt, and pinned the badge above the breast pocket, he was also slipping into a role whose lines were mostly already scripted. There was relief in that.

But when he walked to his truck the chain mail of his commission was pierced again. A slip of pink paper fluttered under his wiper blade. He yanked it free with something like fury—for violating this needed respite. Same Cooke City general store, date yesterday, cash receipt, this time for a knife. There it was, in probably Carol's cursive: *Bowie knife 10" $229*. Nothing penned on the back, but there didn't need to be.

That was a threat. Clear and concise. Canny, because not as blunt and legally admissible as Hilly's simple *Better Off Dead*. He crumpled it in anger and then reconsidered and opened his fist and smoothed it on the hood of the truck, and folded it, and slipped it into his breast pocket.

He would not let it rule him. Him, her, whoever this was. Sometime today he would drive into Cooke City and talk to Jim and Carol at the general store and ask them who had bought the knife. It was not a small item and they would surely remember; also, whoever it was had been in twice now in a week. "Fuck you," he murmured to air. "I'll deal with you later."

He drove first to Wolf Watcher Hill, where he counted over forty vehicles. The first had arrived in the dark, but now, just after nine, more were pulling over, the lines of cars extending down the edges of the road. The tops of the two mounds were crowded with spotting scopes on tripods. He hit his bar light and worked around the traffic to where a black Range Rover was canted across both lanes, as if the driver was trying to decide where to pull over. He was not really in the mood. Ren set the parking brake, lights flashing, and got out, approached the driver's window. The morning was warming fast, probably already near sixty-five, but the tinted windows were up. Ren tapped. The window hummed down. A woman, fortyish, in large Prada sunglasses turned to look up at him. Her glossy black hair was pulled back tightly, and she wore full face makeup. In the passenger seat was a girl, mid-teens, with a mass of unkempt curls and a pair of Leica binoculars around her neck.

"Morning," Ren said.

"Good morning, Officer," said the woman. She had a strong accent.

"What are we doing?" Ren said.

"I'm . . ." She searched for the word. "We are *presos*."

"*Presos.*" Ren took a guess. "You are stuck."

"Yes! Yes," said the woman as if she had just nailed a question on a game show. "We are stuck!"

"You don't look stuck." Ren made himself smile, to let the woman know that she was not in big trouble. "Do you have a license?" he said.

"Yes, yes . . ." The woman spoke to what must have been her daughter in some rapid Spanish-sounding language that Ren realized was too wrought in the vowels to be Spanish, and too exuberant in the plosives, and the girl undid her seatbelt and dove headfirst into the back seat, where she rooted around in a pile of down coats and fur hats, and came up with a shout of triumph, holding up a Louis Vuitton handbag like a diver coming up with a pearl. Ren was a bit out of the loop on women's fashion, but he did recognize the signature pattern on the turquoise leather.

"That's all right," Ren said. "The license is from Brazil, yes?"

"Yes, São Paulo," the woman said. "No! I am mistaken. We have the international license."

Ren held up a hand. "That's all right. Let's get you un-*preso*."

"Oh. Okay, okay. Okay, great."

She had a full four feet at either end of her SUV and Ren gave her hand signals and she still managed about a fifteen-point turn, and when she was finally in the lane and pointed back to where she had come from, she let a smile flutter and said, "*Obrigado,* Officer. We will park now. It is our first time, you know, Yellowstone. My daughter knows all the wolves. By number." She turned her chin. "Show him the picture," she ordered. The daughter was suddenly extremely shy and Ren didn't know why, but though the traffic was backing up in both directions he let the girl reach under her seat for a satchel shoulder bag and unclip it and bring up a large sketch pad with a full-face portrait of a magnificent male wolf. A gray. Done in ink. "It is 382," she said shyly. "From the pack here." And she pointed out the back window. "Today I hope to see him in face—in person."

"Good luck," Ren said and waved them on, and he meant it.

After Wolf Watcher Hill he drove up to the Lamar River Trail parking lot on the bluff. The lot was already full. He could see hikers crossing the river on the footbridge below. Farther on, two groups were rounding the spur at the base of the ridge. A gorgeous mid-September day in Yellowstone—what else did he expect? This is what the trails and bridges and signs were for, to funnel visitors through an experience of the park that was rich and safe, and to keep them from damaging more of a fragile ecosystem than had already been ceded. This is what gave him a job and, frankly, a home. So quit feeling aggravated, you never respected a complainer, ever.

I'm not complaining.

Well, you are something. Get over it. Whatever's in your craw.

You know what's in my craw.

It's not just Ingraham. It's deeper than that. You've been sailing under a false flag for years.

You think so? Well. In other news, everybody around me is itching to kill each other or looking the other way.

He got out of the truck. It was a good day to stretch the legs. Almost any day out here was. He took his daypack out of the back seat, grabbed an evidence kit and a fleece, a bolt cutter and a bottle of water, and set off down the steps to the trail.

◀

Ty had said there was no point in establishing a crime scene because in his estimation there had been no crime. Not in relation to Hilly. There was trapping in the park, but that was Ren's jurisdiction and he could handle it any way he wanted. Ty told Ren he'd never find a print on the traps, not on the one in Hilly's meadow, and not on the ones along the creeks. Hell with it, Ren thought, there was due diligence. And he wasn't just going to leave the trap out there to traumatize Hilly if she wanted to go back. He was sure she would. And he also knew her well enough to know that next time she would surely carry a firearm, probably her Winchester .30-06, which did not shoot darts.

He took his time this morning. He was in uniform, and so the oncoming hikers returning from short walks instantly stepped aside to let him pass and waved and said, "Good morning, Ranger," or "Officer," or just "Sir." No one really knew what to call him. One afternoon at home in Denver, when Lea was still alive and he used to paddleboard around the lake by the house on summer evenings, he came over the bank carrying his drip-ping board and there was a Hispanic family on the path, all talk-ing Spanish, and a little boy in a crew cut, maybe seven, saw him and blurted, "Hey, Commissioner!" Ren had laughed so hard he had to put down the board. After that, for months, that's what Lea called him: Commissioner. Worked for him.

After half a mile he turned off on Hilly's track across the meadow to the far woods, and in less than an hour he was at the pocket shielded by boulders at the edge of the trees. The wolves were there, mostly curled and resting in the long grass after a night of hunting. They must have sentries, Ren thought; were they designated by the pack? He'd have to ask Hilly. Because three out on the edges—one closest to the river and two upstream, nearest him—stood stiff-legged and turned to him and raised their noses. And decided to leave him be. But he knew they would have an ear or a nostril tuned in his direction; all of them would now.

He set his pack on the grass. The first thing he did was take a GPS reading and pin the location. He also noted the coordinates in a memo pad. Then he took two dozen photos with his phone. The sprung trap lay in the wild strawberry and fescue where he had left it. He took photos of the chain, the base of the tree, the padlock. He took close-ups of the flattened spot on the jaw where the serial number had been ground off. Then he snapped the lock with the bolt cutter and put on rubber gloves and took out a mid-sized evidence bag. He reeled in the chain from around the tree. As it snaked around through the leaves and grass, he caught a flash of color he hadn't noticed before: a small red ribbon on one of the links, in a neat bow.

When he left, two of the closer wolves stood again and watched him go. At two hundred yards they seemed very close. One of them shook himself, and they stepped forward with calm deliberation to face him, as if to say, *We knew you were there all along.* Ren found himself saying, "Be good. See ya," and when he did, the ears came forward.

It was on the walk back that he decided. He, like Ty, knew that he would never find a fingerprint. The ribbon was a taunt, which was an invitation. It might have come with a card that said "RSVP." So he would—pay a visit. But to whom? Who first?

Chapter Eight

After Ren knocked down the French teacher, he was suspended for a week, with expulsion under review. He had only been at school for two weeks, so a return to break didn't seem like a giant interruption. But he would miss a crucial week of soccer practice. The JV team was just beginning to gel. And it would mark him within the entire school, and probably in the town as well. He knew it would, but he wasn't sure how.

Pop, perhaps sensing the fragility in his son, took the week off from work. They spent the week cutting wood together, thinning the sugarbush above Florence's. It was simple work, at a beautiful time to be in the woods. The nights were getting cold, and the mornings took their time warming up, and when they did, and the turning leaves flushed in sunlight and the two stripped to T-shirts and worked along the felled length of a yellow birch and tossed the chunks of wood down the hill . . . the rhythmic knock echoed along the ridge, and Ren lost himself as he did fishing. They sat on the tailgate of the truck and ate cheese sandwiches for lunch, and Pop told Ren stories of all the jobs he had had before he decided to go to design school. He'd been a lobster-boat deckhand and a beehive builder, a museum tour guide and a bartender. Ren wanted to be told a story. He wanted anything that would take him away from the absence he would feel when they stepped into the house that evening. It had only been eight months since his mother left. And Ren knew his father was hurting, too; he saw it sometimes when Pop let off the trigger of the chain saw and straightened to take a breather and looked down through a gap in the trees to the reddening hills of New Hampshire, how his eyes lost focus. Pop was a problem solver, and the loss of his wife was one problem he couldn't solve.

Ren had heard that alcoholism is a disease and that it would ravage a life to get what it wants. Was his mother an alcoholic? He thought so. And so he reasoned that maybe the death of Ed Hedges was just the disease's excuse for her to isolate and hit the bottle. He told himself that again and again. In that case, no one could bring her home. His father could try every tactic and never breach the defenses of the sickness. It could drive a person—especially one who loved deeply—mad.

Not madness but anger: what Ren felt when he stopped long enough to feel anything. And so the hard work in the woods was a balm. For a few hours he forgot the shock of having a loving mother and then a handful of cold ash. He even forgot school, which had been so exciting in the first weeks. He wouldn't have minded if the woodcutting with Pop had extended, had gone on into October, into the season when a falling tree would loose its crimson leaves on the way down and they would have to wear wool hats in the mornings. They could start a woodcutting business and he would never have to go back to school and face whatever censure awaited him.

And then Monday morning came and his father had coffee ready when he came down. He was not in a wool shirt and stained canvas pants as he had been the past week, but in clean jeans and a neat button-down. Ouch. There was frost on the grass, which the rising sun began to blazon. His father asked if he had all the books and notebooks he needed in his pack, and Ren realized that he hadn't thought about it, that he had ignored the e-mails from his buddies sending assignments; he had simply e-mailed back, "Thanks. See you in a week." He was now a week behind in all work, which was like a nightmare, but he answered his father: "Yes. I'm good."

"Okay," Pop said. "I've gotta head down. You'll be all right." And he kissed the top of Ren's head and left.

Ren took Ed's four-wheeler up and across Putney Mountain and down to Four Corners and up Lee Hill to the school. He parked at the edge of the ball fields and walked in; he wasn't sure why. He was a freshman, a day student, the lowest of the low, this wasn't going to be fun.

And it wasn't. Fun. But it surprised him. He wasn't met with opprobrium, or, worse, ostracism. Geordie and Jeremy and Will were crazy glad to see him, they were like Labrador retrievers, they said they lost to Deerfield *and* KUA, they just couldn't get in sync without him. And the rest of the school seemed mildly respectful, which for an at-best-invisible freshman was a significant shift. Wherever he walked on the hill there were slight nods, curious backward looks. Even the teachers he met with after class to discuss his catch-up plan seemed helpful and forthcoming rather than disapproving or wary. After a strenuous soccer practice that afternoon, in which he shook off the lingering sadness of the week, he drove home through the dappled woods. They were so warm with color it was like driving through honey. He thought that it was all upside down, that he probably shouldn't be rewarded for knocking down a teacher. He would try not to take any of it to heart, he would try to do better.

But he didn't do better. His grief and anger were oxygenated by the extra care he saw his father trying to muster. It threw his mother's absence into relief, and the impossibility of respite or repair made him crazy. In the next four years he would make more mistakes, probably as bad as hitting Monsieur Blanc.

◗

Ren was pissed now. Someone had nearly killed his friend and marked the trap with a bow like a brag. Like counting coup or cutting a notch in a belt. Same taunt as on the illegal trapline. He shoved the pack and evidence bag with trap and ribbon into the back seat of his truck and backed out of the trailhead parking spot. He didn't even know which way he was going to turn when he hit the park road. He turned left. Apparently, whoever had bought the bowie knife could wait. Right now he wanted to drive down to Slough Creek and talk to mountain man Kyle. Who was not only crapping his own nest by having an affair with his campground host but was apparently mouthing off about attending the meetings of a very secretive group of men. Ren understood that Kyle might know a lot about wildlife in the park, but he was certain the man wasn't the sharpest tool in the box.

He followed the river downstream and twenty minutes later pulled in to the Slough Creek road. Tenner wasn't at the restrooms this time, or at the campground—too bad. Ren could've used a few minutes of Santa's cheer. He waved at Robbie, who was chatting with an older couple at one of the water hydrants, but he didn't stop. He drove straight to the only mini Airstream he could see, a small rounded trailer backed into the shade of a narrowleaf cottonwood on the bank of the slow stream. He could see why a tour guide might want to spend his days off camped here, especially if there was a pretty, already married host-with-benefits who wouldn't screw with his long-term plans. Kyle's white pickup was parked next to the camper. Good. And the thing wasn't rocking, also good. The curtains were drawn, and Ren banged on the aluminum door.

He waited. Nothing.

"Kyle Balkus?" he called. He had done due diligence and looked up the dude's last name; the formality of its use might put Kyle in the right state of wakefulness. Ren followed up with "Officer Hopper here, park enforcement." The door cracked open, and Ren was hit with the full skunk of nonedibles. Then a mass of hair, under which was a groggy, puffy, weathered, and bearded face that was not fully awake.

"Yuh?"

"Step outside, please." Ren was winging it now.

"Outside?" The man shook his head. John Colter, Jr., was not at all swift.

"Yes, step out. Keep your hands where I can see them, please."

"*Hands?* What the fuck?"

"Now!" Ren commanded. Kyle tumbled out. He was wearing only flip-flops and boxers with a pattern of blue-and-red ray guns all over them. Not exactly elk hide. He blinked in the shade of the big tree as if it were bright sun.

"Are you aware that possession of marijuana in a national park is a federal offense?"

"I . . . What the hell?"

"Have you ever been in a federal prison?"

This was heavy-handed. The wildlife guide would never get jail time from any judge for smoking a joint in his own trailer. But . . . it was just a question.

Kyle swallowed and looked at Ren with true mountain-man hatred—as if he wanted to scalp him. Ren could see the Adam's apple moving under the lower beard. He was big and heavily muscled, and Ren made sure to stay back.

"Where do you get off, coming here like this?"

Ren thought he better cut to the chase while he had the mountain man on his back flip-flop.

"Why are you attending Pathfinder meetings? You own no property and are basically homeless."

"Homeless? I . . ."

"Are you attending the VIP meetings at the ball field, or only the lower-level ones?"

"*Lower*-level? Where do you get off? I'm an honored member and I go to the ones at Zach's like everybody else. I don't know who you've been talking to." Bingo. What a fucking idiot. Zach's was a nearly legendary barbecue joint with a terrace above the river in Livingston. Friday and Saturday nights drew locals from up and down the valley and remote ranchers from every drainage within an hour.

"Sorry, *not* honored member, you don't go Tuesdays."

"Tuesdays?" That stopped Kyle in his tracks. He looked confused. "I go Saturdays. Every second one, like all the others. Fuck you. No way there's more meetings." But he wasn't so sure.

Ren shook his head. He was truly baffled that anyone who could probably identify a goshawk could be so stupid. "Listen to me," he said. "You might be right. I guess it's the Wild Boys that have the tiered meetings."

Kyle said, "Fuckin' A, what I was telling you."

Ren said, "You mention to anyone that you talked to me and I'll run you in for drug possession. They can take away your truck and your sweet little Airstream. Understand?"

Kyle stood on the patch of grass and looked at his truck and then his trailer as if they were already on the flatbed.

◗

Ren knew he had to move fast. Because Kyle would certainly end up telling somebody. Well, today was Friday, wasn't it? He checked his watch. And tomorrow was the second Saturday. He drove out to the main road, parked, and hiked the hundred yards up to the mound of boulders where everyone went to get a cell signal. He called Zach's.

"Do you have a private room I can reserve for a larger party?" he said to the chipper woman who answered the phone.

"Sure," she said. "We can seat up to thirty. No smoking, though."

"No smoking?"

"The cigar club booked it last year and we had to close down for two days."

"Jeez."

"I know! Were you thinking tonight?"

"I was thinking tomorrow."

"Lunch or dinner?"

"Dinner."

"Sorry, it's booked at seven. Wanna try lunch?"

"No that's okay, it's an evening meeting. Maybe next month."

"First or third Saturday works!" she said.

"Okay, thanks."

That sense of being overwhelmed. Of enemies, visible and hidden. Of some context or territory beyond his sight that he could only guess at, but from which he felt a vague threat. Or smelled it. He thought often of the wolves: how they lived season to season on the edge of survival and how, waking in the dark at the top of some meadow, and lifting their noses to test the air, they might smell the birth of a buffalo or a coming storm, but could not know that U.S. Fish and Wildlife had taken them off the endangered species list, or that pressure was building in Idaho and Wyoming to lift limits on hunting. They could not know that their lives, and the lives of their pack, and the existence, really, of their entire world—the forests and rivers—were at the whim of people who mostly cared little about any of it. He was not a wolf, and he had never been shy of a fight, but he needed to know whom he was fighting. He drove to Cooke City.

He barely waved to Donna at the entrance gate as he drove through, too fast. He was not cross-commissioned in Park County, he was not cross-commissioned anywhere, so whatever he did out here, aside from meeting with Ty, was on personal time. He was as out of the park and as off his turf as any wolf that wandered across the boundary.

He wasn't exactly sure where Les Ingraham lived, but he knew it was deep in the woods along the creek, because he'd seen a photograph of the place. It was when he was investigating a big-game poaching case two years ago, and Ty had given him a photo screenshotted off Instagram of an eight-by-eight trophy bull elk hanging from a crossbar outside an equipment shed. It was deep shade, an inferno twilight of dense trees, spruce and pine; a man stood beside the animal, unmistakable in his bulk, his features not clear but the whiteness of teeth in a grin the brightest stroke in the picture. Les had already been visited by a Montana game warden and he claimed he had shot the bull up on Beartooth Pass; it was in season and the carcass was legally tagged, and so the matter was dropped. But everyone knew that such a monstrous bull could have only come from the park. And again Ren had wondered: why would any poacher post his trophy on Instagram? Another taunt, a skating along the thinnest edge. It was almost as if Les enjoyed visits from various law enforcement agencies, as if he relished the attention. And why was the hide still on the elk, who hung upside down? Any experienced hunter would skin the animal right where he'd field-dressed it, or just after, while the carcass was still warm and the hide would tug down and off with not much more resistance than a tight wetsuit. Maybe because Les didn't care about the hide—because what he'd been paid for was the head mount.

A lot of maybes, which seemed to be how Les liked it.

There were two dirt streets that ran from the highway south into the woods and toward the creek, one just west of the general store and one up by the gas pumps and five-slot "casino." Ren turned off at the first, by the shop. And pulled over. He shoved out of the truck and trotted into the general store. The worn planks of the floor creaked under his boots as he made his way past the fly cases, the racks of T-shirts, shelves of grizzly-bear coffee cups and freeze-dried food. It was a long, narrow room flanked with floor-to-ceiling shelves, like an Old West dry-goods store, and a woodstove was cricking and groaning in the back. Carol was at a counter halfway down, behind an antique cash register that sat on a glass case filled with multi-tools and knives. She wore a wool skull cap over her graying straw-colored hair, and an unlit cigarette hung from her slack mouth. She had bruised crescents under her eyes, and she looked exhausted. She registered Ren and clamped off the automatic smile.

"Carol," Ren said.

"Ranger," she said. Flat. She was neither adversary nor friend. Her husband, Jim, trapped in the winter, and Ren suspected he was in the resent-the-park-but-grudgingly-grateful-for-the-income-it-provided camp. "Here for your weekly fridge magnet?"

She was trying, Ren appreciated it. He heard a scrabble of dog claws, and Mocha, Carol's nearly spherical chocolate Lab, trundled around the counter, tail wagging. She stood at Ren's feet and looked up at him with wet, deeply imploring eyes. She was beseeching him for something profound, but he wasn't sure what. Maybe just love. He rubbed her soft right ear, and her tail wagged furiously, and then she simply leaned her heft into his right knee.

"Mocha!" Carol snapped.

"It's all right," Ren said. "Need a light?"

"Can't. Not in here." She waved with the cigarette at the encroaching merchandise as if it were listening. "I just suck on it for an hour and then toss it."

"Why don't you chew, like everyone else?"

"I tried. It wasn't a good look. What's up?" she said curtly. Her energy for banter was spent.

"Did someone buy a bowie knife yesterday? Ten-inch. Do you remember?"

She winced down her eyes as if resisting smoke from the unlit Pall Mall. She snatched it out of her mouth and held it to one side as if it really were lit. "We sell a lot of knives," she said.

Ren looked down at the glass case. There were practical Kershaw clip knives, Spyderco folding survival knives, a few Buck hunting blades with iconic black handles, two evil-looking double-edged gut-pullers, and a section of red Swiss Army pocket knives with corkscrews and scissors. The thickest one, the Champ, sat like a proud brick of self-sufficiency above a tag that said "49 Functions!" Ren always wondered who in the world actually carried one of these—someone, he imagined, in tweeds who wanted to be the go-to handyman in, say, the tiny village of a model railroad set. To each his own. All the knives were accounted for, except an obvious lacuna above a label printed with "Colter Classic Bowie 10" $229."

"You don't sell that many," he said.

"Just got a shipment in."

"Huh." Ren took off his ranger's baseball cap. He rubbed his forehead hard with two fingers, closed his eyes as if in pain. Maybe he was. "Can I have a cigarette?" he said. He said it in a new tone, one Carol had never heard, the one a young man uses when he has lost maybe more than he can handle and is overwhelmed. It was unguarded, and it touched a chord. She hesitated, said, "Sure," and reached for the pack under the counter.

"Thanks," he said and took it. "Wanna actually smoke one with me?" he said, replacing his cap and looking toward the front door.

She hesitated again. "God, yes," she said with decision. "But not out front. I don't want to make small talk with one more single A-hole. Hold on." She shrugged into a ratty down jacket, came around the counter, and locked the front door. "Mocha, lie down," she ordered, and led Ren back, and they stepped outside. There was a wooden deck there that doubled as a loading dock, and below it Carol's twenty-three-year-old 4Runner, and a dumpster. She squinted around at the trees that backed the alley, the cold blue sky, as if she hadn't been out in the prison yard in a long time. She stuck her hands in the coat pockets and Ren lit the cigarette in her mouth, lit his own. "Thanks," she said out of the side of her mouth, not moving her hands. Ren hadn't smoked in weeks. Once in a while he shared a smoke with Tenner. Ren would catch him at one campground or the other, and Santa would bang down the tailgate of his work truck, and they'd sit on it and light up a Viceroy. He told Ren, "I heard Tom Waits do that live version of 'Phantom 309.' You know it? Where the hitchhiker climbs up into the cab of Big Joe, the ghost trucker? And Waits is forgetting the lyrics, I think, getting a little lost, but he's such a genius he just starts ad-libbing and sings, 'That dashboard was lit up like the Madam La Rue pinball . . . and we rode and talked the better part of the night . . . and I smoked up all his Viceroys . . .' Well, after that, what else could I smoke?" In August, Tenner had pulled out two Havana cigars that a camper had given him in appreciation for a fishing tip. "Hell," Tenner had said, snipping the ends. "I just told him to use a purple Plan B. Kinda like saying, 'Helps if you use toothpaste, you know, brushing your teeth and all.' Jeez. Said he'd had the best day fishing ever."

Now Ren was grateful for the thin smoke. On a fall day when more than the birds and the leaves seemed to be shifting. "I'd just like a little peace," Ren said.

"Amen," Carol said. She didn't look at him, but at a crow skimming the tops of the spruce. "Two weeks, most of the fall fishermen will be gone."

"Yah." They stood on the deck, smoked. Ren didn't think he'd ever spoken more than twenty words to Carol, but out there in the late morning sun he felt some kind of balance, like the equilibrium of a seesaw finally coming to rest—with both sides equally unmoored and off the ground. In the cold he felt a tear on his cheek and wiped it away with the back of a hand. If she noticed, she didn't say anything.

She coughed once and tossed the butt beside her Toyota. She took the softpack out of her coat pocket and tapped out another. "One more?"

"Sure." He tossed his and lit hers. This time she leaned to him and cupped her hands around the lighter, nodded a thanks. He lit up. She said, "The knife thing is personal?"

"Yes."

She inhaled, nodded.

"Where's your help?" he said.

"Jim? My supposed husband?"

"Uh-huh."

"Trapping. Or fishing."

Ren glanced at her. He thought he heard distinct air quotes around the two verbs. She blew out smoke, and her jaw had set. "He's not?" Ren ventured. She was still looking at the trees across the alley, but maybe not seeing them.

"I honestly don't know what he's doing. You know that woman who opened the little wildlife-art gallery just past Silver Gate?"

"No. I mean, I know where it is." On the way back into the park, past the little cluster of log buildings that was Silver Gate, was a sign on a painted cutout of a wolf's head that said "Jules Cramer Wildlife Gallery." A steep dirt driveway climbed into thick trees. Ren had never stopped in. With his interest in art, he wasn't sure why. Probably because he already knew what he'd find.

"Yeah," Carol said. "Jim goes 'fishing' right across the road. Parks his truck in the pullout by the fisherman's trail, but, honestly, I don't know which side of the highway he takes his rod." Her mouth tightened at her own bitter joke. She turned now and looked straight at Ren. "I never wanted to be a girl," she said.

Ren's mouth might have dropped open. He closed it around the unfiltered cigarette, took a drag. "No?"

"The boobs that get in the way, the periods, all the unwanted attention. Coming up, all I wanted to do was run in the woods, hunt with my dad. I like to fish as much as *he* does." She meant her husband. She winced at Ren through the smoke, waved it away. "I didn't want to be a boy, I just didn't want to be a girl.

Waiting around for someone to poke me. So where the fuck does that leave me? Know what I mean?"

Ren shook his head. "No. Sort of."

She nodded as if that was the best she could expect. She tossed her cigarette, turned. "The kid who bought the knife was five eight, one eighty. Maybe twenty. Wavy brown hair over his collar, light beard, tattoo on the back of his hand of a headstone with the words 'MOM R.I.P.' Couldn't forget that. Seemed like a sweet boy. I gotta go back to work." She turned abruptly and went through the back door. A frisson of recognition or pain shot up through Ren's diaphragm. He stood there with half a cigarette. He finished it and let himself calm down, and then he went around the back of the building to his truck, started it, and continued down the side road to where he thought Les Ingraham had his house and sheds.

◖

Focus, he thought. *Deal with the note, the kid, later. Stay present.* He passed Todd's on his right, a lot cleared out of the trees with piles of firewood, a wood splitter, an ancient half-ton Harvester International farm truck with a caged bed for cordwood. Then, on the left, a two-story slab-wood shack in what Ren always thought of as Hippy House style—crude but sturdy carpentry, a clerestory to catch sun, a round porthole window in one end, and a glass greenhouse with broken panes off the other. There was nothing green in the hothouse, just some stacked flower pots and a dirt-colored stuffed recliner. At the end of the road was a mailbox with "Ingraham" spelled in gold-on-black sticker letters curled at their edges. And the predictable bar gate chained to a post. A metal sign read "No!" Underpinned by a graphic of a tactical pump shotgun and the words "Trespassers: Please Carry ID So We Can Notify Next of Kin."

Ren let the truck idle and got out. He heard dogs. No surprise. One barked a deep warning, the other a high yip, as if the guards were the golden retriever and a Yorkie. Maybe they were. No lock on the chain. He stood on dirt covered in dry pine needles. What was he doing here? He didn't really know. Responding to an invite. What was the point? He'd already told the man he might go rogue if he caught him again. What more was there to say? He was merely reacting now, which is what he did in his life when he was most off his center, and it always got him in the most trouble. The moment he opened the gate he'd be trespassing. It'd be awkward to get a call from the Park County Sheriff Department, which would come from Ty. He could just hear the weary voice: "Nothing I can do, he's pressing charges." That is, if he and Les didn't get into a firefight halfway to the house. Which, the way shit was going, was not implausible. So Ren fished a business card out of his breast pocket and yanked open the obstinate mailbox and left it in the empty maw. Then he drove away. He didn't know what else to do.

❯

He fetched a flat white from the Perk. He wanted to drink it slowly, to stand in the sun at the edge of the porch, as he had often done, and let the sun warm his back, and close his eyes, and not think of a thing. Just for a minute, or two, or ten. But that wasn't going to happen now. He knew himself. There was that sense of too much incoming; he knew that he had to bat one away, and the next—start clearing some breathing room—or he'd hyper-accelerate and get out of control. *Deal,* he thought. *Deal with one thing at a time, start with the one in front of you.* He walked up and across the street to Gateway Gifts and Spotting Scopes. He would get a present for Hilly. She would hate that he went to a souvenir shop for a gift; had the roles been reversed, she would surely have given him a wolf's tooth on a neck string, or the tail feather of a bald eagle, which would violate at least three statutes. Ren hadn't even thought about Gretchen Waggoner Ingraham, but there she was, opening boxes on the counter with an X-Acto knife. Her bangs were cut straight across and her straw-colored hair did not reach her shoulders. She was short, strongly built, with a broad, round face, pocked cheeks, simple silver stud earrings shaped to the capital letter "I." A thick Norwegian sweater.

The door jingled as he closed it and Gretchen looked up, ready with a Hello Tourist smile, though at the end of a long season those muscles were pretty played out, and what she displayed was more of a grimace. The pain and profit of one more transaction. But when she saw it was Ren, she said simply, "Oh," and went back to unwrapping a bronze Charles Russell reproduction of a standing grizzly ready for battle. Ren knew the sculpture and hated it; the bear had a pig's snout and forearms that drooped with muscle. He wasn't much pleased with Gretchen's greeting either.

"If you're looking for Les," Gretchen said to the bubble wrap, "he's not here."

"Not at home either."

Her head came up. Her eyes blazed, and he would not want to be in her crosshairs. Maybe he already was. He remembered Pete saying that she had come to work more than once with bruises on her neck. The woman he was facing did not seem at all like someone who would take an ounce of abuse. He also knew that with marriages, or any relationship, nothing might be as it seemed to outsiders.

"Stay out of our business," she said. She was breathing hard, maybe winded. She turned away from him, seemed to be catching her breath.

"I'm pretty much in your business," Ren said. "Whether I want to be or not. Fact, there's no place I'd less like to be, but oh well."

She turned back. She was pale, with two red spots high on her cheeks. "You think 'cuz you're in a federal uniform you can bully people."

Ren didn't respond. He'd heard that before, usually from drunk drivers. "I'm here to get a gift for Hilly. You know the wolf biologist? Who was caught in a leg trap? Set right by her observation nest? The woman who almost died?"

"Don't know her," Gretchen said, and picked up the box with the bear rearing out of it. She turned her back on Ren and walked straight back to the stockroom door. "We're closed for lunch," she said over her shoulder.

He walked back down Main. He was on the covered boardwalk passing the Beartooth Cafe when he decided a skirt steak and fries would be good about now, so he pushed through the door. Pete's daughter, Aliya, was at the register, and she brightened when she saw him. She worked a few lunch shifts between hours of homeschooling. "You here to eat?" she said. "Sure," he said. "Can I sit outside? Is it too much trouble?" "Yeah, no prob at all, go ahead, I'll be right out. You want a root-beer float?" Her smile was both pleased with herself for knowing his weakness, and a little embarrassed, as if she'd just broadcast a secret. "Oh, yeah, definitely," he said, and stepped back out.

The boardwalk had been widened just enough to accommodate two tables looking over the road. He sat. Across the street, Benjy Allen's blue-heeler mix, Pounce, slouched between gas pumps and went to the glass doors of the convenience store. ICE COLD BEER FISHING TACKLE said the sign above the entrance. Pounce tipped up his nose and seemed to be reading the words, then sniffed at the crack between the two doors as if sampling the savor of smoked sausages and franks Ren knew would be turning slowly on the rollers of the self-serve grill. He'd had the idea of tagging one the way you might a lynx to see how long an individual hot dog remained in place. Better not to know. Pounce backed away suddenly, and a hulking man came out the door carrying a fistful of Slim Jims and a Big Gulp soda in a plastic cup. Les. Just then, Aliya stepped onto the deck with a tall red plastic cup bubbling over with vanilla ice-cream foam. "I got you two straws, the way you like it," she piped. But he was already standing. "Hey, thanks," he said. "Al, can you leave it? I'll be back in a minute." Before she could answer, he was already off the planks and onto the road, angling toward a forest-green Silverado. Les was leaning into the front seat, settling his drink into the console before he climbed in.

"Thanks for the present. I mean the little bow," Ren said.

Les jerked straight, whirled. "Fuck, man! Spilled my drink." He shook the drips off his right hand, blinked. "Oh. You." What Ren had been getting all morning. The grievance evaporated. He held the wet hand away from his body, but now it looked cocked to strike. "Dudley Do-Right. Ever find that gun up in the woods?" he said. "Didn't think so."

"Did you go poaching in the park and leave me a present?" Ren said. "And almost kill a woman?"

Les's mouth twisted, neither frown nor smile. "You're not talking to me, 'cause I can't understand a thing you're saying." He turned his back. Again, as he had in the meadow. He reached under his driver's seat. Ren stepped back and dropped his hand to the butt of his .45. Les faced him, holding a red shop rag. He wiped the soda off his hand and forearm. "Sticky," he said. His eyes when they met Ren's were a hard blue-gray and completely calm. Which was more unnerving than if they'd been shooting flames. "You a little jumpy? Oh, yeah, your name's Hopper."

Ren didn't move.

"Well. What were we talking about? Right . . . poaching. Say we were talking to somebody else. Who, you know, knew about shit like this. That somebody might say that if he wanted to kill someone with a trap, he'd do it. First time out, like a pro. Which this guy is. He'd say that if he put it out in the open along the river where no people ever go on account of wolves, and someone went and stepped on it, he'd feel kinda bad. But that person should really get better at watching her step."

Now Les looked straight at him. He was angry but there was something honest in the heat of it.

"That red ribbon was for me," Ren said. "I took it as an invitation. You have something you want to say?"

Les shrugged. "Not really," he said. "But I do have a question."

Ren waited.

"You a mama's boy?"

"Wha—?"

"Is the Last Great Ranger a mama's boy? Just a hunch. Still trying to decide."

Les hitched a boot onto the running board and grabbed the wheel.

"How'd it happen?" Ren said.

"Huh?" Les twisted around, ready to be amused.

"How'd a guy who dove into an icy creek to save three teenagers end up like this?"

Les was halfway into his truck, and that's where he froze. Like he didn't know whether to climb up and slam the door or to put his boot back down in the gravel and turn around. Folks who came to live in Cooke City mostly left their pasts behind. It was an unspoken norm that nobody dug too deep.

While Ren had him pinned he said, "Who's Dudley Do-Right, really? Like, for real? For real enough to get the Butte Civic Hero Medal or whatever? Me, I'm just kinda stumbling one day to the next. Honest to God. Gun and a badge? They kinda keep me between the rails, that's all." Ren tipped his cap. "See ya." He turned and walked back across the road to a float that had melted down into the cup and was just the perfect consistency of cream and soda.

Chapter Nine

He drove down to the general store in Silver Gate and bought Hilly a T-shirt. He would not think about the kid with the MOM tattoo, because right now he knew that he did not have the emotional reserves. He *would* deal with it. Later. The shirt had a graphic of two grizzlies in a forest standing behind a red SUV with a stick-family decal in the rear window. There was Daddy stick and Mommy stick and four kid sticks in descending order. One bear was pointing and saying, "Hey, look, a menu!" Just as he climbed back into his truck, his radio crackled. It was a call on the radio from Jan, one of the Pebble Creek Campground hosts, about a fight between two families over a campsite. She couldn't break it up and it was getting heated. He was twenty minutes out, driving fast. When he arrived, there was a Mog military-style expedition camper truck and a tall cab-over pickup RV backed into the same spot, looking over the clearing where a bull bison was grazing, unconcerned by the ruckus. The trucks were butt to butt at an acute angle, and the Mog was canting over its monstrous rear left tire, which had gone flat; Ren could see two half-inch drill holes in the upper sidewall.

That was a first. A young man who was apparently its driver was pointing a six-inch-barrel chrome revolver at an older man who was trying to hold a lunging German shorthair on a tight leash. Ren bet that the handgun was a .357 Magnum. Both men were yelling. The young one with the gun wore an Arcteryx soft shell, brushed sage. The older man, fortyish, with paunch, wore a Carhartt canvas vest. California plates on the Mog, Minnesota on the pickup. Bumper stickers all over the Mog—"Baja 500," "'19 Sahara Expedition," "TransSiberia." On the pickup was one decal of a horse in profile, probably American Quarter Horse Association.

Perfect, Ren thought. *Class warfare*. Minnesota's two kids were huddled by the picnic table crying, under the wing of a woman, apparently their mother, who had a Shania Twain feathered perm and was also screaming. Had to be one more player. There was. At the rear corner of the Mog, Ren saw a young blond woman in a wool beanie and down vest holding a . . . *speargun*. Cocked, with double bands stretched to the notches. Jesus.

He saw all this in a flash and hit the bar lights and jammed the blast horn once. That got everyone's attention. He hit the "On" button on his body cam, switched to PA, and unhooked the mic on its rat tail. He had found that his vehicle in full blaze often commanded more authority than a single man on the dirt. He turned up the volume. "Drop the weapons!" he blared.

Kid Mog did what Ren thought he might do and turned bodily and swung the handgun toward him. Ren understood that this was probably less of a threat than a startle reflex, but in any city in the United States it would be enough to get him plastered all over the tree trunks by law enforcement. "DROP THE GUN.

NOW!" Kid Mog looked down at his hand and dropped it in the dirt. "That's a three-thousand-dollar tire!" the kid screamed.

"Hands up! Step back! You! With the speargun. Drop it and step out. NOW!" The girl hesitated. What the fuck? Did she think she was in a James Bond movie? Enough of this shit. Ren shoved out of the car and in the same motion drew his .45 and brought both hands to the SIG and leveled it at Speargun. "Drop it!" Whoa, was that defiance in her eyes? "Not joking," Ren said loud enough, but perfectly even. "You can die right here. Right now. Up to you."

She tossed it. No shit. Like a baseball player tossing the bat after a strikeout. "Come around to the side next to boyfriend. Good. Both of you, turn and put your hands high and up against the truck." Ren was pissed. He keyed the mic on his left shoulder and called the ranger station in Tower. He never called if he could help it. They were way understaffed and had enough to worry about on the roads to Mammoth and to West Yellowstone. "Inky," he said, "Officer Twenty-two. Yeah, Ren. At Pebble Creek, campsite four. Can you get someone over here? Got an altercation, weapons, multiple parties. Controlled, yeah. For now. Thanks." It'd be forty minutes, so Ren kicked the feet of the two twenty-somethings apart and was not at all gentle. He frisked them and hooked them up, one each to the oversized military-style pipe handrails on either side of the rear door, which was about six feet off the ground. So he handcuffed them hands forward, and their arms were now over their heads— good, they could stand like that until one of the other rangers got here. Ren now turned to the overweight father with the dog.

"Put him in the truck," Ren said without preamble.

"But—"

"Don't make me draw my weapon again."

The man shook his head as if trying to clear it and, with an aggrieved spit to the side, he hauled his growling bird dog to the front door of his pickup and whistled him up. The dog jumped in with no fuss. At least someone was behaving. The man turned back and stepped forward, already talking.

"Stay!" Ren commanded, as if talking to the dog. The man was confused; he put his big hands up, palms out, and took another half-step. Ren tugged out the Taser at his thigh and pointed it at the man's chest. "Don't make me. *Stay!*"

The man was not used to being on the wrong side of anything. He stopped, but with reluctance.

"You drill holes in the kid's sidewall?" Ren said.

"Sure, but—"

"Not in the mood. Turn around. Hands to the camper. Like the kid." Ren patted him down and hooked him. This time wrists back. He took a pair of zip ties and fastened the man to the campsite's rusty standing grill.

"That little prick told me to get my fat-ass kids out of the camp-site," the man said.

Kid Mog craned around on his hookup and shouted, "The host lady down there gave us dibs!"

"Not in the mood," Ren said to fat man. And he wasn't. He turned to the mom. The kids stopped crying as if on a switch. "You have any weapons? On you or in the truck?"

Shania Twain nodded.

"I'd like you to stay at the picnic table and tell me what they are and where they are."

The woman nodded. She looked like a zombie.

"Well?"

She glanced at her husband. Ren said, "Look at me, not him. *Look* at me! Good. I am not. In. The. Mood. Backup is coming right now. You mess with me once and I promise you serious jail time."

She opened her mouth, shut it, then began to recite the locations of a shotgun and two pistols. *America on vacation,* Ren thought.

This was turning into the longest day ever. He had begun it seeking respite in simple work, but nothing would stay simple anymore, and now all he wanted to do was sit on a porch and not move, ever. He was a little surprised that he wanted to share some of the stories with Hilly, and that he was relieved when she answered his knock.

She yelled him in. Her cabin had a big picture window, and it opened south through the pines to the valley, and it streamed sunlight. She had a fire going, and inside it was warm and bright. In lieu of a dining table she had a broad oak desk covered in field notebooks, microscope, binders; and a drafting table under the window on which lay thirty-six-inch sheets of wolf family trees. The open room smelled of toast, wool, and something musky—wolf, maybe.

"Taking a break?" she said. She was in a stuffed chair angled to the woodstove. A book lay open on her lap. Her cane leaned against an arm.

"Knocking off. I'll be writing reports tonight."

She didn't ask. Again Ren marveled. Who else on the planet wouldn't have taken that opening? "Want tea?" she said.

"Okay."

She tucked a waxy yellow aspen leaf between the pages and closed the book.

"I'll get it," he said.

"No, I've gotta move."

"Why? It's just a bad bruise."

"Mental health."

"Oh, that."

"In short supply out there, huh?" She waved her hand in the general direction of the valley and the road. "Take off your coat and stay awhile."

He did. She got up and limped over to the kitchen, in the corner under the big window. She ran spring water into the squat Japanese steel kettle and brought it to the woodstove. She pulled a chrome lever on the stove forward to give the flames more air, and they responded with a fluttering rush. She caned back to a shelf over the sink and took down two mugs. One had a yellow Tweety Bird, the other Sylvester the pussycat. That surprised Ren. He figured her cups might feature fabled wolves; you could buy them in any of the park gift shops. She caught him watching.

"I like to think of the conversations they have at night on the shelf," she said. "Also, it reminds me that life on the food chain is always a crapshoot."

Ren took the bentwood rocker, and they drank Lapsang souchong. He handed her the shirt with the two bears. As soon as she unfolded it she began to laugh. "You have no idea," she managed to say. "I really hate those stick-figure families." She had to set her mug down, because her laughter was rocking the tea over the lip. "I mean, I can't stand 'em. Why don't we just go around bragging about our contribution to overpopulation." She patted the tears at the corners of her eyes with her sleeve. "The ones with everybody's name underneath really kill me. Johnny, Suzy, Holly. Mom and Dad are just Mom and Dad; they never get proper names, because of course they only exist to pump out more little stick figures."

"Have you seen the ones with the families of guns?" Ren said.

"Oh, yeah."

"Where'd you learn to shoot?"

"Deer hunting. Northern Minnesota."

"No shit."

"Shit." She refolded the T-shirt and picked up her mug.

"I grew up on a farm," she continued. "We had sunflowers, soybeans, oats, cows, and Dad drove a truck, just day trips. Hunting was a religion. I mean, we lived as rural as you can get, pretty much, and Dad still had a hunting cabin with four friends. This thing was spiff. Two of them, Dad and Calvin, were closet engineers, and they built a solar-powered hoist station to hang deer, with a rail system that ran into a cold shed. They had a fridge just for lager set to thirty-seven degrees. Not kidding. And a smoker that Dad built, for which they kept a small grove of white oak the way some people have a sugarbush. The wood-shed was divided that way: a cord of oak always on hand for smoking, and the rest for everything else. The cabin had a shop off one side with one bench pretty much just for gunsmithing and reloading. Off the other side was a shed for two ATVs. This was serious business. Dad lived for it. So of course I shot my first buck when I was eleven." She sipped her tea, glanced back to Ren. "What're you staring at?"

He didn't know. Was he staring? Hilly had never, in the four years he'd known her, run so many sentences together. Well, she had probably not sat still indoors for so many hours in a row in all that time either. Within her range, she was a restless traveler, like her subjects.

"Were there wolves?" Ren said.

"Oh, yeah." Hilly straightened in her chair and cocked her head as if she'd heard a summons. "I heard them at night, singing, since I think I was in my crib. Our dog, Jib, would howl back. Most children I think were afraid of the sound. I mean, it can be pretty eerie. My older sister certainly was—she became a Realtor in Orange County, BTW. I was never scared. Mom said that when I heard it on an early-fall night when the windows were open to the screens I would crawl to the door."

"Damn."

"I know. When I first saw them I was twelve. Dad and I were on a hunt together. We liked to hunt right from the cabin—we didn't have to drive anywhere. This is Minnesota, so a quarter-mile away was a lake. Pretty big, only two camps on the shore, at the far end. This was timber-company land, was why. We walked slowly down a long meadow heading for a copse of birch and hemlock on the shore. Where we'd wait. Uncle Bill had killed a nice buck just yards away the night before. We were coming down the hill, slowly, like I said; there was a heavy frost, and I remember the whisk of the stiff grass against my pants; and then Dad put out a hand against my shoulder and stopped me. He held his breath. I followed his gaze. There, against dark water that smoked with mist, were two wolves. Timber wolves. Huge. Feeding on Uncle Bill's gut pile. I wonder if they heard my heart thumping, because they lifted and turned their heads and I could tell they were drinking in the scents slipping down the hill, and then they bolted. Turned together and ran flat out along the shore and into the pines. No sound. Like two ghosts. Like they were made of the fog drifting off the water. I don't know how long it took me to breathe again. It was the most beautiful thing I'd ever seen. Not even beautiful, more than that. Like you couldn't name it."

She stopped. Her own eyes were smoky. Ren didn't say a word.

Finally, he said, "Did you study them in high school?"

"I tracked them. To study. I think they got to know my scent, as these do here. Our neighbors used dogs. The pack would kill a calf in a neighbor's field, and the men with dogs would go out and kill a wolf. Almost like an honor killing. I hated it. They had half a dozen dogs and one or two rifles, all against one hungry wolf. Didn't seem fair to me at all. I would never let Dad do it. When Calvin killed a nursing female, I stopped talking to him. Never talked to him again."

Jeez. What was *he* doing in high school? Driving to the bar in Bellows Falls. Getting into more trouble.

Hilly picked up her cane, and with the tip of it she shoved the vent lever on the woodstove forward and shut it down. The fluttering of air in the stovepipe throttled, and the stove wheezed and ticked. After the rush of conversation, she and Ren were happy to cool a little, like the stove. They sat and drank their tea. Ren thought how, aside from being at the library with Karen Logan, he hadn't sat beside a woman indoors for this long in a couple of years. He liked it.

He glanced at the famous wolf biologist drinking tea, and tried to see the passionate teenager teaching herself to track them. Preparing the ground for a life of study. What had he been preparing for at the same age? Stumbling from one disaster to another. He had almost been suspended again for getting in a fight with the captain of the lacrosse team, who had been bragging about screwing a very drunk freshman at a school dance.

Ren cricked back in the rocker and sipped the tea, which was like liquid smoke. His eyes traveled from the squat green kettle to the apple crate left of the stove, which held split kindling.

"Excelsior Orchards" in fading stenciled letters on the slatted wood. He wondered where that was—Colorado or Washington or Vermont—and how it ended up here. On the floor beside the box was an old red Folger's coffee tin with no lid, for matches probably, but . . . he rocked forward and looked more closely. Inside it was a bottle of Karo corn syrup. The same stuff used recently to destroy an outfitter's engine. When he glanced back at Hilly she was watching him, willfully expressionless. But her eyes met his and the tiny gold flecks there seemed brighter, like embers in a wind.

He was trying to decide if he should say something—probably not—when he heard boots on the porch steps and then a rapping at the door. If Ren thought he was done with campground drama for the day, he was wrong. Hilly set her tea on the side table and picked up her cane, but now Ren put a hand on her shoulder. "I got this," he said. He rose and opened the door.

It was Tenner. The usually merry Santa was not jolly. He took a step back to let Ren onto the porch and his breath rasped. His eyes shone and his cheeks above the snowy beard were flushed, but not with good cheer.

"What's up?" Ren said, alarmed.

Tenner took a sec to catch his breath. "You know," he said, "when you're my age—" He coughed into his fist.

"You think you've seen everything?" Ren said.

"What the hell is going on in this valley?"

"*What?*" Ren said.

"I tried calling you on the radio." Tenner was having an unusually hard time gathering his thoughts.

"Yeah, I left it in the cabin. Sorry. Tenner, what happened?"

"Okay, you know about the Kelli-Robbie drama and all that—"

"Kelli hooked up with the mountain man."

"Right. Well, it gets worse."

"Oh, no."

"Oh, yes. So listen. She wouldn't come out of Kyle's trailer to do her job, do anything. She'd wait until Robbie took the truck somewhere, and then she'd come out and go for a hike up the trail, get some fresh air. Mr. Mountain Man told Robbie to his face that she was *his* squaw now. I mean. So Kyle goes off to guide the next wildlife group from Jackson Hole. This afternoon. So she's, like, Fuck it, I'm going to town. I'm a Baptist and all, but I sure as shit need a drink, and I'd kinda like to be back at the Motel Eight when Kyle returns from dinner with his clients. It's where the group stays, and Kyle, too, while he's guiding. So Robbie, he's stinging pretty bad, as you can imagine . . ."

"Crap."

"Oh, man, you'll never guess."

Ren thought of the sweet, goofy kid. Kid—he was probably thirty, a few years younger than Ren was. "He takes the dirt bike into town behind her and tries to kill himself in front of her?"

"Oh, no, that'd be just about normal."

"What, then?"

"He breaks the lock on Kyle's Airstream and leaves six cans of tuna fish open inside. Opens all the windows, too."

"Oh, crap."

"Right. Guess who comes to dinner within an hour?"

"705."

"Oh, no. No, we're talking a special honorary visit."

"God."

"Gimme a chew. Please."

Ren snagged the can of Copenhagen out of his breast pocket and handed it over. Tenner pinched out about a quarter of the can, stuffed it under his upper lip. Now, even under the white mustache, it looked swollen, as if he'd gotten into a fight. He turned and spat over the rail.

"689."

"Oh, boy."

"He trundled into camp . . ." Tenner checked his watch. "Less than an hour ago. I was at the restrooms and I heard the shouts. He turned that trailer into a marvel of shredded aluminum.

Looks like a goddamn art installation. Robbie's got more smarts than I gave him credit for—he put each can in a special hiding place—the fridge, the closet, the oven, the bathroom . . ."

"Anybody hurt?"

Tenner shook his head. "You know this griz. He's mean and he takes no shit from any being on the planet, four-legged or two-legged. On his way out he ate some camper's yapping dog. I think just 'cuz all the whiny ruckus ticked him off."

"Jesus. Where is he now?"

"Hightailed it over the ridge. *We smelled, we came, we trashed the place.* You going after him?"

"Hell, no."

"Can't blame a bear for being a bear, right?"

"Right," Ren said. "Was the dog off leash?"

"Yep. Size of a breadbox, and went after that grizzly like he was a squirrel."

"Okay. Nobody will blame the bear. How old is he? Like nineteen, right? I doubt he'll repeat. Hope not. It's not like he's gonna start hanging around campgrounds now. He's way too smart, and he's lived this long."

"Good," Tenner said. He looked truly relieved. He said, "So I went out on the rock pile where there's reception and tried Kyle's cell. Also the Super Eight. Lance at the desk said he's not picking up in the room." Tenner shook his head. "We won't mention that to Robbie. Fuckin' A."

"Hold on, I'll get my coat," Ren said. He half closed the screen door. "We gotta stop at the cabin, pick up my belt and radio."

Tenner knew he meant his gun belt, and cuffs. "You gonna arrest Robbie?"

Ren stepped onto the porch again. He cocked his head as if listening to a thought, looked straight at Tenner.

"I've gotta get my stuff. You're going back there right now, right? To tell everyone I'm coming."

Tenner eyed him, nodded slowly.

"The most I could get him on is vandalism. For breaking the lock. He didn't take anything. And since he was making one of his rounds and he smelled gas coming out of the trailer, that was his civic duty. And he knows not a thing about tuna fish—he hates the stuff, right?"

Now Tenner nodded slowly, holding Ren's gaze, and for the first time that afternoon Ren saw a flicker of merriment in those wise old Santa eyes, and a glimmer of a smile.

Ren thought he'd sleep hard that night. It was utterly draining, keeping the peace in one remote valley. He banked the stove and shut it down so he'd have embers in the morning and the cabin would cool in the small hours to near freezing but wouldn't freeze. He unfolded the third wool blanket. Then he unhooked his down coat and stepped outside. A clear night. No wolves singing now, no sounds at all but the rustle of aspen and the runnel of Rose Creek below them. In a month, the high dark would sound with the barks of geese skeining southward. But now no shadows moved against the silent constellations. He looked eastward up the valley. Beyond the Baronettes and over the Beartooths, a crescent moon rocked off a sharp ridge. Waxing, but not bright enough to dim the stars.

Still. Hold still, Ren thought. A night like this is all you need on earth.

Was it? He would stretch out in his bunk alone. He would crack the window above him, to feel the thread of cold air. He would hear the stove tick and listen for the call of a wolf or the hollow, questioning moan of the great horned owl who sometimes perched in the pine behind the cabin. He would speak to Lea, as he often did, and ask her how she was on this fall night, and tell her that he loved her still, and hope she had peace.

Now, on the porch, he held his breath and listened.

Nothing. He thought that this was how the valley had sounded for decades and decades. The last wild wolves were killed in 1924 up Soda Butte Creek, a few miles from here. Two pups. And then the silence reigned. Not silence. The pitched moil and yelps of coyotes, night birds, but not the timbered rising songs that had ringed the valley for centuries, and had shaken the stars. They were gone. And then, in 1995, in winter, three wolves from Canada were relocated and penned right here, yards from where he stood, and acclimated to their new home. A black female, her brown pup daughter, and a big bold gray male. The two adults mated, and all three were released in late March, in snow. The pregnant female, R9F, whelped eight pups, and founded the famous Rose Creek Pack. That was the simple version.

But nothing was simple. Her mate, the handsome gray, was shot illegally north of the park by a bear hunter. Near where she had denned. He died because a wolf does not read a surveyor's boundary. R9F was recaptured with her pups and moved back here, and helped along in the enclosure until another release, in mid-October. And was joined by a roving black male who had been freed from another reintroduction enclosure at Crystal Creek, and who now led the new pack. Which thrived.

Nobody thrived on their own. That's what Ren thought as he watched the rockered slip of a moon rise off the ridge as if on a tide. You could try. And even with help, and a mate, there were no guarantees. Because people, and wolves, died young. Tough. It was a tough world. Easy to say it. The word itself like armor.

◀

He did stretch out on the bunk with the window cracked open, and he did listen to the night, and he willed himself not to think. He pulled up the third blanket. When the wind was right, he could hear the faint burble of the creek. *Don't think, don't think, just listen.* But he did think. He thought about the boy with the MOM tattoo, as he had maybe dozens of times. He knew now who was leaving the notes. At first, wildly, he had thought it might be Aileen, the crazed evangelistic ex-nurse in Putney who hated his mother for robbing her of Ed, her one and only convert. He'd heard she still lived in Putney and had gotten more wild-eyed and vocal about the killing and lack of justice. But that's not who it was. Of course. It was a boy who had been orphaned, as he had been.

Last year, on a summer night, he had been called to Pebble Creek for a disturbance. When he pulled in, it was nearly midnight. Jan waved him down outside her RV near the entrance, and he could see her tear streaks in the headlights.

"He's just crazy," she stuttered. Ren had never seen her so out of sorts. This was a woman who shooed bull bison out of campsites with her clipboard, saying stuff like "You *know* you are better than this. C'mon, honey, c'mon, let's get a *move*." And they did. But not tonight. She said that tonight it was a young man who had pulled in by the creek and was high as a kite; he was blasting his speaker and keeping the whole camp awake and upsetting everyone. It was escalating. Ren told her to climb in, and he followed her directions to campsites seventeen and eighteen. Across the dirt drive was the creek, and an old Ram truck with a homemade wood camper on the back was pulled up to the bank. He hit his bar light and pulled up slowly. His headlights swung against a small crowd of campers, adults and children, and when he stepped down he heard "Gin and Juice," Snoop Dogg, at probably volume eleven, and he heard children wailing. The crowd had been focused on a dwindling fire beside the pickup and a figure sitting on a log there, and they now pivoted to Ren. The first thing he wondered was why at least three of the families had their little children in tow, half of whom were bawling. Were these vigilantes or spectators? Ren knew the line between them was often blurry.

The object of everyone's attention was sitting up straight, the hood of his sweatshirt over his baseball cap, staring into the low flames and fluttering embers and nodding to the song as if no one else were there. He was probably eighteen or nineteen. His eyes were glazed, and Ren saw in the firelight that they held a distance that made him shudder. In the kid's right hand was a two-foot length of rebar. The group fell silent when Ren walked up; even the children forgot to cry and followed him, wide-eyed.

"Bastard tried to kill me with that thing," a big man in a plaid shirt yelled.

Ren glanced at the man. Deadpan, he said, "Did you approach him?"

"Well—"

"Did you try to grab him or hit him?"

The man shut his mouth.

"Hey," Ren said to the kid, over the music. "Hey!" The kid swung his head, swept Ren up and down and turned back to the fire. "Hey! Can you turn that off? Turn that off so we can talk about this?"

The kid didn't look up. "Fuck off," he said, loud enough for all to hear.

"Hey!" the big man yelled. "There are children here!"

Ren pursed his lips. He said, "If you shut it down now and turn in, I'll go back to bed, where I'd way rather be."

The kid didn't respond. But then Ren saw his free hand come up slowly with raised middle finger.

Ren shook his head. He was cutting the kid slack and it wasn't being appreciated. "Turn it off," he commanded, louder now. "I'm Officer Hopper. I'm an enforcement ranger—that's 'cop' to you—and I'm telling you to shut it down. Last chance."

"Fuck the fuck off." The kid didn't even bother looking this time, the ultimate dis, but when Ren stepped forward the kid twisted, quick as a snake, and swung at Ren with the rebar. And Ren jumped back and pulled his Taser and shot him. And as he fell over and convulsed, the crowd actually cheered and the children resumed bawling.

When Ren finally got the young man to his feet and frisked him, he found a baggie full of pills that turned out to be fentanyl. Enough probably to kill a herd of elephants. Tory Jaeger was booked for felony assault and drug possession, and was treated with uncommon lenience by the judge in Mammoth because it was his first offense, and because the boy's mother had died the day of his arrest. It came out in the brief sentencing hearing that Tory's mother had been suffering the trials of pancreatic cancer and chemo and that her son was her only caretaker. They lived in Emigrant, south of Livingston, and it was also revealed that the father had left when the boy was two and that the mother had taken her son every summer since to this very campground, to hike and to fish, in an effort to give him what there was no father there to give. The two were extremely close, and the day he went to visit his mother for the last time she told him that they would camp in a place just as beautiful, by a creek as clear and musical, when she saw him again in heaven. He was cry-ing so hard he thought he'd pull himself together and went to get her a cup of chicken bouillon, and when he came back to the ICU she was dead. He didn't know what to do. He tried to unhook the IV and heart monitor and lift her in his arms to carry her out of the awful hospital in her thin gown and take her to Pebble Creek one more time, but the nurses yelled and the guards stopped him and he bolted from the hospital and fled. He had the fentanyl in his truck ready for this day, and he thought he'd drive to Pebble Creek then and join her. And so he made a fire, as they used to do, there across from their favorite campsite, and he took one of the pills, and it hit him right away and he forgot to take the rest. He thought she would come. He was sure, sitting there by the fire, that she would come and sit beside him on the log and put her thin arm around him and ask him if he was all right and did he want to fish first thing in the morning.

Jaeger got ten months in prison and five years probation. He'd have a felony conviction for assault *and* drugs. It would be hard to get any kind of good job. Now or ever. Ren lay on the bunk and thought for the nth time that he was just a kid that night who was out of his mind with grief and lost to the world and wanted somehow to get back to his mother, and also not to feel, and to just be left alone. And Ren had thrown the book at him, or allowed it to be thrown, and the boy's life was wrecked. And now, apparently, he had a yearning to wipe Ren off the map.

◖

That night, he dreamed of the house in Denver. He had come back. In front of it, where the lake had been, there was barren grass and dunes. The house itself had changed shape: it had been added on to. His key still worked, but when he stepped inside he saw scaffolding, exposed studs, a vaulted ceiling where none had been before. And he called out for Lea and no one answered. Maybe she was with the horses. In the dream they had horses. Where were they? There should be five. Or four. He went back outside and followed a track into the grass and sand hills and called and called. Had he asked his neighbor to take care of them? It had been over a year. He had the vague memory. There was his neighbor's rail fence, but no horses. He woke in a panic. He must have slept for hours, because when he raised his head and looked out the window, the narrow boat of the moon was drifting in the west, down-valley, unperturbed by the clamor in his chest.

Chapter Ten

Kelli, it turned out, had driven up to Cooke City for R and R; and Lance, who worked the front desk at the Super 8—who was sweet but not the swiftest—gave her a copy of mountain man Kyle's key so she could surprise him and . . . she did: surprise him. Kyle was giving personalized guiding service to Geneva, a nineteen-year-old wildlife enthusiast from La Jolla, whose parents and brother were poring over guidebooks on the floor above.

Do not double-cross a serious small-town Baptist who has thrown over her high-school sweetheart and business partner for your charms. That could be the moral that Kyle took away from the next five minutes. The claw marks to the girl's back would heal over; the broken lamp, TV, tiny coffee pot could be replaced . . . but to observers in the parking lot, Kelli's screams, and the sight of Kyle fleeing out the back door to his truck clutching a bundle of buckskin, could not be unheard or unseen. Nor could the lawsuit by the La Jolla family be retracted. They found grounds in "trauma caused by a person in a position of trust," and it may have been thin, but it didn't really matter what they sued for, the fancy tour company in Jackson Hole was happy to settle yesterday to make the thing go away. Kyle returned to his Airstream with a plan to move it up to Pebble Creek for some peace and quiet, but found it well ventilated and reconfigured by a grizzly bear.

There was no cell service at Slough Creek unless you hiked out to the rock pile down the road, but Kyle had his VHF radio, which all guides carried to stay in touch with the wolf-watcher chatter, and so he had no trouble getting a message from Lance at the motel saying that Jackson Hole Wildlife and Rafting had called to say that he was fired and they were sending another guide tonight to take over, and he'd be hearing from their lawyers. Well, grizzly bear number 689 had at least been considerate enough not to slash the trailer's tires, so the thing still towed, and the last anybody at the campground saw of Grizzly Adams Kyle was his truck and shredded camper hauling ass to the campground exit and taking the right turn toward the park highway, much too fast.

Ren had already left Slough Creek before this last chapter unfolded. He had taken Robbie's statement, which the poor kid, who was congenitally honest, could barely get out, and only while studying the far-off rise of Specimen Ridge. Yes, he had only broken the lock on Kyle's camper because he had smelled a gas leak. Thought he had. No, he has never owned a can of tuna, which he reviles. Etc. All this while Tenner stood beside him, shoulder to shoulder, and practically poked him in the ribs and whispered in his ear. That was that.

Tenner had caught Ren heading down the driveway and related these last developments. They were idling, truck to truck, window to window, which was the way a lot of important news in the valley was passed on.

Now, just after sunrise, Ren waved to Tenner and drove up to Wolf Watcher Hill and checked to make sure no one was doing anything inordinately dumb. There were already maybe forty spotting scopes set up on the two mounds. One benefit of these dedicated *Lupistas* was that they generally possessed an excellent wildlife ethic and, as a group, prevented on a daily basis the uninformed tourist from causing too much collateral damage. The father and son Ren had caught stalking the pack the other day had clearly been too quick for the watchers. Also, if you slotted in and set up your own scope in the firing line, and proved yourself not to be a complete idiot, and you were generally quiet and respectful, the group tended to ease you into the fold. Because, Ren decided, the daily currency of these recreational biologists was awe. Both given and received. How cool was that in a cynical age? So the communal gasps that went up when a squad of hunters brought down an aging cow elk in full view of the Swarovskis, or the squeaks and irrepressible guffaws that went up when a big female and four pups tumbled together in play, were as sincere as any hymn; and the naked admiration of the newbies when shown the iPhone camera adapters, the video clips of bear meeting wolves, or when told that the big black wolf there was nine years old, more than twice the life expectancy . . . the awe of the newcomers fed and nurtured the veterans. Ren noticed that the more reverence was spent on the elders, the more good information and wolf lore was shared. It was too bad, then, that all that collective wolf awe could not be consumed by the wolves themselves, and turned into muscle and bone.

Another thing Ren had noticed was that this culture of devotees attracted a certain subspecies of the lost and vulnerable. Most of those who came like bees to honey were simply crazy about wolves. They came in every size and stripe. Many of the seasoned wolf watchers were retirees, many were couples. They loved the outdoors and could no longer make the long hikes, the backpack or canoe trips, and so they came here where they could connect with wildness and daybreak and weather fronts and one of the most elusive predators on the planet, and it only cost them a fifty-yard walk up a well-trammeled hill. That was one subspecies. Another was composed of professional wildlife biologists, photographers, and naturalists. But another comprised those whose lives, for whatever reason, had fallen apart and who were casting about for a direction, if not a life ring. So Ren had remarked a host of divorcees and empty nesters, both women and men, who climbed Wolf Watcher Hill almost gingerly, as if each step might be somehow catastrophic, and who set up a new spotting scope with a timidness, the way a novice holds a gun, and who were, morning after morning, painfully shy. The proprietary and high-minded elders might glance sideways from their scopes now and then and after a while finally relent, and say gently, "This is your fine focus, here. And it's easier to get your bearings off a landmark with your naked eye first and then sight in . . ."

Never, ever, count out the old folks, Ren told himself.

Once, about a month ago—or maybe it was late July—it was—he and Hilly were having daybreak coffee on his porch and she told him that wolf biologists were beginning to understand more about the division of labor in a pack. "So, you know," she said, swatting at a rare mosquito, "average age of a Yellowstone wolf is three-point-two. Median age is about four."

"Whoa," Ren murmured. He'd had no idea.

"Pretty compressed. Pretty steep learning curve, too. So, by two years old, both males and females are on a hunting team. Here's the thing: Those young ones are light and fast. The fastest in the pack. But as they get older, the females stay light, and so keep their speed, but the males add muscle and bulk and slow down. So a typical hunting party might comprise three two-year-olds of either sex, an older female, and an older male. This brings what I call the wisdom factor. The older ones have a ton of experience and they know how to spot the most vulnerable available prey, and how to do the calculus: risk versus reward. Is the risk of attacking a certain animal worth the potential reward—how badly do they need the kill? So there goes a group of cow elk. It's summer, the leanest time for wolves—"

"Why?" Ren said. He'd had no idea about that either. He picked up the stainless-steel thermos beside his chair and reached across and poured Hilly a refill.

"Because in winter the deep snow makes it really tough on the ungulates—the elk and deer and bison. They have a hard time moving through it, and so that's one thing. And it's a lot harder pawing down to browse, and so the weaker ones become much more vulnerable. Also, in summer the wolves have the added stresses of rearing pups."

"Ah, got it."

"So, anyway, the hunt. There goes five cow elk, one is older, one is a yearling. And so the two-year-olds and the older female lead the chase and cut out the older cow. And turn her. And then the older male, who could not keep up in the sprint, now leaps and makes the kill. He's got the bulk and the strength."

"Wow."

"Yeah, and another thing. A grad student at Wisconsin published a study recently that showed that, yes, in territorial battles between wolf packs, which can be life-and-death, the packs with greater numbers have an advantage. But even more significant, statistically, in winning the fight is the presence of an older wolf, six years old or older."

"Kidding."

"Yep, your odds in a fight, pack versus pack, go way up. Kira called it the 'old wolf effect.' Again, biologists are extremely averse to anthropomorphizing their subjects, but I think it's fair to call it the advantage of wisdom."

Ren turned and studied Hilly. She was in profile, looking out at the valley that was both her lab and her home. She wore a black tank top and a light sun-shirt unbuttoned to the waist, long sleeves rolled up on her tendoned forearms. Strong slender neck and a few wisps of escaped hair playing on her temple and ear. Her thick braid lay over her shoulder and touched her collarbone. It was threaded with silver-gray. Ren thought she was beautiful; if her features had a purity it was because, he thought, the light that burned inside her was pure. And he kind of wondered why, this morning, she was telling him these stories. She was only five years older than he was.

Ren often got lost in memory and thought, even on patrol. This morning, after shaking off the unsettling dream, he was thinking about Hilly's stories and the pack across the river, how this was their hardest time of year, and he wondered if any were starving. He cruised slowly by the gathering crowd of watchers and their vehicles, and waved to three or four he knew. He drove on, in no hurry, and turned in at the Lamar River Trail lot and cruised through that, too, swinging wide around couples opening the hatches of their SUVs to pull out daypacks and hiking poles.

At Pebble Creek he took the turnoff left up to the campground. The resident bull bison was still in the little meadow, head down, still unconcerned, and still patched all over with ragged strips of hanging fur and looking like he needed to be reupholstered. Ren pulled up to Jan, the campground host, who was checking in the last of the new camp arrivals. She wore a teal-and-fuchsia scarf the way the French do, and had a voice that was laden with humor and carried a great distance, and Ren was often reminded that she was a triple threat: she could dance, act, and sing, and had worked on Broadway and in Las Vegas. When the shows got too exhausting, she became a process server and a bouncer. At the Savoy Club in Carson City she was known as Auntie J, and she had a calming effect on troublemakers, whereas the larger bouncers with Y chromosomes tended to still the waters by knocking guests unconscious. Jan was highly valued by management because she did not incite lawsuits. She might also jump up onto the bar when begged and perform a number from *Chicago*. Now in her mid-sixties, she had "common-lawed"—her words—old Ansel, who used to manage ranches in California and now spent most of his days rereading the Russians. Chekhov, Turgenev, Pushkin. Ren had once asked him why he loved them, as he himself found the going mostly too dour.

"I don't love them," Ansel had said.

"You don't?"

"Nothing worth serious study is lovable."

Ren had burst into laughter, surprised at the candor. Maybe the truth of it. Was it true? He wasn't sure. Not for him, maybe. He had stifled his laugh and Ansel had regarded him from his lawn chair as if he were a horse that couldn't turn right. Now Jan patted her latest check-in, a rumbling RV that was the size of a rock-and-roll tour bus. She sang, "That's right, number twenty, the loooong straight pull-in along the creek. It'll handle you just fine." Singsong. And she walked up to Ren's window.

"Any more drawn guns?" Ren said.

"Lord, when I saw the speargun I knew I was out of my depth. That's saying something."

"Pete pick up the Mog?" That was the super truck belonging to the rich kids.

"Yes, and you know what? That sweet homeboy from Minnesota drilled into the spare tire, too. And guess what?"

Ren shook his head.

"Those tires are made in Hamburg. Have you ever been to Hamburg?"

Ren opened his mouth. His elbow was out the truck window and she put a hand on his arm. "Don't answer," she said. "It's better to imagine you on the River Elbe." She shook off her reverie and said, "Eight weeks for new tires, at the soonest. The kids posted bail in Mammoth and they asked the judge if they could travel to Belize while they waited for their court date. They want to dive the Blue Hole. I just love young people who think big."

Jan's dancing, nearly black eyes, shut momentarily with pleasure, and Ren wondered for maybe the tenth time what she and old Ansel talked about in their folding chairs on a warm evening.

The radio crackled in his truck, and he told Jan he'd better get to work.

"I thought this *was* work," she said. "Now that I know it was pleasure, I'm really tickled."

He waved at her and pulled back out to the campground entrance and idled. The radio coughed, and he unclipped the mic and keyed it. "Hopper."

"Hey, Ren, it's Inky. You got a call from Kat Tooley, assistant DA in Butte. Hold on, I'll patch her through. Channel one nineteen."

"Thanks."

"Hi, this is Kat. I looked up the record of arrest of your Les Ingraham. I wasn't here then, but I took the liberty of pulling the file on the case. Apparently, there was a big senior-class keg party on Water Tower Hill, and there was a dispute over a varsity letter jacket."

"A letter jacket?"

"Well, the real dispute, I guess, was over a girl. Nothing changes, ever."

Ren liked Kat Tooley already. "Then what?" he said.

"Well, it was Ingraham's jacket, which he had of course given to a sweetheart, and then some other boy was wearing it and . . ."

"He beat the crap out of him."

"Pretty much. DA decided not to prosecute, because the conviction rate in this county for high-school fights is near zero. Juries have no stomach for it."

"Boys will be boys."

"Girls, too. My God. These days it's about half and half, no kidding. The victim is a Nils Jansen. He sells medical implants, and he and his wife have a horse property on Rocky Creek, east of Bozeman. I found his cell number; would you like it?"

"Wow. Sure. Thank you. Thanks very much."

"Aim to serve. Here you go."

She gave him the number and wished him luck. He turned off the truck and set his memo pad on his thigh. He didn't need to call Jansen, didn't really need any of this information, but he wanted it. Wanted to know what had happened and if there was a murderous or inordinately cruel streak in Les Ingraham.

What would Ren's own record in high school look like from this distance? It wasn't exactly unmarred by violence. There was the fight with the lacrosse dude and the incident with the French teacher. But the worst thing he did—the one he regretted sometimes at three in the morning—involved no blows and happened at a high-school dance. It was mid-May. Fine warm weather, and the committee had decided to hold the event outside, on the wide dining-hall patio. The school's very own R&B band, the Contenders, were performing. Ren had, for three years, nourished a crush on an art student in the class behind him.

Melissa Rhodes rarely said a word, and she was, Ren thought, the consummate introvert. She had one good friend, the serious equestrian Elizabeth Hinckley. Who was usually on her horse when she wasn't in class. So Melissa carried with her an aura of calm self-sufficiency. Her love was weaving. Not just blankets or shawls that somehow captured the gradations of blue in an evening sky, but tapestries and soft sculptures that told stories and created environments that were immersive and tactile and sometimes gently witty. He had often passed the window of the weaving studio and caught a glimpse of her bent to the loom, her soft hair swinging on her back as she moved to the rhythm of the shuttle, and of course he could not help but mythologize her as they read the *Odyssey* in sophomore English.

He had dated an older girl for two weeks at the end of his junior year. Nia had taught him the fundamentals of lovemaking without ever pretending that she loved him, and when she left he felt empty and relieved. Now Melissa seemed like the matter to Nia's antimatter. Her smile was hesitant but real. She never overreached. She was contained, and her calmness somehow soothed him. Most of the time Melissa seemed to be listening with one ear to some music wreathing in air, as if the choices and beauty in her weavings were coded in measures no one else could hear. Nobody else Ren knew seemed so attuned, or had the patience to listen.

So, though they had never engaged in more than a handful of conversations, he invited her to the spring dance. The surprise on her face and the flood of gladness in her eyes were checked swiftly, but he'd seen them. She had never been to one of the dances. No one had ever asked.

His mother called the night before the party. They had no caller ID on their landline, or he wouldn't have picked up. His father was working on a deadline project, so Ren was alone, eating a reheated rectangle of delicious lasagna that Pop had made a few days before. His mother called to invite Ren fishing. She was drunk. She said the Ausable was running low, as clear as a Swarovski lens, except she couldn't say "Swarovski," though she gave it three running starts. "The fishing is fab'lous," she said. And then she broke down and cried and told him that she was dead to him, wasn't she? She would never see him again. Fuck that. And then he hung up and would not pick up again, though the phone rang and rang.

The next day, Ren felt like whatever goodness he carried in his chest had been scrambled. Where it had been cool it was now hot. He picked up Melissa after the school dinner at the girls' dorm called Huseby but instead of being excited, he felt tense and so angry at his mother, and he couldn't shake it. It seemed lately that she always called at the very worst time, as if she knew somehow and was trying to sabotage him.

Melissa wore the biggest, unhindered smile, and a cornflower-blue country blouse and snug jeans she had patched all over with scenes from comic-book fabrics—*Wonder Woman* and *Spider-Man*—and Ren thought she was devastating. Beautiful. Why did he have trouble catching his breath, not in appreciation but from some frisson of grief? He made himself laugh and compliment her—why make himself? she was gorgeous—and he gave her his arm and they walked up the winding stone paths of campus toward the glow of the lights strung over the patio and the bunches of wildflowers tied to every post.

Melissa was nothing if not sensitive, and she sensed right away that something was not right. Had it been a hitch in a weaving, or an unsuited color in the weft, she would have patiently reworked it, or left the unexpected anomaly alone to enrich the piece in a surprising way. But boys were new. Boy. She had little experience and no confidence in the materials at hand, and so, of course, she thought it might be her. Why Ren was acting strange. He tried. He forced smiles and she mirrored him and tried to bring back the joy she had felt when she greeted him. But her own smiles fluttered to her lips and died. Ren commented on how great the band was, how Arnold had gotten into Juilliard. They danced. But there was no harmony, their rhythms were off, and finally Ren led her to the tropical-punch bowl and filled her plastic glass, and said, "I'm sorry, Melissa. I think I ate something bad. Can you hang alone?" Of course she nodded. What else could she do? And he left. He turned back once and saw that she had stepped back into the shadow, but not shadowed enough, because he could see that she was crying.

He tried to talk to her the next day, but she was remote. Not cold remote, but scared remote. She shook her head rapidly, her eyes entreating, seeming to say, *Please, please, don't make it worse, don't wound me, not again, I just can't.* And he—too angry at things he could not name—did not have the words to untangle anything, and so he walked away.

But. He had never been intentionally cruel. Ever. Had Les? He picked up the mic again and asked Inky to patch him through to Nils Jansen's number.

⟩

Jansen answered after the first ring. "Yah, hello—hang on." A thud, a "Good girl, here ya go," the rattle of a gate, then, "Sorry. Jansen here."

"Hi, hope I'm not interrupting. Sounds like chore time."

"Ha. Horses are chore time all the time. Who's speaking?"

Ren introduced himself as an enforcement ranger and said, "I was wondering . . . did you go to Butte High School?"

Now the man made a slight cough away from the phone. "Yeah, I did."

"Did you happen to go to a keg party with Les Ingraham?"

Silence. Ren could almost hear the wince.

"I'm sorry to stir up the past. I just wanted to know what happened that night."

"Why?" Jansen's voice was no longer neutral. "Long, long time ago." It was almost a plea.

"I know. I . . ." Ren, without thinking, snagged the chew tin out of his breast pocket and pinched out a dip. "I'm having some dealings with Mr. Ingraham."

"I'm sorry about that." Jansen let that hang in the air of the barn or corral or wherever he was. He sounded sincere. "Just a sec." Ren heard the heavy slide of a wood door, maybe to a tack room. He heard it cluck shut. "Okay, it was mid-May; I guess you know that."

"Yes."

"They had broken up, like, over a month before. Avery and Les. I'd never had a girlfriend and I was . . ." He stopped, and Ren heard the hard swallow. "I guess I was kind of overwhelmed. I don't even know why I wore the jacket. The one he had given to her. Wasn't thinking. I guess to please her. I had my own letter jacket for cross-country." Again the silent wince. "Four years at the state championships." The way he said it, it was modest, more like a confession. "We were all drinking on the hill. We had a keg, big moon, kind of end-of-the-year tradition; the cops weren't going to hassle us if we didn't do anything crazy. I wasn't even thinking about Les, I was just so happy to be graduating, to be accepted to university at Bozeman for the fall, to have a girl." A hitch of emotion. Ren felt for the man; this wasn't easy for Nils Jansen.

"I climbed up to the keg with our two cups, and the boy at the tap straightened and turned and . . ." Nils stopped. A second while he gathered himself. "Les. He turned, he was laughing about something, and saw me. I can't adequately describe it. It was—you know the way a summer storm can come over a ridge? Just like that. Mid-afternoon, and suddenly the cloud bank comes across and everything goes dark and the gust blows off your cap and the thunder cracks?"

Ren nodded in the truck, to himself. "Yeah, sure," he said.

Nils sucked in a breath. "It was like that. Like his eyes, his face, were storm. And he just dropped the full cups and swung. Total blindside. I had no chance. Knocked me back flat on the grass, the beer in my eyes, and then he was pulling and tearing off the letter jacket, his jacket, sure—I would've gladly given it to him, I didn't want the thing anyway. He ripped at it so hard he dislocated my shoulder and broke my arm. I heard a roar like some kind of animal. And he must've kicked my thigh, 'cause he broke that, too. And then, somehow, I wiped the beer out of my face with my good hand, and my broken arm was all twisted back, and I looked up. God. There was plenty of light—the party was planned for the full moon. And he was standing over me, holding the goddamned jacket, and he was blinking down at me. He was sucking air and blinking down, and it looked like he was crying. Like he started to *cry*. Like the storm had passed. 'Oh God, oh God,' he said. I remember that. And I must have blacked out. But they told me the next day that he picked me up and *carried* me off Water Tower Hill. Carried me down like a goddamn keg, and he got me into his truck and drove me to the ER. And he came into the hospital the next day, after he bailed out, and apologized. Took his frigging cap off and held it in both hands and said he didn't know what got into him, he had no business being upset anyway, they were broke up, et cetera. And he pleaded with me to press charges."

"He *wanted* you to press charges?"

"Yes."

Ren could imagine Jansen's face, thin, a lifelong runner—the dismay and pain and wonder of the memory playing over it. "I didn't—press charges—nor did the DA. I've come to find out that very few people on the planet know how to give a real apology. He did."

God. Ren thanked Nils Jansen and started the truck and pulled back onto the park road.

He turned east, figured he'd stop in at the gatehouse; he hadn't checked in with Donna and Ray for a while. He liked it there; it was no more than a shack, or dollhouse, but they always had coffee on and they were always glad to see him. It was like docking at a tiny island where they were eager for news of the wider world. The last few days, it seemed he was always speeding through.

He took his time driving now, enjoying the open road and fast-warming air. Focus on that, he thought. He might have been about to hum, but then he saw the traffic jam ahead and finished his thought: *Maybe I'm in the wrong job. A fireman probably shouldn't secretly wish the whole neighborhood would burn down . . .* He knew even before he hit the lights and pulled over beside the line of traffic that this was gonna be all about Mrs. Moose.

Dense woods on the right side of the road, but on the left were open groves of mostly lodgepole and fir in thick grass along the creek. The moose loved it. Mrs. Moose had been hanging around with her calf. Which created stellar photographic opportunities and one of the trickiest human-wildlife dynamics in the park. Because it's a fact that moose are one of the most dangerous animals in the United States, injuring many more people than, say, bears, and a mother moose with calf can be particularly tetchy. This was a big female, and she had been, all in all, pretty laid back about the crowds. But there were limits. Ren zigzagged between cars stopped in both lanes and became alarmed when he heard what he knew by now was the collective hum of a score of visitors murmuring to each other, "No way! Are you *seeing* that?" He squeezed himself through a line of photographers at the edge of the pavement and had to take at least a split second to digest the scene.

Down in the thick grass, halfway to a stand of pines, were a mother and a father. He knew they were parents because their daughter was ten yards ahead of them, holding out an apple. She was about six. And about eight yards past her was the gangly calf, all legs and ears and little hump. Her long ears were twitching forward and back and her neck was extended, her wet nose inhaling the sweet aroma and wavering toward the apple as if it possessed agency of its own. Cute. Mom and Dad thought so. Look, two little ones, reaching across the human/wild-animal barrier. Dad had his camera up, probably on video mode, and Mom was urging on her own calf: Ren heard, "*Aow,* so cute! That's right, honey, just like the horsey, remember?"

Well, it wasn't just like the horsey. Mrs. Moose had her own ears flat back and the fur on her hump was raised, a bad sign. He could hear a low grunt. The little girl was in mortal danger, no exaggeration. Ren processed it all in a single second and then jumped and slid down the steep bank.

He went straight for the little girl. He didn't give a shit, frankly, about the parents, except that it was probably no fun being an orphan. His dash frightened the calf, who shied back, thank God, and bolted toward her mother. Mrs. Moose had already been triggered, however, and Ren knew that once a moose gets an idea it's very difficult to dissuade her. She lowered her head and half stomped, half pawed the ground, and grunted again, and Ren scooped up the girl and without breaking stride veered right back past the parents so that they would form the first line of defense. The girl shrieked, which was a perfect response. But his priority was to get her clear of all danger, and so he did not unholster his pepper spray or try to make himself the object of Mrs. Moose's ire. He didn't stop until he had charged up the bank and set the girl on her feet and told a woman in her forties who held binocs and whose mouth was open, "Here, take her hand! Do not, under any circumstances, let go. Understand?" He squatted beside the girl, level with her face, and said, fast and as gently as he could muster in his haste, "What's your name?"

"Eva."

"Okay, Eva, you stay right here for a minute with this nice lady, okay? I'm going to get your parents, okay?"

She nodded and he was off, jumping down half the bank. Too late. The parents stared at the huge animal—who snorted now and bunched—and they turned back toward their daughter, confused, alarmed, terrified—one second they had the perfect Instagram shot, the next their kid had vanished in thin air, and now . . .

Mrs. Moose charged. She bunched and shot forward, head down like a battering ram, but Ren knew that that was not what would maim or kill these people. It would be the sharp and flailing hooves. From the road, from the couple, came a cry, part gasp, part shout, and the moose, who might as well have been breathing fire, closed in a flash to within twenty feet of Mom and Dad and . . . skidded and stopped dead. Dad was in front of Mom—gotta give him that—arms up as if crucified, his mouth an O of terror—and she was crouched behind him, shrieking, arms over the back of head and neck in nuclear-attack position. But the moose had stopped short. A bluff charge. Her hackles were stiff and straight up, and her head lifted, and for a moment she was a picture of outrage, her muscled hump and chest and shoulders dark with sweat and shining in the sun. And then she reared back and turned and trotted toward her baby, who was back in the shadows of the trees, not certain what all the fuss was about but certain there was a fuss.

Ren called back to the nice woman holding Eva's hand and asked her to hold it for one more minute. He loped across the grass. Mom and Dad were still partially paralyzed and in semi-shock. In just a few seconds they would catch sight of their child and nothing he said would reach them.

"Look at me," he ordered.

They did. It took a second for their eyes to focus.

"Are you okay?"

They both nodded like zombies.

"Good. That was close, right?"

Nod, nod.

"Too close. Way too close. Did you know that there is nothing in this park more dangerous than a cow moose with calf?"

The woman nodded. The man shook his head. His jaw was slack.

"They cause many more injuries in the U.S. than grizzly bears. I believe your little girl was in mortal danger. She could easily have been killed."

He let that sink in. The mom started to shake.

"Okay," Ren said gently. "Please, don't get close to any wildlife again. Rule of thumb in the park is a hundred yards. Okay?"

They both blinked, as if staring into sun, but the sun was behind them.

"Okay, go get your daughter. She's probably a little traumatized. Go on."

They went. He had spoken calmly but he was more than pissed. Had the moose truly charged and made contact, she would probably have been put down. The calf, too, because she was still nursing. How many innocent lives had been lost in service to Instagram? He waited until the couple had clambered up the bank and disappeared, and then he walked back to his truck.

Why did he ever think he could do this job? The appeal was that he could live in a wild place, be out in it every day, make a living. Well. He should have been an offshore fisherman or a surveyor. Or a biologist. PR, which is what he spent the rest of the day doing, was becoming less and less his forte.

He continued on to the gatehouse and shared a Mountain Dew with Donna and Ray, who kept a mini-fridge next to the desk. Then he turned around and dove back into the park, cruising the road all the way back to Tower, directing traffic at the jams, stopping where tourists with spotting scopes had gathered off the road, answering questions. He made a valiant effort. But it was the anger again. He couldn't quell it. He conversed with visitors while his spirit begged him to flee. He could not flee. People waved him over. They asked directions, they asked about the caching behavior of grizzly bears—there was a boar on a bend of the river feeding on a cow elk—they asked how to tell the difference between a vulture and an eagle, they even asked where was the closest cold beer. He could relate. He wondered himself if he'd rather be in a dark, cool bar with an iced longneck than out on this road. Rather be anywhere else. The anger was a tightness behind the sternum he could not shake. Its source was manifold. He could not point solely to an ignorant couple with a child and an apple, or entitled rich kids with a three-hundred-thousand-dollar camper truck and a speargun . . . or to poachers, or even to Les Ingraham. It was all of them and more, and deeper, and the reasons ramified. He really needed a break. There was no break.

Whining again.

Not whining.

What, then?

I feel like I'm choking.

Aw, poor guy. There is a classmate of yours fighting fires in California right now on his third month who will not be home to help his wife give birth to their son. There is—

Not helping.

Suck it up.

He did. He drove to the Tower Ranger Station and picked up his mail. The envelopes held a Trout Unlimited membership renewal, an electronic paycheck deposit receipt. There was a postcard from his dad. His father had remarried—the Putney property assessor—nine years ago and they were, apparently, on vacation in Zihuatanejo. The card featured a Corona on the arm of a beach chair in the foreground, and a breaking wave with a rocky island behind it. On the back the scrawl said simply, "There's a reason that guy in *Shawshank Redemption* always dreamed of coming here. We'll all go together next time. Miss you, Ren. Pop"

We'll all go together next time. That would be nice. He missed his father, too.

Something about the promise. We'll all go. Did his father know he was lonely? That he was always lonely, no matter how many people he had around him?

Tower was pretty much just an intersection with a compact Park Service–brown building and a gas pump. Inky was in; the other two enforcement rangers were on the road. She was behind the counter, where she would sell park fishing licenses and hand out maps all afternoon. Nobody loved the job, and the three traded off.

"Zihuatanejo looks nice," she said.

"Everything looks nice in mid-September."

"Right? I was even dreaming about visiting my sister in San Antonio."

"That sounds fun."

"It's never fun. Her husband is the biggest mansplainer on the planet, and we always get in a wicked fight, and he always kicks me out before my flight home."

"Damn. Where do you go?"

"Well, it costs two hundred fifty dollars to change the flight, so I always figure I'll just keep the return ticket and spend that money on a few nights at the Alamo Inn—there's three of 'em—and I sightsee and read, and meet my sister for lunch without Josh. Did you ever sightsee in San Antonio?"

Ren shook his head. He felt a little better already.

"They have this historical movie they play on the side of a church. It's really cool. Not being sarcastic." She smiled. "You've been busy lately."

"I guess."

"Those kids with the Mog and the speargun really pissed off the judge. They wanted to go on vacation, too, I guess. To Belize, to scuba-dive. Vacation from vacation. They started whining about it."

Ouch. Is that what he'd been doing, in his head? "I heard," he said.

"He made them spend two nights in jail."

Ren fist-bumped her and thanked her. He checked his watch: 4:15. Good. From here, going straight north through Mammoth, he'd make it to Livingston in under two hours. Plenty of time to have a barbecue dinner at Zach's before his date with the Path-finders. Shouldn't be too many folks so early; in fact, tonight it shouldn't really get crowded until seven o'clock.

Chapter Eleven

Dinner at Zach's should have been on the Park Service. He was working, after all. But he had told no supervisor about his investigation into the group, said nothing about his suspicions. If anyone in Special Investigations was alarmed by the increasing incidents of vandalism and poaching, and the mounting evidence that they were organized, it would have been news to the rangers on the ground. So he was on his own.

"Hey, I'm going to use Cell Block Six to change," he had said to Inky. It's what they called the small back room where the station's rangers wrote their reports and played cribbage.

"Be my guest," she said. "Promise I won't look."

And when he emerged in jeans, dress boots, and a flannel snap shirt, and settled the black Stetson on his head, she whistled low and long. "Someone's gonna get lucky tonight," she said.

He waved. He honestly hoped she was right.

He'd been wrong about the crowd. When he pulled into the sun-blasted gravel parking lot at five-fifty, the place was already packed. Rows of pickups, flatbed ranch trucks carrying water tanks with coiled lariats hung from rifle racks, stakebeds with goosenecks and loops of orange baling twine slung from the rails, and, at the edges, in the shade of the cottonwoods along the river and up along the ball fields, the duallies hauling four- and six-horse trailers. A day riding the range wasn't going to keep anyone from Saturday barbecue at Zach's.

He drove past slowly and looped back toward the town center and parked in deep shade at the edge of a lot belonging to a closed craft store. He walked back the half-mile; he could smell smoked meat for most of the distance.

Zach's was a low log building with a narrow porch and potted geraniums hanging from the eaves. As soon as he pushed through the double glass doors he was hit with more than the roast of barbecue: there was the toasted sweetness of fresh-baked pie crust, the heady aroma of French fries, a tannic whiff of iced tea. And the noise: clatter of plates hitting wood, the steel ring of a spatula knocking the grill, the call of waitress to her cook, ting of the counter bell, and beneath it all, like a groundswell, the clamor of conversation. It was festive, almost celebratory. Why not? It was Saturday, end of the week, the summer had brought rains, the fall was coming clear and crisp, and dishes piled with maybe the best barbecue on earth were hitting the tables in an almost syncopated rhythm.

From where he stood he could see two rooms, the red-check-covered tables almost all full with what looked to be families, ranchers in sweat-stained cowboy hats just off rides checking stock, a men's softball team in purple jerseys, couples of every age. Ren understood immediately why people came from all over the county to eat here. And why the place worked for semi-clandestine meetings: everybody was already here; a convergence of trucks would attract little attention, and a back room amidst the hubbub would be almost as secure from eavesdropping as a sound booth.

A young woman, maybe college age, in blue apron and carrying a tray with baskets of fries, breezed by so close and fast he felt the wind, and as she did she half turned and said, "Be right with ya!" She came back, the tray now full of half-empty iced tea glasses; she blew a strand of hair off her face and said, "Just one?" He nodded. Another girl was passing, heading for the kitchen, and the first handed the tray off seamlessly, and without a single word; Ren thought of a relay race in track. He loved watching a pro, whatever the work. She swept a menu off a rack without looking and over her shoulder said, "Follow me," and he did.

There was a small table, just cleared, in the corner. She handed him the laminated menu. "Tea?" she said.

"Sure."

"Sweet?"

"Sure."

She breezed off. He twisted in his chair. Above him on his left was a black-and-white photo of "Main Street Livingston 1892"—rutted mud in the road, wagons, boardwalks. The mandatory false front advertising "Dry Goods." It didn't look like much fun—there was no Zach's, no softball, no sweet tea. No Pathfinders. He checked his watch: 6:28. Plenty of time. A sweating plastic glass appeared on the tablecloth. "Ready?" she said. She was smiling down at him, head cocked to one side, studying. He was dressed like a rancher or a hand, but he didn't really look like one. He had deep crow's feet at the corners of his eyes and his hands were dark and weathered, but. There was something about him. Ren read the question in her eyes, and an alarm bell sounded. He was relieved that he hadn't tried anything cute like gluing on a fake mustache. A round tray was tucked under her arm, and she held up an order pad and a pen.

"Sure," he said. "Whatever combo you recommend."

Her smile remained but she narrowed her eyes, quizzical. My first mistake, he thought. Or maybe second, or third. Maybe I shouldn't have ventured out into open ground. Maybe I should have ordered straight off the menu. "You been here before?" she said.

"Nope," he said. Best to stick to true things. "But I heard it's the best anywhere." He was bracing for another personal question, like did he work on a ranch in the valley, but her eyes were steady and they roved over his face, and then she said, "I wouldn't know. Never been to any other barbecue 'cept Pete's in Bozeman and, between you and me, it sucked."

He laughed. "Pete's my brother," he said.

Her eyes widened, and she put the hand holding the pen to her mouth. "Oh! Jeez. Sorry!"

"Just kidding."

She blew out, snorted. She was laughing and she wanted to slug him in the shoulder; he knew that if he were her relative he'd have a bruise right now. Okay, good, he had derailed her curiosity or suspicion for the moment; now they were buds.

"Pork ribs, brisket, chicken," he said.

"Works for me." She wrote it down, tongue in the corner of her mouth. Then her eyes came up, lit with play. "My mom says it's better to be decisive, even when you're not sure. The world likes you better."

"Right," he said. "Well, I've decided to use the restroom." She pointed behind her, to a narrow hall on the same side of the room, shook her head, and hurried off.

He had already seen the sign. And he had seen the solid double door in the south wall, river side, which could only be the private-event room. It was on the way to the bathrooms. He pulled out his iPhone, tapped the voice memo app, hit the "Record" button, and felt for the small roll of electrical tape in his chest pocket. Around it he had wound a strip of Gorilla tape. From the outside it looked just like a can of chew in his shirt. He slid his chair back and rose and made his way along the south end of the room. He took his napkin and made to wipe a sauce stain on his snap shirt, distracted as he walked, and when he got to the double doors he didn't look up but grasped the lever door handle and pushed through.

Not a hall, but a sizable room. No one else in it, thank goodness. Three long event-tables arranged in a U, the head table against big windows that looked out over the river, which was green in the long sun and flurried with riffles. He went straight for it, the table where the VIPs would be sitting. Not red-checked tablecloths here, but white linen. He crouched fast, lifted the skirt of the cloth. The tape was already in his hand, and he pulled off a foot-long strip, tore it in three with his teeth, and taped the phone to the underside of the table. Stood and walked briskly to the door and almost ran into a young man carrying a heavy tray of iced tea pitchers up on one hand.

"Oh, sorry!" he said. "I thought this was the bathroom!"

The kid looked just out of high school; he had raw pimples on his jaw. He beamed a goofy smile and said, "Happens all the time. I think they should move the stupid sign further down."

"Good idea," Ren said, and made his way to the real restroom, where he really did have to pee. He hadn't downed his tea yet, and so it had to be nerves.

All in all, a delicious meal, which he would have appreciated more if he hadn't had his eye on the double doors and the men who walked through them. He wished he had another phone to snap their pictures as they came through the crowded rooms; as they stopped to chat with this family or that, raise a raucous laugh, tip their Resistol cowboy hats to what looked to be newly-weds at the far side of a table; as they shook hands with an ath-letic high-school boy who must have just made varsity, or leaned down over their wide rodeo belt buckles to peer at a baby still in a car seat. What struck Ren most of all was the deference—the clear appreciation the families and couples had for the attention of these men, and the obvious respect. Whatever the Pathfind-ers were, they were composed, in part, of valley royalty.

Others came that were not ranchers or hands. There were two men still in mechanic's coveralls, one balding, one with hair hastily slicked back, their oval name patches in cursive on each breast, which Ren couldn't read. A young kid with a black beard and stained green Gore-Tex anorak who looked like a climbing or fishing guide. And a lumbering barrel-chested biker with a long gray rat tail and a leather vest. At least he looked like a biker—Ren bet he would see a Harley, probably chopped, parked in the shade of the porch when he left. And by the time he was halfway through his coleslaw and had drunk a refill of sweet tea, here came Krebbs and Chesnik together—Krebbs again in his Livingston Archery windbreaker and Chesnik in the Carhartt. Ren tipped his head down over his plate, and his own wide hat brim covered his face.

There was no sign of Les Ingraham. No Kyle either. Good.

At six-fifty-five, the trickle of attendees stopped like a closed faucet. And Ren watched as what must have been the entire waitstaff left off their general duties and began streaming through those doors, ferrying trays mounded with barbecued meat and baskets of fries and bowls of beans and slaw. Clandestine meeting or not, these men felt so at home here, so within their perimeter—their castle walls—that they saw no need to disguise anything except what was being said. At five after seven, the intrusions of the servers ended and he'd bet money the door was locked from the inside. Ren felt himself humming like a radio receiver on a strong signal: the timing of all of it suggested the group was highly disciplined.

He lingered over the cherry pie, asked if they were too busy for him to take up a whole table with a cup of coffee—to which the girl replied, "I am *buying* you a cup of coffee."

"Why?"

"Because you're Pete's brother."

He laughed. She might have been twenty, much too young, but he liked her sense of humor and felt the frisson of flattery, and forgot for the moment the real danger of being here. Not that anyone would probably attack him in Zach's, but if they discovered him, Ren knew his life in the park would become more difficult and scary. At five after eight, he paid the bill, tipped his hat to the girl, and left. He walked—not too fast—to his truck in town and drove it around to the edge of the ball field and took up his binoculars and strolled across the empty diamond. No wind. Smell of the river and cut grass. Dark now, and the sky dense with stars.

He sat in the outfield and glassed the front door of the restaurant. It was all patrons leaving now, an early crowd. The stuffed and contented diners fanned out to their vehicles. Headlights blinked on, and the thrum of starting engines and crunch of gravel carried over the grass as they pulled out and headed home. Ren wasn't sure why, but he felt a certain peace, a happiness for them all, and for the warm night on the cusp of autumn. Maybe it was the ribs, the pie, the coffee, the joyful ruckus of families together at the end of the week—maybe it was the knowledge that this was not always a zero-sum game. It did not have to be these people versus the wolves; Zach's on the one hand, or the Lamar Valley with its herds on the other. Or did it?

At eight-forty, it had been ten minutes since anyone had exited and there were only about twenty-five vehicles left in the lot, almost all pickups. The lot was lit, if dimly, by the windows of the restaurant, and Ren ambled over to first base, where there was a better angle for the binoculars, and he jotted down as many license plates as he could see. He got to the end of a line and scanned back. Maroon Dodge Ram with a homemade wooden camper on the back. His heart kicked into a canter. The kid. Who was threatening him with who knew what. A ten-inch bowie knife. Made sense that he would drift into the Pathfinders' orbit: Ren remembered that his mother was from Emigrant, not far from Livingston, and the group was the perfect foil for the entity that had wrecked his life. Also, Tory was an orphan, and the appeal of an instant family of brothers would be irresistible.

At nine o'clock, the door opened and the ranchers in their hats, the mechanics in coveralls, the biker—yes, there was the Harley—came out under the lights of the porch and dispersed. The kid in the anorak emerged, talking to a tall cowboy in a cream Stetson, maybe the leader. He climbed into the Dodge with the camper and drove off. At nine-ten, Ren tapped on the locked door and the pimply boy opened it, and recognized him. Ren said, "Hey, in the confusion of getting lost before, I think I left my phone in that big room." His waitress, he was relieved to see, was nowhere in sight—probably sorting silverware in the kitchen. "Have at it," the kid said. "Just let yourself out."

He did. He went swiftly into the back room, which had already been stripped of tablecloths, reached under the main table, and unstuck the phone. It still lit when he tapped it, and the voice memo was still recording.

Chapter Twelve

The boy from Emigrant lost his mom as I did. What Ren thought as he drove back up the Yellowstone. It was at the end of his first season that he got the call. He was driving. It was a night like this: clear and warm and swarmed with stars, stars moving over the valley in schools as thick as ocean minnows—he was thinking that and remembering their trips to Maine when he was a boy, out to visit his mother's cousins on North Haven—how the light sprayed down into green water and schools of translucent minnows, and how the popweed clung to the pilings of the pier and swayed with the swell. The ferry horn blasted, and there was that excitement of leaving the mainland for an island. An island. How islands became for him, in one form or another, a sanctuary. Yellowstone was an island in a way, and so was the Lamar Valley. This was two years ago, and he was driving. He was remembering the ferry ride, how the pilot navigated between the flotillas of lobster buoys in the bay, and he was feeling some gladness, some peace, when the radio erupted with his call sign. It was Inky, and she said it was his father, and she patched him through.

"Hey, Pop."

"Hey. Are you driving?"

"Yes."

"Maybe pull over."

"Okay." He was just beyond the Baronette pullout, the mountain-goat-viewing pullout, and he slowed and stopped in the road and backed up into it. The great dark cliffs were above him, bulked against the stars. In their light he could make out the swaths of rockfall on the slopes. He waited, tense.

"I'm ready," he said.

"Your mother died about an hour ago."

Did the constellations shudder? The bulwark of cliffs, the spurs and rock ledges, blurred.

"Oh," Ren croaked. "How?"

"She was driving back from Lake Placid. There was a bar she went to, I guess. She hit a tree."

Ren did not say anything. He had nothing to say. He stood in the empty parking strip with the mic stretched out the door. He didn't think to switch to the radio on his belt. He shook.

"Ren?"

"Yeah."

"You there?"

"Yeah."

"The service is Sunday in Lake Placid. Do you think—"

"I'll be there."

"Okay. Do you want to come home first and drive together, or fly into Burlington?"

"I better fly in. I'll have to request the days."

"Okay. I look forward to seeing you."

"Pop?"

"Yeah."

"Was she—?"

"Yes. Very. Like point-one-nine."

"Okay. I'll call you." He clicked off. He never had to tell his father he loved him. His only thought as the tears dripped off his chin onto the pavement was that he would never share a sandwich beside a river with his mother again. With their rods leaning against the branches behind them. With her hair blowing across his face.

A night like this. Two years before. Now he played the radio loud to keep himself awake. He kept his speed ten miles over the limit. He got to his cabin in less than two hours. It was a few minutes to eleven. Way past his bedtime. And he knew he wouldn't sleep, and so he made black tea and sat at his tiny desk and played the recording.

◖

"To Mr. Recurve. Social-media outreach. Any progress?" Voice older, authoritative, rough at the edges like a frayed rope.

Clearing of throat. " 'Bout how it's been going. Steady. Got three guys in Escalante. Different story there." West Tennessee, less drawl than Arkansas or the Carolinas. It was Chesnik—Ren recognized the voice from the Perk. Recurve. They must all have snazzy call signs. Cute. Like a bunch of fifteen-year-olds, Ren thought. Except that their actions were not at all kid stuff.

"How so?" said the moderator, or president.

"Well, the Monument won't let 'em dig. But it's not gold nor uranium, it's fossils. They say they got triceratops in there, complete, worth more than the whole damn town. Guess who *is* allowed to dig 'em up?"

Murmur in the room, anticipation of outrage. Ren knew they were talking about the Grand Staircase–Escalante National Monument in Utah. There were hills and ridges of flowing blue mud stone rich in fossils, both plant and animal, with layers before and after the asteroid wiped out most of life on earth sixty-six million years ago. Findings in the place had added much to the understanding of how ecosystems and biodiversity recover from a mass extinction event. His friend Kirk was a paleobotanist and had once invited him on a dig there.

"Museum in Denver," Chesnik continued. "Buncha doctorates from Yale and cute little interns from Colorado." Laughter. "So these three are on board. Full on. They're done with getting run off. I gave 'em Tops and Rex. Seemed apropos."

Apropos. Chesnik was a sleeper, talked crick-and-hollow but was well educated. Ren bet most of these guys were.

"Anything else?"

"A guy in Bozeman. Runs a sawmill. Pretty fired up about the beetle kill off of Bighorn Pass. Says they're mismanaging the crap out of it, what else is new, and the whole thing's gonna burn. Not good burn, but hot enough to scorch roots, kill the soil. He's not saying clear-cut the park wholesale, he's saying let him go in and thin it, the standing dead. He's been petitioning, writing letters, the usual bullshit, and they look at him like he's some kinda worm. Dude's got a master's in forest management."

Rising chorus of excoriation.

"I gave him Saw." Ren heard fists pound the tables in affirmation. He was in his cabin, at the small work table against the south wall, listening to the recording on his phone. A cold wind shook the windowpanes and brushed the limb of the big pine against the roof. Radically different weather up here from the Indian summer down in Livingston.

"Good," said the MC. "And while we're at it, on the north edge of the park, I'd like to commend Mr. Sackett on the vehicle countermeasure." Ren guessed he was talking about the slashed tires on the park ranger truck. Sackett was surely from Louis L'Amour.

"Sure as shit poked the hornets' nest," another voice asserted. Young and smooth, sounded local, Montana. "My source at HQ says they're pretty ruffled. Enforcement rangers have started patrolling in pairs." Ren frowned. That was news to him. So was the presence of sympathizers in the park administration.

"Speaking of countermeasures, our newest member is Stack. For Stack Time. He's a local boy, and he's young but motivated. Already had a significant run-in with our friends in the park. Stack, why don't you stand." Light applause. "He's ready for his first exercise. Aren't you, son?"

"Yes, sir." Swallowing the words. Cowed by the attention. Some drumming of the tables.

"Like I've said before, we don't do initiation here. You walk in that door, we figure you're serious and we count on you to be stand-up."

"Yes, sir."

"Okay. Sit down, son."

Son. The kid. "Stack." Surely this was the young man whom Ren had put away and who was now harassing him. His first "exercise." Nice euphemism. Did the plan entail burying the bowie knife in Ren's back?

"Brings me to Mr. Red." The resonant, sanded, charismatic voice of the leader. The murmuring ceased. "Hasn't been to a meeting in . . ." Beat while he probably checked a roster. ". . . three months. While we appreciate his initiative lately, the man is a lone wolf. Things almost went sideways the other day." Pause for emphasis. Silence in the room. "I hear he almost killed a biologist. That girl from the Rose Creek station. I don't need to tell you men how bad that would have gone. One PR stumble like that . . ." He let each man imagine his own repercussions. Ren heard the clink of ice in a glass. Maybe the man was sipping his iced tea for effect. Yes, there was the clack of the glass coming down not softly on the table.

Red. Ren shivered, not from cold, but almost the same rush as when a big trout hit his fly and ran. The biologist, Red, red ribbon—first direct link. Scary and reassuring at once: someone in their group had set the trap, *and* they did not plan or even support it. Rather, they were *against* it. So the Pathfinders drew some kind of line. That meant, probably, that the boy was not planning to kill him.

"The man's gone rogue," the leader said. "Frankly, I can't say I didn't see it coming."

Les. Not a place he traveled he didn't cause consternation.

"Thing is," the leader said, "our appeal is growing. Among regular folks up and down the valleys. Who see that locking up millions of acres for the enjoyment of a few rich folks in Sprinter vans is not what this country is about. Who maybe live on the edge of Yellowstone, our backyard. Managed well, we could graze our cattle and *improve* the soil, the browse. Log it, thin it, like up on Bighorn, and prevent the kinds of megafires we've seen. They're worried about elk overpopulating; we know how to take care of that. Think of what a hunting season could do . . ."

Chorus of hoots and drumming of tables. "It's a damn no-brainer is what it is. But we're disrupters, aren't we?" Applause, some shouts. When it died down he said, "We raise awareness, we get folks involved. We're not killers. We end up killing some-one and half those folks who just want a better life for their families will turn away. We are decent men. That's what the Pathfinders is founded on—common decency and common sense." Another long pause while maybe he looked around the room, man to man.

"Someone needs to have a talk with old Red," he concluded. "And I mean right now."

That was the nut of it. Ren rose stiffly and drank cold water from the faucet and stepped onto the porch for some fresh air. He shook the tension out of his neck, his shoulders. These guys were committed and disciplined, they had roots in the sur-rounding communities, maybe in the park itself, and they were spreading the gospel. And Ren thought it was bullshit. Greed disguised as Good Samaritanism. There were few places left on earth where large areas of habitat were wholly protected and mostly intact. Whenever and wherever the protections were lifted, these remnants were always destroyed. Couldn't humans leave the few remaining tattered patches alone? Voracious. Most voracious predator on the planet.

Ren spat off the porch. These men, he knew, were going to be a pain, and dangerous, for a long time to come. Like an endemic disease. And if one member had already gone rogue, it would happen again. But it was reassuring, at least, that violence against others wasn't in their game plan. They would just keep harassing, keep vandalizing, keep making the park's job more difficult.

He turned his head and heard far off, upstream, a single wolf raising a circular repeating howl. It was thin, carried on the wind, insistent, undaunted. That didn't happen every night, not close to it, and he always felt lucky to hear the affirming cry—*I am here, I am here.* Tonight it sounded like a prayer.

He went back inside and sat again and tapped "Play." There were two hours of recording, all the usual scaffolding of official meetings—the reading of minutes, agenda, report on fund-raising; another report on countermeasures against the increasing use of drones by park enforcement and U.S. Fish and Wildlife, said countermeasures consisting of the timely application of a twelve-gauge shotgun by a shooter in a mask. There was mention of FreeTheParks.org, which they would develop as their public face, which would raise money and sue in the courts and lobby and support sympathetic politicians. But what interested Ren most was that these seemingly reasonable men preferred direct action to any of that, and that each act of subversion was associated with a single call sign and a single man. And that Red had to be Les Ingraham. Ingraham, who could not be held accountable even by a radical terrorist group. Which—let's call a spade a spade—they were.

He finished the recording, transferred it to his laptop and then to a memory stick, brushed his teeth on the porch, and went to bed. He lay on his bunk for a long time, thinking about the wolves. And the unpeopled mountains rising around him in the dark, and the valleys and towns beyond them. What was anyone, wolf or man, supposed to do with a life?

He thought about 755. *Return. Try one more time.* That's what the old wolf did. As he aged, as his stare hollowed with loss. Widowed and widowed, driven away, he always came back. Until, on a night probably like this, he wandered alone across the park boundary and was never seen again.

Because for the old wolf it was more than breeding. It seemed to be about love. And creating a small pack. Ren thought about his own life. What could he create? A story. A web of friendship. A solitary song. He lay on the bunk and drifted with his thoughts like a boat tossed on a rolling swell, because, surely, there was no solid ground.

Chapter Thirteen

At eight, the radio crackled and woke him. A fierce old boar grizzly, 692, had attacked a wounded twelve-hundred-pound bull elk in the middle of the Madison River, drowned him there, and rolled him like a barrel to the far bank, away from the road, while a hundred vehicles stopped dead and emptied themselves of visitors. All night the bear tore up the mud bank and covered the elk in an attempt to cache it, and fed on the carcass intermittently, and then lay over it and napped, rising reluctantly to fight off the wolves and coyotes that came to scavenge. Videos taken at dawn were already going viral, and the traffic jam comprised hundreds of vehicles. HQ asked Ren to head down to help manage crowd control.

Ren made a cup of extra-strong coffee, poured it into his thermos, ate a banana and two nut bars, and dragged himself down to his truck. He was so groggy he had his hand on the door handle before he noticed: he had no windshield. Or windows. And his boots crunched crumbs of broken auto glass as he stepped. What the fuck? He jolted back as if the door were electrified. He was wide awake now, and breathing hard. He breathed.

He walked around the poor old pickup—that's the way he felt, almost as if someone in a feud had deliberately injured an innocent horse. The truck had done nothing to anyone. The headlights were smashed out and the taillights broken. Jesus. The tires had been left untouched. An added humiliation, he thought: now you have to drive down the highway in a wreck, drive through crowds who will gawk and gossip. Folded into the far forward door, like a traffic ticket, was a pink receipt from the general store, this one unmarked. Fuck.

He felt the anger rise like bile and shook himself. *You cannot spiral,* he said to air. *You cannot spiral now. Keep it together, you're a pro.* He climbed into the shattered truck and drove.

He ignored the dumbstruck tourists all along the route and swapped for a new truck at Tower and headed south and west. He stayed on the Madison into mid-afternoon, answering questions and directing traffic, and was relieved at two o'clock by Angie from Mammoth. By the time he ran the gauntlet home, it was almost time to knock off. As he pulled into the drive below the cluster of buildings, he thought he'd go back to the cabin and catch up on incident reports, and maybe, after five, he'd go on into Cooke City and buy Pete a beer.

But first he wanted to check in with Hilly. Needed to, he wasn't sure why. Tell her about Kyle's big surprise visit from Kelli and his hasty departure. About Robbie's inborn sweetness, his near inability to give a statement that wasn't true, how the words stuck in his throat crosswise and how Tenner poked them out of him. She would laugh so hard, he could see it—a rare eruption—she needed a good laugh. He wanted to tell her about moose versus family. This was a new sensation for him—pulling into the research-station parking spot and wanting to head up to her cabin before he stopped in at his own.

Careful, boy, he thought.

He wouldn't mention a thing about Livingston or the Pathfinders. She was involved, certainly; he could not unsee the bottle of Karo in the coffee can, the same stuff left on the hood of the outfitter's truck that had been ruined with corn syrup.

Her pickup was beside his, and when he got out he could hear her engine ticking. Still cooling down. She'd just got in. He doubted she could walk far with her cane and badly bruised shin; maybe she'd gone to town to check her texts and e-mail, and had enjoyed a rare restaurant meal.

He made himself bring his daypack up to his place, and he unbuckled his utility belt and hid the gun behind the fridge; and he made himself set a kettle of water on the stove and wait until it whistled. He poured it into a travel mug over a teabag of Earl Grey and stirred in honey and a dollop of half-and-half. Then he shrugged on his Carhartt and walked up the track.

She wasn't on the porch, which she often was on an early-fall afternoon—catching the warmest part of the day before the sun dropped and the wolves got active. He knocked, waited. After a few seconds he called: "Hilly?"

"Yuh." He heard it barely. Her voice sounded strange. He thumbed the latch and opened the door.

She was at her desk near the window, head down on her arms. Not turned to the side, but buried. Her cane lay on the rag rug as if suddenly dropped.

"Hey," he said. "Hey. What's up?"

She didn't lift her head. He saw her shoulders bunch and release in a single heave.

"Hilly, hey. You all right? What happened?"

He went to her and put his hand on her back and felt the waves of her sobbing. He let his hand rest on the broadcloth of her blouse and felt the heat of her skin through it and the judder of her breath. He spread his fingers as if to somehow broaden their solace and just let them rest. If his palm imparted comfort, it received pain; he felt he might sob, too, though he wasn't sure why.

Bad, he thought. *This one's going to be bad.*

For a while, neither moved but for the quiet crying. He looked at the rug and at the cane lying there, dispossessed of use.

"Hilly," he said. "Do you want to tell me?"

Minute shake of the head, not enough even to move the braid curled on her shoulder. But she said, "My phone." Her phone. He saw it on the oak desktop next to a field guide to Rocky Mountain shrubs and grasses. He reached for it with his free hand and placed it next to her elbow. She lifted her head enough and thumbed her fingerprint. The screen opened and lit on her text messages. "The recent one," she whispered.

The top message was from an area code he didn't recognize. He pressed it. No text, just two photos. The first was a grainy shot of a rumpled figure in brown grass, curled around herself in fetal position: Hilly, for sure. There were the dark field pants, her fleece sweater—and there was the iron clamp on her leg and five visible links of chain. Ren's insides turned to ice. Next pic: A large fawn wolf—Ren recognized him—paler, brighter somehow than the others. The big runner in the pack that had lined out the other morning at daybreak, one of the four scouts who broke from the rest to survey the bison herd from the rocky ledge. In this photograph he, too, lay on his side in grass, but stretched out, head back, eyes half closed, tongue lolled into dirt, a red spray of blood in the beautiful tawny fur behind his shoulder.

Inside Ren, the ice slipped and scalded.

)

He became aware that under his hand now were tremors but no heaves. "831," she said. "We're not supposed to give them human names, but I did."

He didn't ask. Hilly, he could tell, was reeling herself back in, her resilience.

"A three-year-old male, big, but still fast. A lethal combo, indispensable. He was alpha material. And something else: in two documented fights with much smaller packs, he didn't kill the vanquished. He prevented the others, too. He had *mercy*."

Mercy. What some of us need now.

"Oh," Ren said. Then, when he had recovered his wind, he said, "I'm sorry. I'm so sorry." And he wiped his face on his sleeve before she could lift her head.

He had asked her if she wanted to sit on the porch and she shook her head no. It was as if she couldn't bear to be in the same open air as the pack across the river who would now be grieving. She had told him once that they knew. They knew somehow—usually—when one of their own had been killed, knew when it was not a lighting out for new territory, a solo scout, or a hunt. Anyway, solitary hunters were very rare. 06, the legendary gray female, had often hunted alone. She was one of the few Yellowstone wolves ever documented taking down adult elk all on her own, and more than once or twice. Hilly had told him how she would bestir herself and stand from the resting pack as if she were saying, *Okay, I'm gonna go get an elk. See ya later.* And off she'd trot. And she would. Kill an elk. Extraordinary, given the average odds of success for any individual wolf on any kill attempt. She was a super wolf. Ren loved the fairy-tale part of the story: how suitors came from valleys all across the land, from other packs and territories, to woo this glorious alpha female. She was courted by big, handsome males who were alphas in their own right. And she eschewed them all. Instead, she chose two gangly, callow young brothers who didn't know squat, and she trained them to hunt and mated one and whelped four litters, and successfully led the Lamar Canyon Pack for six years, and then she strayed over the border and was shot by a hunter in Wyoming.

A story that was repeated in unending, sad permutations, year after year. Now starring Hilly's big fawn, whom she had named.

Hilly had one worn upholstered chair, which sat against the log wall. Ren helped her into it and repeated the ritual he had just enacted at his own cabin. He filled a kettle and heated it and brewed tea. This time in a Japanese teapot with a sisal-wrapped handle. He let it steep and scalded two cups—Tweety and Sylvester—and poured in the chamomile and brought them to her. He set them on the side table under the standing lamp and retrieved one of the rockers and sat beside her.

She sipped and let her breathing smooth out and finally looked at him.

"Do you recognize the phone number?" Ren said.

"No."

Ren nodded. He hesitated, said, "I met Les in town. He told me, in so many words, that he did not mean, necessarily, for you to step in that trap."

Hilly sipped and looked straight ahead. She had turned, partly, to salt.

"I believed him for some reason," Ren said. "Shame on me."

Chapter Fourteen

He needed to talk to Ty. Ty first. If he brought the new photos to District at Mammoth, they would ask if there was any evidence that the wolf-kill pic was in the park. The photo of Hilly they would take more seriously, but they would explain to Ren that there was no federal duty-to-aid law. And they would look at Ren as if the simmering and continuing trouble in his area were somehow his fault, and stemmed probably from some character defect.

Ty might give him the same legal perspective, probably would, but he would understand the seriousness of what was happening. He wouldn't just file it in the "It's a Politically Unappetizing and Crazy World" folder and forget about it.

Ren and Hilly finished their tea, and he made her Texas toast with honey and peanut butter—one of her favorites—and said, "You okay for a while?"

"I'm okay," she said. He could tell she wasn't thinking at all about herself now. Her spirit was ranging, and if he knew her as he thought he did, it would be hunting. His own impulse. He wanted to neutralize the threat so badly. But he knew this had to stop.

He left her. He picked up his badge and gun again and climbed into his truck and drove to Cooke City. He had a much better chance getting a clear radio signal from there over to Livingston, because there were booster transmitters in the Beartooths. Also, he could ask Pete, or Sandra, or half a dozen others, to use a landline.

By the time he got to town, the sun was low in the valley of the Lamar, a level bore that threw the truck's shadow ahead on the frost-heaved two-lane, and gave little heat. The day had cooled fast, and now the chilly autumn evening presaged a hard frost and winter coming. He pulled a U-turn by the convenience store so he could look down Main, but stayed back of the gas pumps. He flipped down the visor to keep the last sun off his face; the Baronettes would put the whole town in shadow in a few minutes. He unclipped the mic on its rat tail and keyed it and called for Ty. Who was probably in Livingston now, ending his shift. Or out on a call in the Yellowstone Valley. He didn't pick up. Well. What should he do? He was rattled. Both texted photos were horrific, but the one of Hilly lying in the grass, close probably to death—it shook him. That someone could have snapped it from the edge of the woods. It was taken from uphill; the vantage and angle placed it in the lower reach of the trees. That someone had lurked there, right there just within the cover of the pines. That they had coolly snapped the photo while the woman—his closest friend here, admit it—lost so much body heat she had stopped shivering, and drifted in and out of consciousness, and had stopped fighting the jaw clamped to her badly bruised leg. Had curled up and waited to die. What kind of ice in the veins? What kind of monster?

He was thinking it when he saw a sliding reflection off the glass door of the gift store across the street, and he shifted his gaze and saw the door open, and Gretchen Waggoner Ingraham stepped out of it. And before he had any idea what he was going to do, or say, he was out of his truck and heading across the road.

She was just locking the door when he got to her. She turned, surprised. That's when he saw the oxygen cannula looped over her ears. She snatched it from her nostrils and tucked it into her coat. And he noticed the concealer not quite concealing a bruise spreading on her neck and throat. A sudden rush of compassion bloomed in his chest; also white-hot anger.

"Sorry to startle you," he said.

She was breathing hard, still hunched from where she'd turned the key. She looked him up and down. "You leave me alone," she said.

"I—"

"Why can't you just leave us alone?"

Because your husband is a monster who needs to be caged, or worse. He didn't say the words, but he felt himself harden.

"I need to see your husband," he said. "Now."

"I'm sure he is not concerned about what *you* need. Neither am I." She straightened and began to move.

Ren put his hand on her arm. She was startled. "Look, Mrs. Ingraham," he said. "He came this close to killing a biologist the other day. Left her to die through a cold night in a leg trap. And I'm pretty sure he just shot a wolf in the Lamar Pack. It's going way too far—"

She held up a hand. Her eyes narrowed. He thought she might spit at him.

"Yes, he shot a wolf," she hissed.

"What?" Did she just say that?

"It's wolf season in Montana now. Did you even know that? He got a permit. He shot him just outside the park."

Ren was speechless.

"Do you know why he shoots wolves? And traps every day he can? Nights, too? Do you think it's for fun?"

"I—" Ren had nothing to say.

Her chest was heaving; she was breathing rapidly. She stopped, made her breathing slow, sucked in the evening air.

"You see this?" she said. She stretched her head away from him, bared the side of her neck and throat. With one hand she tried to wipe away the threadbare concealer. "See it? The bruising? Do you know what that is?"

"He. He is rough—"

She winced. Found her voice. "*God!* Is that what you think? *Really?* Les would never, ever lay a hand on me. Never has. He doesn't even have it in him. You righteous prick." Tears tracked her cheeks now.

When she caught her breath again, she pulled the clear tubing out of her coat and rehooked the cannula over her ears and positioned it. Her hand was shaking. When her shining black eyes found his, he could barely meet them. They were large and held depths of suffering and they were angry. "I have acute lymphocytic leukemia. It causes bruising, shortness of breath. Do you know how much my chemo costs? Seven thousand a month. My cost. Do you know how much he can get for a tanned wolf pelt? A thousand dollars. That's why he traps and hunts." She turned away from Ren and walked slowly to her RAV4 parked at the edge of the Super 8 fence.

There was a split-log bench beside the gift-shop door, and Ren sat on it. He watched Gretchen Waggoner Ingraham make her way to the white car as if she were walking into a headwind. Which, he understood, she was. Every day. He watched her open the back door and place a paper shopping bag on the seat. She placed it with care, and he thought of a baby seat, placing a baby in the back, carefully, and how she had never gotten to do that. Maybe she'd had the disease for a long time. Maybe Les had married her knowing that she had it, that she'd need long-term care. That they could never have kids. *God. God* is right. And then he felt Lea in his chest again. The grief again, for her, as she told him that they could never have children. And that she would deteriorate over the years, her condition would, that she would be gone maybe by fifty-five. Ren sat on the bench and hoped no one could see him. He did not have it in him to stand, to stride back across the road, to resume. He felt the cold night air pouring off the pass. It funneled down with the growing dark like a tide and chilled the town and sometimes brought rain or snow. He wished it would rain now, rain hard, wet his shoulders and face. That he could sit here and get soaked by a fall downpour that slashed into the covered boardwalk.

Les was a bad man. He was. He would not have texted those pics otherwise. He would not have set a trap in the park otherwise. Right? Right? But.

It did not rain. It did get cold. Ren tipped the brim of his cap low over his face and sat until he was shivering. Then he stood stiffly and walked across the road to the Crooked Moose, from which he could already hear "Free Bird" seeping out the heavy door.

He sat at the bar on a high stool and ordered a pizza from Lauren. She pushed through a swinging door to the little kitchen and came back with two frozen pies in cellophane, holding them up shoulder-high and flat-palmed like a real Italian pizza chef. She clattered them onto the bar like two land mines. Which, Ren thought, is exactly how his gut would feel after inhaling either one.

"Frisbee one or Frisbee two?" she said. One seemed to be lumpy with a brownish topography that Ren took to be sausage, or maybe meatball; the other was flecked with shades of olive and what might have been actual olives, and a black paisley pattern that had to be mushrooms—better be.

Lauren pressed her palms on the bar and leaned forward. Her hair was down tonight—it wasn't busy yet, and she hadn't corralled it all up into a pony tail—and he could smell the coconut in her shampoo. "What'll it be? And what to drink?"

She wore no makeup, but her lips were pink; he'd never noticed the light sprinkle of freckles below her eyes. Ren felt his heart galloping again. She had trampolined him straight out of his melancholy, which he'd known she would. And she didn't wait for him to answer. And he didn't follow her with his eyes as she walked to the taps in very tight jeans and the tight faded blue T-shirt tucked into them; did not follow the sway of her hips. Tried not to. She pulled him a Cutthroat Ale, slid a coaster as she came back down the bar, set the tall glass carefully on top of it, then leaned over the varnished wood and kissed the corner of his mouth. Her lips were soft and full, and the kiss was neither fast nor slow. She pulled her head back, said, "That's instead of the shot of bourbon. You need to hydrate, I can tell."

Ren, for maybe the third time that day, was speechless. Her eyes danced. He looked down the bar. There were three other drinkers, and they were cross-talking and were in no mood to notice. He didn't know what else to do, so he reached for his wallet. She stuck up an index finger, wagged it. "Not tonight."

"Why?" Ren stammered.

" 'Cuz."

"Well."

"You're a YouTube star, for one."

"I am?"

"That stunt swooping up the little girl just before Mama Moose charged, it has over thirty thousand views." The bar had Wi-Fi, and, like most folks in Cooke City, Lauren was regularly on her smartphone. She pinched her phone out of her waistband, where she kept it because her jeans were much too snug to use the pockets. She tapped the screen a few times, said, "Nope, forty-two thousand. You're trending, lovely."

Lovely. That was a very British thing to say. Or not. They didn't say that. Ren felt the untethering of vertigo. She held up the phone and he waved it off with a "Thanks." Once, on a fishing trip with his mom, he had gotten seasick on the Lake Champlain ferry; it didn't take much. Lauren was watching him closely. She put a hand on his arm and said, "You relax. It's been a rough week. Plus, the pressure of stardom." She pivoted and snatched a rag off the faucet as she went and, in a wobbly dimness made more murky by the thumping jukebox, he heard her call, "What're you guys up to? Talking P-O-L-I-T-I-C-S? Which you know is *verboten*. C'mon! Who wants another?"

◀

Ren ate the meat pizza—it had fewer ingredients and less suspiciously shaped toppings. He drank a second beer and drove home in the dark. The night was clear, with a quarter-moon floating high, and after he passed the gatehouse and hit the first long straightaway he switched off his headlights and let his eyes adjust to the pale road, the slopes shadowed with woods, the reach of stars bright enough to pulse through the moonlight. He slowed way down. He didn't want to be the guy who hit another buffalo, or anything else. He opened the window and set his elbow there and turned up the heat, as the night was already near freezing. He hummed the Jamey Johnson song "In Color." He didn't sing the words, but the tune evoked the scene, and he loved the setup: the grandfather showing his grandson a handful of snapshots—of great suffering and great joy, war and marriage. He hummed and wondered: What snapshots would he show his own grandkids? Would he even have children? He had wanted them—them, or one—with Lea. But after Lea the world did not seem like the kind of place where he would want to raise a child. It was colder, harsher. It was lonelier and more brutal. But maybe the world itself did not change that fast.

He pulled in to the cabins and checked his watch. Only nine-ten. He needed to check on Hilly. She would be asleep by now. Unless she was crunching numbers in a statistical analysis for one of her studies, or swept up in writing a report. He should have thought of that earlier, how she often hit the hay with a book by eight-thirty; he should have kept track of the time. He walked past his cabin and up the hill and could see from a hundred yards away that her place was dark and still. He continued up the path. The steps creaked, as did the sprung boards of the porch itself, but he nearly tiptoed. Eased open the screen and the door. Leaned his head inside. Listened. Her cabin was bigger than his, and her bed was in the back, behind the screen of a single wall that shielded it from the main room. He thought he heard her breathing. Good. Then he heard the voice, husky, nearly a whisper.

"Ren?"

"Yeah, it's me."

"Oh, good."

"You didn't want to shoot anyone tonight?"

"Not really." He heard her bed creak. "You can come in." He saw a light behind the wall switch on. Not bright. "You can come," she said.

He bent down and unlaced his boots and pried them off—no need to track mud. He padded across the rag rug and turned the corner. She was sitting up in the amber glow of a reading lamp. Her thick, dark hair sprayed down over her shoulders and across the pillow on either side. He had never once seen her hair down. Nor had he ever noticed the sculptural beauty of her collarbone and slender neck. Usually when he saw her she was in a tech T-shirt or synthetic sun-shirt buttoned to the throat. Now she wore a nightgown of ivory cotton tulle; the ribbons had not been tied at the neck, and the fine material was supported mostly by the swell of her breasts. Which he had never noticed either. She smiled. Not her usual semaphoric suggestion but warm and unhurried and sad. Her eyes, he could see, were red from crying, but they were steady. Ren might have stood there for a full minute; he had no idea, he was entranced.

"You look like a zombie," she said.

"That's the second time I've been told that tonight." As soon as he said it he remembered the kiss at the bar and felt a twinge of guilt, almost as if he had somehow betrayed Hilly. Why should he feel guilty?

"Wanna sit?" she said.

"Sure."

He cast around the room. There was no chair.

"Here," she said. She patted the edge of the bed.

He sat. The quilt was thick, and as soon as he sat he breathed the warm scents of lavender, woodsmoke, and something clean and sweet, like wheatgrass, which, by the heat of it, came off her skin. If he felt vertiginous at the bar . . . He placed a steadying hand on the bed. Her thigh was there, under the blankets, and he said, "Sorry," as if it were a hot stove, and he made to move it, but she placed her hand on his.

"That's not where I'm bruised."

"It's not?" he said stupidly.

She made a face. "You really are out of sorts." She removed her hand, and he wasn't sure why but he felt some relief. But the hand went to the ribbon in the V of her neckline, and she loosened it further and then pushed the gauzy material to the side. She crossed her arms, and with the backs of her fingernails she edged and rolled open the collarless nightie onto her shoulders. She did not take her eyes off him. They were steady, sure, and in them he read, *Someone needs to take care of you for once.* Her breasts were bare to the nipples, where the sheer cotton snagged. Why had he thought they'd be modest or tiny? Maybe he had never thought about them at all.

"Help me, will you?" she said.

"I—"

"Haven't you ever seen a girl? You're gonna get this down to my waist and then I'm going to roll over and you're going to rub my lower back. It's killing me. Way too much sitting in the last couple of days."

"Okay. Sure," he said. "Do you want me to turn around?"

"I don't think you can do any of that with your back turned. I'm not shy. Remember, I'm a large-mammal biologist."

He had no idea what that meant. He reached with both hands to her shoulders and she helped him by spreading the cotton off her breasts and then she tilted up her face and kissed him.

It was not a kiss on the corner of his mouth, neither fast nor slow. Duration—time, even—had nothing to do with it. She kissed him and her mouth opened and she tasted of chamomile and honey. He closed his eyes, and then that was all there was. In the world, that taste. For hours maybe; days. Until he felt her fingers on the back of his head, in his hair, and she was pressing him down to her chest and asking to be kissed there. It was enough to be asked. It was all enough. Somehow, leaving her mouth, he sank farther into her. And she pushed him down farther and he had no will at all, and he let himself be led and lost. He was lost. And the more he relinquished, the stronger he felt, seeing nothing, knowing nothing, immersed entirely, pulled on this insistent current, and from some great distance hearing his name again and again.

Ren woke at first light. The window had no curtain, as his had no curtain, and it was five by three, as his was, and looked out

also on the dark trunks and moving filigree of pines, the nee-
dled boughs. And so, when he stirred awake and opened his
eyes, he thought he was in his own bed and turned his head
away from the dawn and felt the flank of Hilly beside him. She
was naked, as he was, and warm, and long, and her hair was
on his neck, and for a moment he thought he was dreaming
and he felt himself growing hard and he had the dream-thought
that he hadn't had a dream like this in a while, it was nice, and
then she stirred and in half-sleep rolled on her side to face him
and he felt the brush of her pubic hair against him, at the tip
of him, and somehow they both shifted and he was inside her
again and they were moving, barely. Again he lost his bearings,
but instead of sinking deep into a dark, warm pool, he was waking into a world in which Hilly was present and fragrant and
beneath him and above him and every cell was alive to her. He
shaped her with his hands and consumed her with his mouth,
and this morning he delighted in all of it. He was not dreaming.
He knew he was awake when she stiffened for a second and
said, "Ow, watch the ankle."

They lay side by side, hands touching thighs, long enough for
the window to fill with light and the pines to throw their first
long shadows, and they didn't say a word. He heard the three
clear notes of a chickadee. Her eyes were closed, and he looked
up at the rough shiplap of the sloped ceiling, following the
ruddy grain in the fir planks, feeling a little like a small boat
again, but this time at mooring, rising and falling in a slight
glassy swell, at rest.

He said at last, "Did you just mate me? I mean last night."

Her eyes blinked open. If there was a smile at play on her lips
she reined it in. "I hope not. Pups are not really in my plan."

Behind the smile was a dead seriousness. Ren could see it there, and he wondered if she was thinking about the dead fawn wolf and what *was* in her immediate plan.

He said, "I mean, did you mate me the way 06 mated with one of those gangly young brothers?"

She turned her head now. She took her hand from his thigh and pushed back a fan of unruly hair. She was smiling. She said, "Or maybe the she-wolf that brought 755 back into a pack of two."

"Which one?" he said. "Which female? Are you going to dump me for a wayfaring stranger?"

"There's nothing to dump," she said, still smiling.

A bolt of pain shot through Ren. And panic. As if his little boat, swinging on the tide, had just struck a rock. She must have seen it. She propped herself up on her elbows and, holding him with the same steady gaze as the night before, she said, "I meant that we're not whelping pups, right? There's no obligation for you to stay here and protect me. But if you want to hang around the meadow, I'd like that." And then she leaned over and kissed him again and the panic subsided and was replaced by something warm and bright. *She has the spirit of an alpha,* he thought. *And no desire to dominate.* It was novel and strange and freeing, and something rose up in him that felt like joy. And then she said, "You hang out. I don't mean today, I mean—"

"I know what you mean," he said.

And her face darkened and she said, "I've got a few things I've gotta go take care of."

Hilly always made crap coffee. So he dressed and sauntered down to his cabin and ground the beans and put on a drip pot and hummed while he scalded the thermos. He carried it up the hill with the sun warming the side of his face. He rinsed out Sylvester and Tweety and left his cup on the plank counter—same wood, same steel sink as in his own kitchen—and brought her the Sylvester mug. The cat definitely ate the canary. She was sitting up, with the duvet to her hips and her dark hair spilling to the tops of her breasts, and he thought her more beautiful than last night. He handed her the cup. "Honey?"

"This is good. I want it bitter." He didn't have to ask. It was an acknowledgment of a surfeit of sweetness. He went back to the kitchen and opened one cupboard, then the second. A glass jar full of oatmeal. The bunch of bananas he had brought her the other day in a bowl on the counter. That would have to do. No milk in the fridge. He hadn't bought her any in Gardiner because she didn't drink it. But there was a carton of almond milk; that'd work.

He found a two-quart pot and lit a gas burner with an old flint striker and put on the water and oats, turned it down to simmer. The cabin was cold—it had frosted in the night—but not that cold. She seemed to like it, too; she had been sitting up naked against the headboard, keeping a reservoir of heat under the quilt on her legs, so he left the pot and shoved his feet into his boots and went out into the chilly sunny morning and down the steps and around the corner of the porch. He could smell the sharp sweetness of aspen turning. Against the wall she had a long stack of cordwood. He gathered an armload and climbed back up and inside and dumped it into the woodbox by the woodstove, but did not build a fire. The oatmeal was bubbling. He turned the steel valve and cut the gas. He unpeeled two bananas already going dark—perfect—and sliced them with a spoon into the hot cereal and stirred and mashed. He drizzled a thread of honey in a loose spiral and splashed in almond milk. Found two heavy blue-glazed bowls on the shelf and served up breakfast and brought it in to Hilly, who had put on a red union suit against the chill. He had no union suit or long johns, so he sat at the edge of the bed beside her, somehow completing a circle from last night.

"A man-cooked meal," she said, raising a full spoon in a toast. "Haven't had one of those in a long time."

A sweet scene. But, raising his own spoon, meeting her eyes, he could sense behind them another engine humming. As if some machine of maybe dark design were idling in a shed, beside some hunting shack her father had built.

Chapter Fifteen

Ren left. Went down the porch steps and down the path. Sharp scents of autumn. He trotted out of the pines and into sunlight, where the melting frost wet the grass. Past a cluster of aspen that loosed a few bright-yellow leaves with no help from a breeze. Tangy smell of them, and wet earth, and the creek that burbled in its cut. He should have felt buoyant, he might have been singing to himself. But he didn't; he wasn't. Why not?

Why not? He thought of Hilly sitting up in her bed eating the oatmeal out of a blue bowl. Her wild hair. Her red union suit with black buttons. The patchwork quilt. Strong light from the window framing the boughs of pines, green needles gleaming in early sun. It might have been a painting by Matisse: strong colors, colors with heft, in juxtaposition and in concert, somehow creating a composition of great energy and lightness.

He felt heavy, though. Why? Fear?

She laid no claim on him, had made it clear. But she was happy to have him around. And when he had thought for a moment that the night had meant little to her, he had been jolted by a frisson of panic. So why wasn't he glad now?

The thing about his work that he most appreciated was the lack of ambiguity. If somebody broke a law or posed a danger to themselves, or others, or wildlife, if someone was fishing without a license or dumping spaghetti off the side of the road, or if they dropped from a heart attack while scoping a kestrel . . . Well. His course of action was very clear. Usually. Most of the time. He had some discretion, which was necessary, but he had a mighty bulwark of federal law and park regs to lean against, and precedent, and training.

He had no training for Hilly. Nor for how his heart would feel when it was cracked open just a little. Or for what his spirit needed or wanted in a lover. With Lea he had always known. Her sureness in all things, her clear love of him, and her acceptance of his abstraction and whimsy—he had known. He didn't know a thing now. Were he and Hilly dating? How stupid. Might as well say that o6 dated the young brothers. Were they in love? Was he? She was his closest friend. She was, it turned out, a passionate lover. And so . . .

He rounded the corner of his own cabin and climbed the steps and turned. There, through the trees, was the valley. Brilliant in sunlight. Amber grass, dark woods, orange aspen. Across the way, the high cliffs of rimrock breaking out of the timber were salmon pink. The river glinted, nearly blue. A day to make the spirit throb. But. In his gut was a tightness. He couldn't explain it. He didn't want to. He just wanted to know what to do without deliberation, the way a trout goes for a bug. To live like that. Could he envy a fish?

And then there was Les. He hadn't mentioned to Hilly his exchange with Gretchen Waggoner. She hadn't asked. In Hilly's mind, he was sure, he had his process and protocols and she had hers. And he did know that whatever surprises he had gleaned from the conversation outside the gift shop wouldn't matter to Hilly anyway. Les had shot one of her pack. Again. It meant little to her whether the selling of the pelt was in service to his wife's survival; whether it was inside the park or out; whether he had a legal permit or not. That fawn wolf was, Ren knew, her family. As much family as she claimed at the moment. And he knew that there was nothing about the woman that would let it slide.

What day of the week was it? He had lost track. He checked his watch. Monday. Shouldn't make a difference in a remote travel destination, but it did. On Mondays, fishers and families with flexible schedules made the drive from Bozeman, local hikers from Gardiner. Vacationers drove down from the Bozeman Airport. Mondays weren't as crowded as the weekends, but he'd have plenty to do, which he welcomed.

What's wrong with me?

He might have added the thought, *And why is my life nettled by that question?*

He thought about Lea and tried to remember the first time they made love, how he had felt then. He couldn't. Remember. And none of that mattered, because he had been so sure from the outset. Is this what happened as life went on? You got less sure about everything?

He was thinking and remembering, and he must have been lost in it, because when he stepped on the brakes for an RV that was in turn braking for a slowly crossing porcupine he realized that he had blown past the usual landmarks and he was almost out of the Lamar Canyon. It was a wonder, that he could have been so abstracted and knew his routine so well: he must have maneuvered through minor and major throngs, maybe waved, probably pulled around stopped vehicles, all without interrupting the flow of musing and memory. It was one of his talents, as Lea liked to remind him.

He waited behind the camper. He saw the little hump of bristles trundle clear of the RV's front end, *oops*, and there was another behind, littler, a mom and kit padding across in no hurry, peering at the world from under a spray of needles; no one was going to bother them. The traffic began its crawl again, and he thought, *What the hell, I'll see if Tenner is at Slough,* then turn around and visit whoever was in the gatehouse this morning. Probably Donna and Ray. Sharing a cup of strong coffee with the two of them was always edifying, and the prospect suddenly brightened his morning.

Which is just when he got the call on the radio. Of course. Out of the gust of static was a man's voice—Landis.

"Ren? Ren? You there?" None of the official "Ranger 22"—this was gonna be bad.

"Hey, it's Ren."

"You near Slough Creek?"

"Very."

"Good. Inky and Jim are way down in Canyon. There's a fire—"

Ren was already pulling wide around a line of three cars and accelerating.

"Where?"

"Specimen Ridge. Sounds like the ranger cabin. A wolfer just called it in. Saw it through her scope across the valley. I can't leave the station."

Crap, it was Mom's. Mom's Cabin. Ren ate up the paved highway in maybe four minutes and took the turn onto gravel on what felt like two wheels. A windless morning, and he saw the column of smoke over the trees as he climbed. Black, like a roof burning—not good. He stomped the gas up the last steep hill and came over the rise with front end airborne and landed, and there was the cabin's face engulfed in flames. The front porch, the door, a maw of fire. He heard the rush and wood cracking and a frantic yelping and whine, Jesus, maybe Lucy the dog, or a squatter, fuck. He was out the door and had the topper open and the tailgate down without a single thought but *Move!* His firefighting kit was on the rear passenger side, right there, and he skipped the protective Nomex coat and tugged out the Indian backpack sprayer pump and shrugged into it. He grabbed the heavy commercial red extinguisher and ran. Not to the front. The porch was gone and the front walls were pouring flames upward and the roof had already caught. A section had caved. With the kit he had he wouldn't put it out, but if there was someone in the back still alive and screaming he'd have a chance of getting there.

The pack tank was steel and five gallons, and it knocked against his spine as he ran. The pitched, terrified keening of someone trapped. There were two plank steps up to a back door that opened, he knew, onto a little kitchen, and he grabbed the pipe railing and kicked it in. Maybe not what you were supposed to do—he couldn't remember—maybe kicking in a door could cause a rush of oxygen and an explosion of fire; too late, he was in. A whoosh of air and the smoke and flame funneled to the front, and up to an opening in the roof—good—the kitchen was clear, the vinyl tiles were empty of bodies, and he went through it headlong. He hit the heat and billow, a roil of white smoke, and the roar and burst of timbers almost drowned the yowling. There was a yowling, someone was screaming. He yanked the collar of his T-shirt over his nose, put his head down, and bar-reled in. As into thick fog. Probably dumb, too; he was not a firefighter, but he was in it, and through the pop and bang of exploding siding he heard what had to be an animal cry, and he followed it left and left, and through smoke there was the gaping dark entrance of what he remembered to be the caretaker's bed-room, and there was a roof beam angled across it running with blue flame and behind it a sheet of burning plywood and roof tar and shingles—he aimed the extinguisher hose and blasted.

Cloud of white phosphate in front, and on his right the fire raged. The heat and smoke were rushing up and out, and when he hit the beam and sheeting with the snowy blast there was a clear opening, and he went through at a crouch and in the light of a crack in a boarded-up window, he saw them: in the corner curled a man in a green anorak trying to hug a brown-and-black brindle dog who shook and whined, and the man was trying to cover her and the four tiny pups squirming at her belly.

Ren blasted their way out with the extinguisher as they rushed the kitchen and out the back steps. The four puppies were in the anorak, clutched like a sack, the bitch in Ren's arm; she had struggled for half a second and gone slack in his grip. When they hit the light outside and stumbled back against the trees, the kid's head came up and their eyes locked and the boy cried out in a stark flash of recognition. It was a bark, more of dog than of man, and the boy was cradling the motile bundle in both arms and he took another step back and nearly fell over a downed limb and burst into tears. The kid's eyes were screwed shut, and the sobs racked his thin frame, and he could barely breathe. Ren set Lucy gently on the grass.

"You shoulda fucking left me," he heard the kid say between gasps.

Ren stepped forward, and the kid's eyes opened and he reared back. "You!" the kid cried. "I got nothing. You shoulda taken the dogs and let me die. I didn't mean to—" He was crying so hard he couldn't get the words out.

"I—" Ren had no words. "I . . . Please."

The puppies squirmed, the boy stood in the sun with the ruddy light of the fire moving on his wet face and his chest heaving.

"Hey! Hey!" Ren urged. "Look at me!"

The boy squeezed the bundle against his chest like a life buoy and wouldn't look.

"*Why?*" Ren said. "Why'd you do it? My truck, I get, but—"

The kid coughed hard against the smoke in his lungs. Coughed and coughed. He finished and breathed and spat. When his head came up his face was a mask of hatred. "*You.* You took everything."

"I—I know," Ren stammered.

"I can't even get a fucking job. I'm a felon, forever."

Ren squeezed his eyes shut against a past he could not change. Then he reached out to the kid, who stood rigid and small against the backdrop of trees. Ren pulled his hand back. He had an idea. He yanked the memo pad and pen from his breast pocket. He scrawled something, tore off the narrow sheet, held it out.

"This is my friend Chuck. He's got a woodshop in Livingston. A good man, and he really needs a hand. Call him. Okay? *Okay?*"

Tory Jaeger coughed. He turned and spat and wouldn't look at Ren, but he took the paper and stuffed it into the pocket of his jeans.

"You got a vehicle?" Ren said. The kid blinked. "Do. You. Have. A. *Vehicle?*"

Not comprehending, but a nod.

"What? *What* vehicle?"

"I—a dirt bike."

"Get it. Get on it. *Go!* You gotta get outta here!"

The kid's mouth opened. He shook his head: was he dead and dreaming? "I was gonna," he mumbled. "Then I heard the dog . . ."

"I know, I know. You went back in. Gimme the pups. I got this. Before you hit the main road, go around. Get into the trees. They'll be coming up. Understand? The highway—get onto it further down, understand? They get you for arson, you're done. *Understand?* And call my buddy!"

All uttered in a rush, and Tory Jaeger stared at Ren as if seeing a ghost; and worked his jaw to the side—not able to digest any of it—and then shoved the sack of puppies at Ren and ran. Down to the trees at the edge of the drive, and Ren couldn't hear it over the fire, but twenty seconds later he saw the young man and the dirt bike rocket out of the woods in a spray of rocks and jump the lip of the steeply dropping road and disappear. And he felt against his chest the frantic nosing and pawing of four puppies.

Landis was the first to arrive. He had called in a wolf watcher who was also a park volunteer to man the Tower station desk. He and Ren sprayed down the clearing and brush at the edge of the trees as best they could, and prayed. Tenner was next, and Ren sent him home with the stray and her new pups. Two fire trucks from Mammoth arrived half an hour later. Pretty fast. They put four hoses on the cabin and had it charred and steaming in half an hour more. Landis cut Ren loose. "Go," he said with a grim and sympathetic grin. "You have about five hours of reports to write."

"Thanks." Ren got into his truck and drove. He didn't write a report. He blew past the turnoff to his place and headed for the Northeast Entrance. The morning owed him a cup of gatehouse coffee, and there was really nothing he'd rather do than sit in the little shack and share a cup with Ray.

He let the adrenaline in chest and limbs settle out and drove and didn't give a second look to the visitors in the pullouts and didn't think about a thing. As he got to the gate he could see a line of vehicles already backed up on the entrance side. Yes, Monday. There would be one ranger taking fees and handing out maps at the window, and one in reserve, ready to sell fishing licenses or answer questions the gatekeeper didn't have time to answer. It was a good system, since it gave the off-window person a needed break. This morning it was Donna checking people through and Ray in reserve. Ray was a vet who had fought in Panama with a Special Ops team, had followed orders at immense personal risk and then been grilled by an unsympathetic Congress upon his return. He had been nineteen then, turning twenty. Now he was gray at the temples and mostly bald and he laughed a lot, almost all the time, even when hungover, and he was one of the most enthusiastic and generous people Ren had ever met. He once told Ren at the Moose that he had to focus on the positive always or his mind would go to dark places, and a mood that was not at all self-love would consume him. Ren got it. Ren might have had a similar struggle, but he never framed it that way; he just knew when it was time to go fishing.

He pulled into one of the four official spots on the park side of the little gatehouse and let himself in the green door. Ray was at the desk, unpacking a box of maps and fishing regulations and placing them in neat stacks on the labeled shelves against the back wall. He looked up and brightened.

"Oh, good!" he chimed. "Heard you had a rough go just now."

"'S'up?" Ren said.

"Coffee?"

"Sure. I'm already shaking, what the hell."

"What the hell."

Ray went to a shelf dedicated completely to caffeine. He took a Pyrex pot off the burner.

"Hold on," Ren said. "I'll get my cup."

"Nah, you get a house mug. You gotta drink it all here." Ray unhooked a heavy coffee cup from a nail. On the white ceramic it said "Number One Grandad."

There were two lawn chairs leaning against the wall, and Ren unfolded one and sat in it. The gatehouse was such tight quarters they had no room for permanent seating, but that wouldn't foil their hospitality. They loved drop-ins. They needed them. Ray sat against the desk, raised his cup: "Love, money, and the time to enjoy them."

"Isn't that supposed to be in Spanish?" Ren said.

"Didn't want to scare you. You all right?"

Ren nodded.

"All right but still not at all smart," Ray said. He balanced his hands in the air. "Your life versus a dog's life. I heard it was touch-and-go."

"Five dogs."

Ray edged one hand down under a phantom weight. "Okay, I take it back," he said. They drank. Ray watched Ren as if he didn't think he was at all dumb. He looked like a proud uncle.

"You been fishing?" he said.

"A little," Ren said.

"Any good?"

"Strictly speaking."

"You run into a bear?"

"Kind of."

"Ahhh. I heard about that, too. Rules of engagement starting to chafe, huh?"

"I'll say."

Ray sipped his coffee, made a face, stepped past Ren, and tossed it out the door. "Cold," he said, and poured another. "Want a warmer?"

Ren held up a hand. He said, "He sent Hilly a pic. Of her lying in the leg trap nearly dead of exposure. Burner number." Ren didn't know he was going to say it until he did. He might have caught the words midair before they'd flown. But it seemed he had to tell somebody, and he must have intuited that Ray was maybe the only person in the valley he could trust after Ty. Because, whatever happened next, Ray would keep this conversation to himself.

Ray's eyes were slate gray. Now they darkened to granite. He studied Ren for a second, and blinked whatever thought away.

"You've got to live with yourself," he said, almost under his breath.

"What?"

"Whatever you do. If you stay within the law you might not have nightmares."

"I—"

Ray's face had hardened. Ren had never seen the affable ranger so serious, and he knew Ray was talking from experience, not easily earned. He was not avuncular now, he was priestly. That's what Ren thought: as if Ray had reckoned that a man's soul was at stake.

"So," Ray said. "Your buddy came through here three hours ago."

"What?"

"Green Silverado with toolbox." It wasn't a question. Not much got by Ray Rossi.

"Crap." Ren set down his mug. "Did he have a dog? A golden retriever?"

"Didn't see one."

"Thanks, Ray. Fuckin' A." Ren stood.

"Maybe he's going on a grocery run."

"Maybe," Ren said. "Probably not."

Ray fixed him with a look Ren wouldn't forget—as if the odds for the good of Ren's soul had just gotten longer—and then he nodded. Ren went out the back door, same way as Ray's cold coffee.

His first thought was of Hilly. He drove back the way he had come, with the same disregard for the watchers at Baronette, the hikers at Lamar. But this time it wasn't abstraction, it was hyper-focus.

He threw gravel as he skidded to a stop at the pullout below his cabin, but no need: Hilly's truck was gone. And it struck him: She might have hopped out of bed and dressed as soon as he left. She had probably been right behind him, damn. So while he was heading down the path in his dreamy funk of indecision or whatever it was, while he was wrapped up like a teenager in the age-old question of "How do we *know* when we encounter true love?," she was concentrating on her own mission, and it raised the hair on the back of his neck, imagining what that might be. She had smiled at him with the blurred warmth of new lovers in the morning, and that was probably real, but she was covering. Hiding the pointed alacrity she would exercise as soon as he got his ambivalent ass out the door. He had no clue what she was planning, but he'd sensed the hum of it, even as they lay in postcoital rapture.

He was about to back out of the parking spot when he had a thought. He turned off the ignition and hopped to the ground and jogged up the path. He had seen her Winchester .30-06 leaning in the corner of her bedroom last night. It was behind a coat tree on which had hung a flannel wrapper, another nightgown. But he had seen it, the walnut stock, the blued receiver and scope peering out from behind the innocuous sleepwear. And it wasn't the dart gun. The tranquilizer gun was a modified Remington and he had noticed that, too, in plain view leaning by the front door.

Now he ran. He did not knock. No point. He pushed through the door and went straight to the back and into her sleeping nook. As soon as he turned the corner behind the wall he inhaled her scent again, the smoke and lavender and musk. And for a second it overwhelmed him. He wanted it, he loved it. *Jesus, Ren, fly level now.* That's what he told himself. And he went along the wall, straight to the nightgown tree, and pushed aside the robe and . . . it was gone. The rifle was gone. Of course it was. He pivoted and flew across the main room, out and down the steps, and let his feet freewheel down the path. Hopped up into the truck and threw gravel again as he backed around.

But. Where? Where should he go?

He had an intuition. Two weeks ago, on a day off, he had hiked into his favorite remote creek for a day of fishing. It was Hornaday Creek, where he had sometimes fished alongside grizzlies. He loved the solitude there, the near guarantee he would not meet another soul that was not on four legs or fins. It was the same creek he had fished last Wednesday, but that time he had decided to fish a section farther upstream, and so did not hike from the back of his cabin but dropped into it farther to the east. It was only a three-mile hike, but straight over the steep spine of the eastern rump of the Baronettes. The way passed through the notch of a narrow wooded pass and then steeply down again through scree field and forest and into the willow-and-alder-choked drainage of the creek. He had been fishing for about an hour when he found traps, and he knew that probably Les Ingraham enjoyed the solitude, too.

So he pushed the truck back again along a careworn route he felt he could navigate this morning with his eyes closed. Past wolf watchers and fishermen unloading gear, into a clot of cars, and around. He passed the mountain-goat watchers going eighty.

The turnoff was just a gap in a grove of old aspen. He jounced into it and into a tunnel of blazing yellow leaves and hard blue sky. On any other morning the colors might have pained him, how they enhanced and sharpened each other. But not now; he was driving the track as fast as he could without hitting his head on the roof.

It was more of a four-wheeler track than a road, and the limbs of trees screeched against the truck as he plowed through—oh well. He crossed a little park of grass and sagebrush and startled two does. They lifted their heads in unison, ears forward, and showed their pale rumps and bolted. Back into woods now, now pines. And he saw sky again ahead and there was a grassy opening in the trees and he bounced into it and there were two trucks parked against the far end, one forest green, one black. A Silverado and a Tundra.

He jumped out. Went straight to Hilly's Toyota, put a hand on the hood. Still warm, engine still ticking. Went to Les's green Chevy. Cool. Okay. Les had been out since dawn, probably, which jibed with Ray's sighting. And she was just here, in the last fifteen or twenty minutes, maybe. Ren checked his watch. 9:47. She hadn't left her cabin right away, and now she was two and a half hours behind Les. Enough time to let him get lost in his work, whatever it was, but not enough time to lose him completely. She was an excellent tracker. The trail here was unmarked and rough, and once Les got through the notch and over, he might veer off and go anywhere. The woods were more open on the other side and easy walking and he could pick his route. But if he was trapping, he would probably want to get down to the creek.

Ren moved fast. Maybe she had located members of her pack in the Hornaday drainage. Maybe the Wapiti Lake Pack was edging north, one ridge over from the Lamar, and she wanted to hike in and see what they were up to—which members had come over; was it a hunting team or a war party? Maybe she had simply moved the gun, stashed it in her truck for some reason, or maybe the reason was Les Ingraham and she had decided to carry it for protection. Maybe maybe maybe.

Because he had never woken up after making that kind of love and felt the woman beside him somewhere else—a part of her, maybe the deepest part. He had never, he had to admit, had a night of lovemaking like that, period. With Lea it had been 100 percent committed from the start. Not committed to a life together yet, but fully committed to the act, to plumbing the heart and spirit of this vital dynamo. She was a force to reckon from the first moments, and he wanted to know her, and love-making felt like the shortest shortcut to knowledge. With Hilly it was almost more powerful. Because he already knew her so well. Because in their relations as neighbors, in the daily commerce of shared coffee and conversations about a place they both deeply loved, in the slant of their observations and the colors of the humor and losses they brought to bear, they were teaching each other: *This is I*. And there had been no propulsion toward a consummation, because it was already happening, not with the force of an eruption but with the ineluctable press of river water. If there had been a circling of sorts, both of them had hidden the movement from themselves. They had kept the possibilities at bay and continued to learn about one another. To know. So, when they did make love, finally, maybe inevitably, it had shaken Ren to the core. It was like traveling into the center of a deep wilderness and realizing you already knew the place by heart.

As he stood beside Hilly's ticking truck, he understood that the shocking wonder of the night was not that he loved her, but that he had loved her already. Why, then, the desperation? Why did he feel he might drown?

He shook himself. He looked at the two trucks parked side by side. She was not on a hike to track wolves. If he knew anything about her he could admit, it was that this morning she was not a researcher, she was a hunter.

He grabbed his field pack from the back, his binoculars from the passenger seat. The pack was already loaded for emergencies, for a day or a night in the woods. There were power bars, a water-purification straw, lighters, a plastic sheet, parachute cord, down sweater, and Gore-Tex raingear. First-aid kit. Even a foldable lightweight pot he could set on rocks over a fire to boil water, and grab with the pliers of the Leatherman he had zipped into the top pocket. He could bivouac if necessary. The pack had a CamelBak water bladder that went to a tube on his shoulder strap, so he could suck on it and drink as he moved. He hated hiking with his utility-and-gun belt, so he now swiftly unbuckled it. He found his shoulder holster under the seat and strapped it on. He left the handcuffs but took a half-dozen zip ties. He unclipped the can of bear spray and slipped it onto his regular belt. He strapped the binocs to his chest, forward of the .45 and below his body cam; then he locked the truck and moved.

The trail to the top of the pass was easy to trace if not well used, and his job was straightforward: hoof it through the pines in welcome shade as he climbed the skirt of the ridge; break out into black rimrock cliffs stuttered with small spruce and occasional juniper; and wend up steeply, trying not to surprise a shaggy mountain-goat mom with the heart of a linebacker. Ewes with kids could charge and head-butt with the ferocity of the rams, and Ren did not relish being the first park ranger to be knocked off a cliff. As he climbed, he was grateful for the cool morning and that the sun on the dark bands of cliff was not turning the path into an oven. At the top, in the crook of the notch, in the shade of one short spruce from which some fool had strung a loop of Mardi Gras beads, he drank from the water bladder in his pack. He turned and surveyed the Lamar Valley and the great tawny meadows stretching westward, and then he went over.

All bets were off as soon as he let his feet scrabble down the pitch on the other side. It was less steep on the north slope of the ridge; that was a plus. Easier going, and soon he would be down to the shade of the woods. He could see a dark-blue slash of the creek in the trees far below. Most of the hikers who took this unmarked and undesignated trail to the top of the pass had pretty much one agenda—to get to the notch and take in the view, maybe be lucky enough to see a mountain goat from above. But those going over had myriad missions. Some were going to fish, and these had a range of destinations. Many animals, including grizzlies, had come over the pass with their own ideas, and had followed their noses down, and so there were many game trails that branched and forked and petered out. So Ren stopped. He'd gone ten yards down the north slope and he stopped, took three steps back up to a flat rock with a clear view of the whole drainage, raised his binoculars, and scanned.

Nothing. The river. A wooded cleft upstream in which he could see the white tatters of a riffle. Gray beach of a gravel bar. The uneven, feathered canopy of spruce and fir. Another bend and a smooth curve of creek revealed, crowded with willows. Downstream, to his left, more woods, and then a crescent meadow of grass making a cove in the trees beside a stretch of water. He scanned back. Had he seen movement in the little open park? He steadied his breath and inched back slowly, letting the lenses slip along the far bank. He took in the part of the meadow closest to the stream, pausing at the clumps of sage and probably rabbitbrush and Mormon tea—no, they were not a person crouched—then glided up to the edge of the trees and—

He stopped again, hedged back. There. Just a ripple of movement, as of a fox slipping into cover. But not fox red or gray, it was olive green, and then he saw a flash. Of sun on glass. He held his breath, steadied and refocused, and saw for an instant the unmistakable angles of two arms and the unbending swing of a rifle. The glint off the scope.

Hilly.

She was not in her usual blue fleece or off-white sun-shirt, she was in camo, and she was settling in for an ambush from the cover of the trees. Had probably chosen a solid firing position over a downed log. She was not using a tranquilizer-dart gun. That was still resting by her front door.

And Ren knew that if she was now setting up to wait, she had already seen Les Ingraham. Had probably scanned with binoculars as he had, had seen the man below carrying traps, probably in and out of thick trees a half-mile off or more, had seen him probably hit the creek and turn, and so she knew he was working upstream and she would wait where she would have a clear view.

And what was *he* thinking? Les? He had not made many friends lately. Was he just going to park his truck at a trailhead and traipse into the woods? It was not an obvious, well-trafficked trail or parking spot, but it was not remote either. Though the Hornaday Creek trail was not maintained and not on the map, it was one of a few traces out of the Lamar and into the backcountry. Any local would know it, and especially someone like Hilly, who would have used it more than a few times to reach new dens. Les would know that she would know, and he would know that she could ID his truck. So what was *his* plan? To sucker her in? To draw her into a tight drainage where there would be no company but bears for miles and finish their argument once and for all? The field of view through the binocs began to pulse with the drumming of his heart.

And Hilly, he thought again. Who as lately as yesterday was hobbling around on a cane. What was *that*? The hike in with daypack and Winchester was not easy. Was limping around with the cane all for show? It was almost an alibi. Jesus. He thought: *They are circling each other. They are both hunters and neither one is a fool.* He clipped the binocs to his chest again and ran.

As best he could, down the loose sand and gravel of the first steep pitch. Faster once into the woods and taking the most trammeled game trail down the ramp that tended westward. He could follow the sloping bench and then drop off it straight to the creek and splash across into the meadow.

As he ran, it occurred to him that the pack on his back still held a flare. Two. He could fire one straight over the narrow valley and let everyone know the game was up. And then he thought: *Wishful thinking.* Because Les and Hilly had maybe more in common than they had their differences: the thrawn disdain—of authority, of convention—their cross-grained stubbornness and iconoclast's temper. Firing a flare might just precipitate what was already in motion. And they would know that it was him. Who else could it be? Hilly might bank on his discretion, Les on him being a witness to her aggression and so the guarantor of whatever self-defense he had in mind.

The trail he was on was well traveled. It wended through the bedded needles of the black timber, finding its own contours, and in the dips that had caught recent rain and dried he saw the cloven tracks of elk and deer, the large, almost human print of a black bear. In one silted hollow where the mud had dried to crust he saw the edge of a boot print, and beyond it the chevron pattern of a Vibram sole. Too big, the boot, to be a woman's, and too big for most men. The track had been made since the recent rain.

Ren was still two hundred feet above the creekbed, but the track put Les already within rifle range. All she would need was a clear line of sight. And Ren made himself steady his breaths and slow to a jog. Because he had no idea what he was going to do once he hit the screen of willows along the bank.

Prayer was always an option. *Please,* he said, to no one, *let me get there before she shoots the bastard.*

You come too late. You always do.

Lea on the kitchen floor. Late to the party. Didn't even know his wife was in mortal pain. Too late to comfort her, to say, *We'll get through this together.*

He ran as fast as he could. Not steep here, not the slide through scree, but a trail zigzagging down fast through woods. Roots snaked across, the game trail divided, and when he lost the view of the clearing below he tried to judge.

He stumbled into a copse of aspen, and downslope he saw a stretch of the stream, stripped of willows; he knew the spot from fishing. The beaver were here in force, had already built three dams, backed up three ponds, and on this stretch they had cleared the bank save a few scattered thickets. And coming out of one, moving upstream cover to cover, Ren saw Les Ingraham. He was not carrying a trap. He moved with the heavy agility of a bear, and he was carrying in one hand a revolver. A .44 Magnum by the size of it, what locals called the Bear Minimum. And he wouldn't have held it unless he had spotted her.

It was not illegal to carry a firearm in the park. You just weren't allowed to discharge it. But. If one was fired upon unprovoked, by, say, a crazy wolf-activist who valued canines far more than humans, well, the rules of self-defense would hold in the park as well as anywhere. And Ren could see it: Les knew. He could see it in the deliberate, grim way he moved. In the ursine determination as he shifted his bulk out of the brush and bent low. He knew where Hilly was setting up. Watching the man stalk, the lumbering grace and underlying calm, Ren understood what had made Les Ingraham a merciless All-State linebacker. Les had drawn her out here; he had let her see him, probably. He knew the terrain better than anyone, every inch of the creek—he had trapped it illegally fall and winter; he had trammeled the banks when no other soul would venture to climb over, had snowshoed in; he knew exactly where Hilly would set up to wait. All he had to do was get her to fire the first shot and he could sleep at night knowing he was, for once, within the law. That he already had his gun out . . . nobody would ever know.

Ren had lost his view of Hilly's clearing, but thought Les was already opposite the downstream edge of it. Damn. Ren cast around, sweeping his grove, and thirty feet upslope was a granite boulder that had tumbled in some century past off the ridge. He sprinted through the ferns, smelled the sharp scent of crushed fronds as he ran, and scrambled up the spine of the rock, and there, with just enough elevation, he could see over the riverside brush to the little meadow. He could see Les crouched and running toward the willows—a brave man: Hilly's skill tranquing running wolves from a chopper were legend. And from where he stood and tried to catch his breath Ren saw the shift at the edge of the trees, a subtle sideways sliding that was not a spruce bough in breeze. For just a flash he was in Hilly's head, he could see the crosshairs of the scope slipping along the bank as she sighted. And he saw, as if in slow motion, Les squat and lift the .44 in both hands, aiming. Forty yards to the trees—not an easy shot, but not impossible. And forty yards, less, from Ren to the man.

He did not think. He thumbed the "On" switch of his body cam and in the same motion yanked the .45 free of the paddle shoulder holster and raised it with both hands and fired.

Chapter Sixteen

He never meant to kill anyone. In his life. His mother had taken care of that part, and though he had despised the act—for what it did to his family, more than anything—he had learned to accept the compassion in pulling the trigger on Ed Hedges. But he had not forgiven her. How could she have so much compassion for a dying old man and not for a young son whom she could so easily abandon? That she chose the bottle and self-pity over him. And the woman he had loved most in the world after his mother had also killed: herself. A dose of compassion in that, too, for her own pain, but not for him. How did Lea imagine that all the questions would not tear him apart? She was in too much pain to imagine anything. The fire-red pain through which nothing can be seen.

And now Hilly. A litany of killers. The morning after they had made love and discovered—he did—the surprise and power of a love already waiting . . . The very morning after, she would seek to kill and probably trash whatever chance they had to hold each other again, to say, *You know, I'm really glad you're in my meadow . . .* She had made her choice.

Well, he was in her meadow now. Or just above it. And he pulled the trigger twice and watched Les Ingraham's legs fly out from under him. He watched the arms extend as if for flight, but there was no flight, and he watched the big man's chest hit the ground and heard the unmistakable blast of his .44 Magnum.

Chapter Seventeen

There was luck. His radio had good range, but the narrow valley of Hornaday Creek was steep and deep. But he called over and over, and he caught Ranger Cam McLeay east of the Baronettes, heading for the gatehouse. Who relayed the message to the chopper in Mammoth. A Bell Jet Ranger outfitted for search and rescue. In twenty-five minutes he heard the rapid thud of the blades as it banked over the west buttress of the Baronettes, and felt in his chest the particular pressure drop of a helicopter descending in a remote valley.

He had gotten to Les in seconds. One shot had hit, and it tore open his right thigh. It was bleeding hard, but not the gush of the artery, and Ren had the tourniquet out and twisted tight before Les cocked his head back out of the dirt and half opened his eyes. They were the blue of murky water, and they slipped like water sideways and found Ren's face, slid back.

"Did you aim low?" he croaked.

"You'll never know."

Ren thought he saw the man's chin dip barely in a nod.

Ren tore a thick square of gauze out of a pale-blue package; he already had a bottle of iodine in his teeth. He said, "Les, you hear me?" The man's eyes opened again, swam back. Now he did see the mouth open: "Yah." "I have you on body cam lifting the gun. They won't be able to prove you were about to shoot at Hilly. Because I saw a grizzly just upstream as I came down. Do you hear me? Do you?"

He thought the chin dipped again. "Do you understand?" Ren insisted.

"A grizzly," Les grunted.

"A big mean-ass grizzly that looked to charge."

"Charge," Les murmured and passed out.

◖

And Hilly. She waded across the creek thigh-deep, with pack and rifle slung, and stood above Ren and the bleeding man. With tourniquet, and gauze taped tight, the wound still seeped blood onto gravel in the shade of the alders, and Les's face was blanched in the shadow and ghostlike. Timing was critical. Hilly stood above him, and when Ren looked up he saw that she was shaking.

She held out a hand, it trembled and sought his, but he was occupied trying to stanch the bleeding.

"What were you doing out here?" he said.

"He was—"

"No, what were you *doing*? Do you have your wolf pack charts? Your field notebooks?"

She stared at him. Through tears. She nodded.

"Okay, so what were you doing?"

He saw her mouth work. It twisted, grimaced. She closed her eyes. "I had a ping from a collar from the Wapiti Pack. From just downstream. I did. I did this morning."

"And what?"

"And I hiked in to check. And when I saw Les's truck I wanted to make doubly sure they were unmolested. I took the rifle in light of everything that's happened. To protect myself."

Ren felt the heat in his face. "And why were you set up at the edge of the meadow?"

"To watch for the pack." She looked back across the creek, and then, as if she were in a courtroom: "It is a typical observation scenario."

Ren said, "Good. Good enough."

Good enough. Was it? No. For a jury, yes, if it came to that.

Hilly didn't know what to do with her hand. She blotted her chin with the back of it. "He would've killed them," she said faintly to no one, to herself. "If he had run across one, he would have killed."

Ren ignored her. He said, "You took an EMT course, right?"

"Yes."

"Check his pulse, please."

She found Les's right wrist and looked away.

"Hilly?"

"It's rapid, thready, uneven."

"Thank you."

Chapter Eighteen

Les was in the hospital in Bozeman for a week. A surgery, two pins for a fracture, heavy antibiotic IV. Not a thing like what he'd been through earlier in his life. Piece of cake. Ren drove up on day three of Les's recovery, after stopping in at park HQ in Mammoth. Internal Affairs was investigating the shooting, but the big boss saw no reason in the initial report to suspend Ren while the inquiry was in progress. Ren had stood in Park Superintendent Pat O'Driscoll's office, overlooking traffic on the loop road and a herd of elk on the lawn. O'Driscoll had said, "You were headed for Hornaday Creek and did not begin writing the report on the Specimen Ridge cabin fire because you believed lives were in immediate danger, is that correct?"

"Yes, sir."

"And you took the shot because you believed the biologist was in the line of fire, and that, given the history of acrimony between her and Mr. Ingraham, you believed he was deliberately targeting her. Is that also correct?"

"Yes, sir."

"The body-cam video, the sightline inferred from the angle of Mr. Ingraham's handgun, and the location of the biologist, which was confirmed by Forensics, support this assessment."

Ren wondered why he called Les "Mr. Ingraham" and Hilly "the biologist." But he said, "Yes, sir. That was their conclusion."

The superintendent shook his head and took off his glasses. It was odd: Ren thought he looked both older and younger without the heavy steel frames. "So," O'Driscoll said, "this is all protocol, but I apologize. We should be giving you a medal for saving a life rather than investigating you."

"No, sir."

O'Driscoll's head swung up. "No? Why not?"

"I may have made a mistake, sir."

"Because he says he saw a charging bear? In the clearing? Pretty convenient, don't you think?"

"I saw the bear, sir."

"I read the report. You didn't see it charge."

"It was in proximity. At the top of the clearing. I didn't see it charge because I was focused on the shooter."

"Good thing, too. Fraction of a second later and . . ." O'Driscoll interrupted himself and studied Ren as if he were about to ask a question. He said, "Forensics didn't find any fresh tracks in the meadow."

"No, sir."

"There were day-old tracks along the bank. Grizzly. Well, they're not professional trackers."

"No, sir."

"I talked to the AG. He's going to file charges on Ingraham."

Ren's breath caught.

"For discharging a firearm in the park. It's a misdemeanor. You said you saw the bear and they can't prove there wasn't a bear, so: Ingraham should have used bear spray."

Ren exhaled.

"The biologist is your friend?" O'Driscoll said.

Ren nodded. "Yes, sir."

Ren thought O'Driscoll looked naked and unguarded without his glasses. He wished he would put them back on. But the superintendent watched Ren closely. He was no fool. You don't get to run the most famous national park in the world by being clueless. "Good job," he murmured, finally. "Take the rest of the day off."

Well, he had a free afternoon, so Ren changed out of his uniform and drove on to Bozeman. What the superintendent did not say, either out of a certain tact or because it was not strictly germane to the investigation, was that Forensics had also determined that the Specimen Ridge fire had been intentionally set, and that the arsonist had fled on a dirt bike, judging from the tracks. And that, given the progress of the blaze when the fire crew had gotten there, Ren had to have just missed him. It was a him, BTW, wearing Danner boots, size ten. But no witnesses had been found who had noticed a motorcycle or a dirt bike in that time frame. Well, two had, but what they'd seen was a heavy older couple in matching leather on a vintage Honda Electra Glide. So, for now, that part of an unusually active day was resolved. What Ren couldn't resolve was the very real threat of the men at Zach's. They weren't going anywhere, and neither, apparently, was he. They might be waging a low-grade war for a long time. At least Les Ingraham did not seem to be a member in good standing . . .

At a Loaf 'N Jug on the outskirts of Bozeman Ren bought copies of *Four Wheeler* and *Sports Illustrated,* and a king-sized box of M&M's and one of Whoppers. On the magazine rack was one last copy of *Guns & Ammo,* but he decided against it. He parked his work truck in the visitors' lot of Deaconess Hospital and took the elevator to the third floor. He stopped at the nurses' station and asked for a Les Ingraham, and an older RN entering data into a computer terminal looked up over her granny glasses and said, "Are you family?"

"Is he in an ICU?"

"No, he simply requested no visitors except family."

"I'm not family."

"Then I'm sorry." She went back to her screen.

"Ma'am," Ren said. He opened his badge. The nurse sighed. "Right," she said. "This happens a lot with gunshot wounds. Three twelve." She gestured down the hall. No smile, no *Have a nice visit*. As far as she was concerned, the machinations of law and order should stay the hell off her ward.

Ren found the door. It was open. He knocked on the frame anyway. A raspy "Yuh!"

It was a double room. The other bed was empty. The big window looked on the Bridger Mountains. The swaths of blazing aspen on the ridges had already lost most of their leaves. Les was sitting up in bed, watching a small TV mounted high on the wall. *Storage Wars*. The thin blanket was at his waist, and instead of a hospital gown he was wearing a wrinkled T-shirt printed with the words "Dog's Best Friend" and a graphic of a golden retriever proudly soft-mouthing a duck. His dark, curly hair was mussed, and there were food stains on the shirt. When Les recognized his visitor he flinched. Ren thought maybe he shrunk back, just a little.

"You," he said. Same response as Gretchen's.

"They let you wear the T-shirt?" Ren said.

"What the hell are they gonna do? Arrest me? Hospital gowns make me feel sick." Same old Les.

"You are sick, sort of."

"No, I just got shot. Remember?"

Ren pulled the one upholstered metal chair off the wall, slid it to within four feet from the bed. "You mind?" he said.

Les's mineral-blue eyes moved over Ren's face, maybe assessing the threat level. "Suit yourself," he said. "Right now, to tell you the truth, shit company's better than no company."

Ren sat. "I got you some stuff." He handed Les the plastic grocery bag. Les dumped the bag in his lap. He picked up the *Four Wheeler*, which featured a canary-yellow new-model Ford Bronco in a boulder crawl. He licked his parched lips. "I had one of those," he said. "The real thing. Desert sand. Hand me that water, would ya?"

Ren reached back to a shelf behind him and gave Les a wide-mouth water bottle with a sippy cap.

"They try to neuter you with a gown that doesn't close at the back, then they give you a water cup for three-year-olds."

Les drank, blinked down at the photo of the truck. "When I committed to playing for UM, the Bronco magically showed up. Driven by what I'm guessing was a stripper. Go figure." He glanced at Ren. "They didn't have to bribe me. I liked the hell out of the rig, but I was kind of insulted." Ren saw the flush on Les's neck.

Les set the cup on the side table. He said, "Why'd you say the stuff about the bear? There was no bear."

"I don't know."

"You said it to me and you wrote it up: you saw the bear. So now they'll probably fine me five hundred dollars for discharging a firearm and call it good." Les ripped the top off the box of Whoppers and held it out to Ren, who shook out a handful and handed it back. "I fucking love these things," Les said.

Ren rolled one into his mouth and sucked on the waxy chocolate marble for a second and then thought, *Fuck it*, and bit into the powdered malt center, which began instantly and wonderfully to dissolve. Whoever invented these suckers deserved a prize.

Ren said, "You were going to kill Hilly. And call it self-defense. Plus, you stood back and took a photo while she was probably dying."

Les was likewise chewing on what must have been two or three Whoppers. His cheeks bulged like those of a gorging chipmunk. He swallowed. He took another sip of water and wiped his mouth with the back of his hand. He said, "Scoped aught-six against a handgun—I don't think so."

"You know the ground like your own yard. You weren't surprised she had followed you in, you had spotted her, and you were gonna work in close and finish her."

On the TV some couple had won the storage unit and there was a fanfare of trumpets and the couple was jumping up and down and yelling and trying to high-five each other and missing. Les picked up the remote tied to his bed frame and switched it off. "Jesus Christ," he said. He turned to Ren, and his heavy face was slack and exhausted, but his eyes were hard.

"BTW," Les said, "whoever sent a pic of her on the ground? They didn't just stand there to watch her die. That was a game camera strapped to a tree. Motion detected. Whoever it was retrieved the memory stick a couple of days later."

Les tipped the box of Whoppers toward him and peered into it, as if checking to make sure none of the malts had escaped. "Why didn't you kill me?" he said.

"I tried."

"No, you didn't."

"It was an offhand shot."

"No, it wasn't." Les picked up the *Four Wheeler* and the *Sports Illustrated* and handed them back to Ren. "You keep 'em," he said. "I don't take charity."

The heat rose into Ren's face. He said, "It wasn't charity. It was ... was ..."

Les watched him, with the same keen focus with which he would watch a coyote crossing a slope. "Decency?" he said.

"I guess."

Les pulled the magazines back. He tore open the king-sized box of M&Ms and handed it across. He said, "They say sugar causes inflammation now. Nothing's frigging sacred."

◖

When Ren got back to his cabin that evening, he walked the path uphill. He hadn't really talked to Hilly since telling her to unload the Winchester and get in the chopper. And since taking her statement in Mammoth. In which she said she was out checking on a wolf from an out-of-territory pack pinging in Hornaday Creek, and had the rifle for self-protection.

It had been three days. She was on her porch, in one of the Adirondack chairs, drinking a can of pale ale. She wasn't even pretending to use the cane; it was nowhere in sight. God. When Ren climbed the steps, she crumpled the can and reached for two more from the six on the planks. He took one. It was ice cold.

He sat, and they both looked down through the trees and over the roof of his cabin to the river and the wide meadows. A large herd of elk were grazing. Neither spoke. The sun dropped below the final ridge to the west. They couldn't see the sun set, but the long shadows faded and a current of cold air rattled the aspen. They finished the cans and Hilly reached down for two more and they popped the tabs.

"You want to try that again?" Hilly said. She was watching the elk, not him.

"Which part?" Ren said.

"You know which part."

"Very casual sex? Or is it friends with benefits? Or some wolf thing where you're passing through. Or I am."

Hilly winced.

Ren said, "If you had ambushed him you'd be in jail now, then the pen."

She put the can to her lips, set it down. "Self-defense," she said.

"Doubt it. Your 'wanted dead or alive' poster wouldn't have helped."

"I made a mistake."

Ren turned finally. She was staring straight ahead. *Everybody makes mistakes,* he thought. *They make a big mistake and then they are gone forever and they never really tell you why.* She was wearing a maroon MSU cap. Her thick, dark braid snaked through the back band and over her shoulder and rested beside her breast. Stray hairs that had escaped it played on her temple. *She is a beauty,* he thought, and the thought stung.

"I don't do anything lightly," she said. "Nothing ever."

She had been willing to throw away her life to protect her pack. Nothing light about it.

She said, "You know that, right?"

He didn't say anything.

"And so, when I invited you the other night, I knew."

Knew what? He didn't say anything.

"I knew what I was doing." She turned. The only time he had seen her so stricken was when the male had killed the litter of pups. "You want me to say that I knew that I loved you."

He didn't say anything.

"I don't know what love is," she said. "I really don't. But it might have something to do with old brokenhearted 755 trying again and again."

She stood, a little unsteadily, and went through the screen door into the cabin. Ren watched the herd of elk, heads down, barely moving in the gathering dusk. He heard the faithful runnel of the creek below and felt the cold air stirring out of it. He closed his eyes. The pines, too, smelled sharp and cold. Any night, it could snow.

It could snow. It was not a lot to be sure of. There was a stream that would mostly ice up; storms that would blow in from the northwest and deepen the drifts; the rusty creak of frozen trees. That was enough, wasn't it? To count these few things? He didn't know.

He got up from the chair. He left the remaining two beers to freeze on the porch and went through the screen door and into the cabin. He heard her call, "Ren? Ren, close the big door behind you, it's gonna get cold. Were you born in a barn?"

Acknowledgments

Many people lent insight and energy to the making of this book. I am deeply grateful to my first readers, Kim Yan, Lisa Jones, Donna Gershten, and Helen Thorpe. Thank you for your astuteness, wisdom, and thoughtful attention. It means the world.

I am indebted and grateful to research biologist Kira Cassidy at the Yellowstone Wolf Project. I had no idea when I sent her the book for review that *she* was the actual biologist who did the study on the Old Wolf Effect that Hilly cites near the beginning of the story. That the novel sailed full circle and landed in her hands felt wonderfully propitious.

Thanks to biologist Doug Smith for a lifetime working with wolves and for a lecture he once gave to college students in Butte. I am indebted to wolf naturalist Jad Davenport for his help, and to the extraordinary wildlife biologist Jim LeFevre. Thanks to LaRae Kangas-Yan for rich stories about growing up with wolves, and to Bobby Reedy, as always, for sharing his knowledge of the outdoors. Thanks also to Inky Ford, Meghann Ford Paddock, Adam Duerk, Lamar Simms, William Bartz, and Sascha Steinway for their legal and logistical expertise. And to Doctors Melissa Brannon and Mitchell Gershten for never tiring of answering medical questions.

ACKNOWLEDGMENTS

It's worth noting that any liberties I took, or errors I made, are my own.

Jenny Jackson and David Halpern were on this journey from the first pages, with spirited brilliance. Such a joy to work with you both.

And a special thanks to Myriam Anderson and Céline Leroy, whose discernment and animation have been a great gift.

It is an honor and a privilege to know you all.

ALSO BY

PETER HELLER

THE GUIDE

Kingfisher Lodge, nestled in a canyon on a mile and a half of the most pristine river water on the planet, is known by locals as "Billionaire's Mile" and is locked behind a heavy gate. Sandwiched between barbed wire and a meadow with a sign that reads DON'T GET SHOT!, the resort boasts boutique fishing at its finest. Safe from the viruses that have plagued America for years, Kingfisher offers a respite for wealthy clients. Now it also promises a second chance for Jack, a return to normalcy after a young life filled with loss. When he is assigned to guide a well-known singer, his only job is to rig her line, carry her gear, and steer her to the best trout he can find. But then a human scream pierces the night. Jack soon realizes that this idyllic fishing lodge may merely be a cover for a far more sinister operation. A novel as gripping as it is lyrical, as frightening as it is moving, *The Guide* is another masterpiece from Peter Heller.

Fiction

ALSO AVAILABLE

Celine
The Dog Stars
Hell or High Water (eBook Only)
The Painter
The River

VINTAGE BOOKS
Available wherever books are sold.
vintagebooks.com